Sapphire Sparks

Katie Dunn

Titles by Katie Dunn

Ancient Elements

Myth Blessed

Four Horsemen

Sapphire Sparks

The Wolf's Assassin

<u>Skor Stone Trilogy</u>
Pirates from Under
Prince of Shayd
Rebel in Skorval

Chapter 1

"Please, please, please!"

"No."

"Pretty *please*!" I may be an adult now, but I am not above begging.

My sister turns to me in exasperation. She is dressed in her hero uniform, with pink and black designs and a large B symbol on her chest. Since she is part of House of Heroes, she is required to dress in ridiculous superhero outfits when on missions. Thank goodness she doesn't have to wear a cape because that would be too much.

Cape or no cape though, I just want to see her in action.

I throw my wavy black hair into a ponytail, grab my tactical backpack and sunglasses, and stand by the door, refusing to accept her rejection. Technically she can't keep me from going but it will be easier on both of us if she just brings me along.

Letting out a long, dramatic sigh she ties her shoulder length blonde hair back and leads me out of our small two-bedroom condo to her car. I let out a squeal and run to the passenger side before she can change her mind.

When we are in the car, she turns to me and points her finger at my face. "If I tell you to run, you do not hesitate, ok?" Her nose scrunches up with authority.

I bite my lip trying to take her seriously but can't help it any longer. I start laughing at her attempt to be stern and swat her hand away.

"Jo, I'm serious." She stares at me sternly.

I force my laughter to die down and huff. "Fine, whatever, I will run if you tell me to." Not.

She gives me one last look before starting the engine and heading to her mission. My legs bounce with nervous energy. I am about to see Blast in action, something I have ever only seen on TV. Well, except one other time but that doesn't count.

"Would you stop? You're making me nervous," she complains after a bout of silence.

I grin at her. "Sorry, I'm just so excited. Do you know what you will be up against?"

She glances at me but quickly focuses on the road again. "No, there were reports about some screaming but that could be anything."

I nod, going over all the information in my head about monsters I have been studying. Screaming really can be an indication of anything. Lots of monsters screamed.

Even people screamed. I frown at how unhelpful her information is. I pull out my phone and make sure it has a full battery then hook it onto my selfie stick and test out the camera. There is no way I am going to be there and not film the showdown my sister is about to partake in.

Sherry makes a disgusted snort, drawing my attention away from the phone. "You know, there is a reason I didn't join the House of Glamour."

"Pshh, this isn't for you," I say, continuing to set it up. Totally a lie but she doesn't need to know that.

Her eyebrow rises in obvious disbelief, but she doesn't push it. Soon, traffic slows, and we have to pull over. We are near downtown and people are rushing about, most in the opposite direction we are heading. Many have their phones out recording the mayhem. People are stupid. Why they would record themselves as they ran *away* from the action is beyond me.

"Stay against the buildings and do not go down any alleys, those often lead to dead ends."

I roll my eyes but nod, knowing she shouldn't be worrying about me while she is fighting a monster. The closer we get to the center of downtown the more I can hear the screaming. Now that I hear it, I know exactly what we are up against. We haven't even seen it yet and my ears are already aching. I quickly pull my tactical backpack around to my front and pull out some ear plugs.

My backpack is my survival kit. It has everything I could possibly need to fend off monsters or treat a wound.

Garlic and wooden stakes for vampires, silver for werewolves, salt for ghouls, and last but certainly not least, ear plugs for banshees. My bag also contains a first aid kit, rope, and trail mix, among other things.

We arrive at the scene in short time. Sherry, or Blast, clears a path and shouts for everyone to get back. I hit record on my phone and hold it up to film the action.

A lady in a ripped gown stands in the middle of the street. She has long flowing black hair, but it doesn't look like it has been brushed in days. She probably would have looked like a normal lady if it wasn't for her abnormally large, pointed fingernails and ear-splitting screams. I notice bodies littering the sidewalks and I walk up to a few to check their pulses. They are fine, just unconscious though a medic should check on them soon. I don't have enough salts to wake everyone. There are some people still conscious hanging around, holding their hands to their ears but either too afraid to move or too intrigued by a banshee this far into the city to leave.

Banshees often stick to wooded areas or small towns, never where there will be too much noise. I like to think it is because banshees enjoy being the loudest ones around. However, annoyingly, that means the House of Rogues is behind this one. I look around, eyeing the shops specifically, looking for anyone using this commotion to their advantage. Rogues are notorious for using monsters as distractions so they can pull heists.

A loud booming noise brings my attention back to Blast and the banshee, pushing the House of Rogues from my mind. Even if I spotted the Rogues, there is nothing I can do. From here I can see Blast's eyes turn pink with her power. She punches out her hands and sonic booms shoot out, hitting the banshee and causing her to tumble through the air. People cheer around me, chanting Blast's name. I silently urge them to shut it, not wanting my sister to become distracted.

The banshee opens her mouth to scream and I flinch, anticipating the sound. However, the sound never comes. Blast shoots out a boom of power again making the banshee crash into a sign at a bus stop, then the sign topples on top of the creature. Blast carefully makes her way over to the monster, kicking away pieces of glass until the banshee is uncovered. I tense, readying myself for a jump scare. The banshee seems unconscious but maybe that's what it wants us to think. I smile at my thoughts. This is not a video game and Blast's…well, blasts, are powerful. I should know, I have been hit with one before.

Blast takes out a set of monster cuffs from her belt, a set that every hero is required to carry as part of their hero kit. The cuffs radiate some kind of electricity that incapacitates monsters, keeping them unconscious long enough for the cleanup crew to dispose of it. How they disposed of monsters was beyond me, but if I had to guess, I would say they took them to the House of

Discovery. I shiver at the thought of being a monster sent to the House of Discovery. That is probably how the alien probe conspiracy started.

Blast leans down and cuffs one of the banshee's wrists. Still the creature does not stir, and I sigh in relief. I shorten my selfie stick, realizing the action is over and put my phone and the stick away in my backpack. As I zip up my bag, someone screams in the crowd. My head shoots up to see what caused it and my chest spikes with fear when I see a wyvern flying down from one of the buildings.

"Sherry!" I scream, panic clenching my chest.

Blast looks up from the banshee and searches me out in the crowd.

I point up and Blast turns in time to see the monster and manages to dive out of the way as the wyvern rakes its claws in her direction.

I have been studying monsters ever since Sherry got her powers, wanting to know every weakness and strength so that I could help her if the need ever arose. I even have a book of monster cards that I created outlining their stats and mythology. The wyvern is a level seven dragon-like creature, but it only has two legs and is a bit smaller than a dragon. I remember labeling the wyvern as a legendary monster because they were rarely seen and were extremely powerful. Not as powerful as a dragon, hydra, or kraken but still up there. These kinds of monsters require at least two heroes to subdue it.

A scream lodges in my throat when the wyvern's sharp tail lashes out and Blast barely deflects it with her power. My sister is talented, but I don't think even she can take on a wyvern alone. People begin running away from the scene, probably realizing they are in more danger with a wyvern than a banshee, but I stay. I press the emergency communicator on the side of my bag, suddenly thankful for Sherry demanding I carry one at all times. Hopefully, a hero will arrive soon. In the meantime, I have to do something to help her. I rifle through my backpack and pull out my gun. It is loaded with silver bullets which I hate to waste but I need something to distract the flying monster. Gun in hand, I edge closer to the scene and fire at the backside of the wyvern with expert marksmanship.

Annoyingly, the bullets do not cause harm and it only succeeds in irritating the monster. The wyvern turns in my direction and lets out a deafening roar. I am thankful no one is around to hear my terrified squeak.

"Run!" Sherry shouts at me then blasts the wyvern in the snout.

The wyvern turns back to Sherry and roars again then swipes at her with its barbed tail. Of course, I ignore my sister and shoot the monster again. Hopefully between the two of us we can distract it long enough for another hero to arrive.

Hurry up heroes, I plead silently.

A terrifying screech rips through the air sending shivers down my arms. If I had not kept my ear plugs in,

I would be among the bodies passed out on the sidewalk right now. My head swivels to find the cause of the scream and when I find it, I curse. The banshee is awake and looks ready to kill. Before I can warn Sherry, the banshee rushes at my sister while she is distracted and shoves her. I gape at the strength the monster shows when my sister ends up flying across the road. I aim my gun at the banshee instead of the wyvern and press the trigger, but nothing comes out.

"Crap," I mutter to myself.

I shove the gun back into my bag then sprint at the banshee, hoping to get the cuffs hanging from her wrist and wrestle her the rest of the way into them.

I spare a glance at my sister to make sure she can handle the wyvern for a bit and smile when I see her pink blasts hit the creature's wings, causing it to fall.

She's got this.

I reach the banshee who is still focused on screaming at Blast and grab her cuffed wrist, yanking it behind her. I almost have the other cuff on when the banshee yanks her arm away and screams in my face. My ears ring and it takes me a second to get my bearings. I think I just went a little deaf despite the ear plugs. I really hope it is not permanent.

I scream back in the monster's face surprising her just as much as me. I fight down the giggles that want to escape and use the banshee's confusion to grab her wrists again. This time I successfully bring the wrists together in front of her but now I do not have a free hand to do the cuffing part. Crap.

The banshee smiles wickedly, actually full on smiles, which is not a pretty sight, then headbutts me.

"Ow, fu-" My words are cut off when the banshee rakes her claws across my chest opening four deep gashes. I collapse to the ground with my head, ears, and chest throbbing with pain.

Yeah, I probably could have thought this through better. The banshee turns back to Sherry and walks away from me. I touch the gashes on my chest to figure out if I am about to die and red stains my fingers. I choke on a terrified sob but pull myself together when I hear Sherry scream. I have only ever heard Sherry scream one time in my life so when I hear her make that noise now, dread floods my body. Clenching my jaw at the pain, I turn over and grab a silver dagger from the side pocket of my backpack. I am glad I decided to put it in a side pocket because at the moment I do not think I could search through it in time. I cry out at the sharp pains in my chest when I push myself to my feet.

Sherry is battling two monsters now and by the looks of it, she is weakening. Red seeps from a gash on her arm but I do not know which monster caused it. There is no way she will survive this attack on her own.

I rush at the back of the banshee, wincing as I push through the pain, and shove my dagger into the banshee's back. Usually it is a big no-no to kill a monster unless it is a level four or higher but seeing as this level three banshee just ripped my chest open and is attempting to do the same to a hero while she fights a level seven wyvern…well, yeah, of course I am going to stab the beast.

The banshee screams, this time in anguish, and claws at her back to remove the dagger. I leave her and focus on the wyvern that is still on the ground. The wings resting on the ground, acting as front legs, look injured. I am pleased that Sherry managed to prevent it from flying. Sherry ducks under the monster's wing and blasts away the snout that tries to bite her. She has tear tracks running down her face and my heart breaks. She is the strongest person I know and if she is crying then she must think there is no hope.

The wyvern swipes at Sherry with the talon on its wing and she turns to face the attack but what she does not notice is the sharp tail rising behind her. I scream out a warning, but it is too late. The tail strikes and I fling out my hands to stop it, though from this distance there is nothing I can do to prevent it.

Desperation fills every pore in my body and my skin hums with an unfamiliar energy. It rises and pushes on me, *in* me, until I feel like I will explode. Needing to get rid of the pressure I yell, and a blue force shoots down my arms to my hands and out toward the wyvern. It takes the shape of lightning and blinds me as it is released followed by a loud thunderous sound that reverberates in the air.

The bolt of lightning hits the wyvern and blue energy zips across its body. I laugh in disbelief and relief when the pointed tail halts a few inches from Sherry's back. She turns around with a frown of confusion then her eyes widen when she sees the tail. She scrambles away, gawking at the electrified monster.

Suddenly, it screeches and starts writhing on the road. The energy does not disappear like I expect it to. Instead, it spreads to cover every part of the creature from snout to tail, from claws to wings. Every scale has blue currents running over it and the wyvern seems to hate it. A twinge of guilt makes its way into my heart as I stand there watching it suffer. If I knew how I did it, I would stop its pain. All I wanted to do was prevent it from killing Sherry.

The monster begins to grow, its tail and talons getting longer as its body lengthens and expands. I gasp at its change. The pained screeching turns to roars and I dart forward to grab Sherry and pull her back even farther. Is my lightning causing it to get bigger? I look at my hands as if they hold the answers. Somehow, I know this strange new power is the cause.

Oops.

When the wyvern finishes with its growth spurt, it gives us one long look that I cannot decipher and takes to the air. I am surprised to see that it can fly again.

So, check for making monsters big and check for healing them. Well, this is not a helpful power.

I hiss at a stinging pain in my chest and suddenly remember the banshee. I look around and see the banshee dead on the ground a few feet away. I solemnly walk over to retrieve my blade. Sherry places her hand on my shoulder from behind and I turn around after putting my dagger away to give her a bone crushing hug. She grunts from the impact and squeezes me back just as hard. I could have lost her today. I don't know what I would have done if she died. Probably destroy the area with a grief filled explosion of lightning. I glance at my hands over Sherry's shoulder and watch as little electric currents skitter across my skin, almost like in a plasma ball.

"Hey, are you girls ok? We came as fast as we could."

I look up to see two heroes running toward us and snort. They are way too late. Sherry needs to have a talk with the Council about the Heroes' terrible response time. I pull away from my sister and she slips back into her role of Blast as she faces the newcomers.

I can see the irritation threatening to crack her professional exterior, but she stays strong. "I'm fine, but she needs medical attention," Blast tells them, pointing to me.

They look at me and their eyes widen at the gashes on my chest. The one in a striped yellow and black hero suit, Buzz I think, brings over a med kit and starts to dress my wounds in bandages and ointment. I hiss at the stinging it causes but it is not the worst thing I have felt today. Buzz lets out a pained shout and shakes his finger before putting it in his mouth to soothe it.

Buzz chuckles after a second and takes his finger from his mouth. "Sorry, I got a little shock."

I don't respond, not really wanting others to know about my lightning power until I could talk to Sherry about it. I look over to where Blast and a hero in camo-wear called Chameleon are dealing with the banshee.

How did two monsters of different levels end up in the same place? Where did the wyvern go? More importantly, where the hell did this power come from?

Chapter 2

The day Sherry exhibited her powers for the first time was the most terrifying and devastating day of my life. We were in the car with my parents heading to a birthday party when a large, glowing, blue and black hole appeared in the air in the middle of traffic. I knew from the news that it was an interdimensional portal. They had been appearing in random places across the world for almost sixty years. Except that one was in the middle of the road and my parents had to swerve to avoid going into it. I don't exactly remember much after that, but what I do remember is Sherry putting her hands out as if that would help her stop the truck we were about to hit and a sonic blast erupting from her thirteen-year-old hands. Sherry helped us avoid the truck, but it didn't stop the car from flipping. I lost my parents that day but gained a superhero best friend for a sister when her parents adopted me. I am glad that I didn't lose Sherry to the monsters yesterday or else it would have been another devastating day.

Sherry places a plate of Pop-tarts in front of me and nods at them expectantly. Instead of taking one like she wants me to do I narrow my eyes at her suspiciously.

"I'm not hungry."

I told her after we left the scene about my weird power display with the wyvern and now she keeps giving me food to replenish my supposed lost energy. Sherry always has to recharge by eating after a mission because her power takes too much energy. However, I do not feel drained at all. In fact, after these powers appeared, I feel energized all the time. Sparks dance along my hands and wrists at the thought of the energy. I have shocked Sherry more than once in the past twenty-four hours, but I found that if I think of something else, the sparks go away.

Kittens. Trees. Glass of water. Pop-tarts.

The sparks disappear and I smile at the little control I managed. "See? No recharge needed."

"Fine. I will have them then." Sherry picks one of the pastries up and takes a bite. "I have something else for you," she announces through a mouthful of cherry Pop-tart.

If she tries handing me one of those energy drinks or power bars I am going to run. From the gleam in her eyes I figure it is something more exciting though. I sit up straighter on the couch with interest. Sherry walks away and comes back a moment later with a stack of mail. I deflate when she puts them on the coffee table in front of me.

"Yay?" I try for an enthusiastic response, but it falls flat. The pile looks like a bunch of advertisements and those are my least favorite mail items.

Sherry rolls her eyes and snorts. "Look closer, Jo."

I lean forward and look at the top of the pile where there is a small pamphlet showcasing an upside-down yellow triangle with a red star in the middle.

House of Heroes.

I squeal with excitement and grab the stack of papers. There are four pamphlets, one for each of the Houses, excluding House of Rogues of course. The Rogues don't exactly advertise themselves.

Sherry grins at my excitement and squeals with me. "I'm so excited to work with you."

We never thought I would have powers but always imagined what it would be like. Now our dreams can be realized. We will both be heroes with cool names and outfits fighting monsters and saving the day. I squeal again in delight. I have practically been training to be a hero since Sherry became one and now I can put all my skills and knowledge to use.

I frown as a thought comes to mind. "How did they even know I have powers now?"

Sherry coughs and looks away guiltily.

"Sherry?" I ask slow and accusatory, but I am too excited to put much bite behind it.

Sherry turns back to me with a guilty smile. "I'm sorry for not telling you first. I got excited and reported the Genesis to the Council," she holds up her hands to fend off any arguments and continues, "and technically it is my job, so you can't hold it against me."

So that was why she was gone so long yesterday. I thought she was reporting to the House of Heroes, but she was actually meeting with the Council. I try to maintain my frown but honestly, I don't care that she reported my Genesis. I am just glad to finally join my sister in the business. However, a part of me can't help feeling confused and curious about the power. It appeared with no warning and it helped the wyvern grow stronger rather than incapacitating it.

"I'm going to call mom." Sherry hurries away excitedly to call her parents, leaving me with the House pamphlets.

I sit back in the couch and flip through the papers. House of Discovery's logo is a blue and green lightbulb made of puzzle pieces. I would rather join House of Rogues then House of Discovery, but I flip through the pamphlet anyway. Pictures of smiling scientists in white lab coats with the House logo on them dot the inside. Next to the pictures are quotes of the members gushing about how great their House is and how much they have contributed to society. Bunch of B.S. if you ask me. I know most of the monsters the heroes take down end up in House of Discovery for experiments and testing. I heard they even test their own members to discover the full capabilities and limits of their powers. I shudder. No way do I want to be under that kind of scrutinization.

The next pamphlet has a purple and silver star trophy printed on the front. I smile, already knowing what I would find inside. House of Glamour is home to many well-known individuals. The whole point of the House of Glamour is to get your name out there and gain as many followers as possible. That is where the Instagrammers, movie stars, Youtubers, and the like are. Well, only if they have powers. They host tons of charity functions and there is almost always one of their members at every major event. While I enjoy capturing videos of the heroes, I am not too interested in having my own name and power in the spotlight. Especially since my power seems to do the opposite of helping.

I flip to the last pamphlet but before I can give it a good look, Sherry comes over with her brows drawn down and biting her lip. "You're being summoned to the Council."

I frown at her announcement. Being summoned to the Council is not normal. Usually they let the new people pick which House they want to join without any input from them. The Council's main goal is to police the Houses and members when they get out of line and to occasionally meet with heads of Houses to get updates about the situation in the world then guide the Houses in the right direction. Sherry met with them to report my

Genesis, but they shouldn't need to see me before I have even chosen a House.

"Why?" I put the mail back on the coffee table and stand so I am at eye level with her. "When?"

Sherry sighs. "Right now. They have a car waiting for us."

I grab my tactical backpack and follow her to the door. "They sent a car to pick us up? Who does that? Again, why am I being summoned?"

Sherry has only ever been to the Council once in her six years of being a hero and that was yesterday. She did not even have to go when she first came into her powers. So, why am I different? Maybe it has to do with our frustration over the Heroes' response time. Worry wiggles its way into my body and twists my stomach made only worse by Sherry's answering shrug. Hence her worry, I guess.

"Well, what should I expect?" I don't like going to places without knowledge of what I will be facing.

Sherry turns to me making me stop abruptly or risk running into her. "Don't speak unless spoken to and don't try to run." With that ominous note, she turns to the door and leads us outside where a black SUV sits waiting in the community parking lot.

No one knows the whereabouts of the Council because they always change locations. It is to keep them safe and prevent assassination attempts, but I think they like being a mystery. Technically I shouldn't even know about the

Council, but Sherry tells me everything, so I have known about them for a while. I shift in my seat nervously wondering where I will be meeting them today. Would it be at an office? A community center? Library? When we pull up to an IHOP, I expect the driver to turn around and say 'gotcha!' then move on to the real location. Instead, he pulls into a parking space and sits there silently. I glance at Sherry with a confused frown. Sherry shrugs as if meeting a powerful Council in a pancake house was normal then gets out, holding the door open for me.

I follow her into the IHOP, and a waitress greets us. "Table for two?" the waitress asks and grabs two menus.

Sherry shakes her head. "We're meeting someone."

The waitress' face falls slightly but she hides it by smiling even wider. "Please follow me."

I glance at Sherry wondering how the waitress knows who we are but again, Sherry shrugs as if the whole situation is normal then leans toward me and whispers, "The same thing happened to me when I met them yesterday, except," Sherry looks around, taking in the pictures of pancakes on the tables and happy families enjoying their meals, "we were in a yoga studio, not an IHOP."

The waitress stops in front of a backroom and waves us forward, indicating she would not be going further but we should. I walk into the backroom and glance back at the waitress who continues smiling though it has become forced and her eyes are slightly wide in fright. Well, that is totally reassuring. Not.

There is only one occupied table and it is all the way in the back, as if a whole room to themselves is not private enough. Three sets of eyes look up and pierce me. My breath catches at their intense gazes, and I stumble but latch on to a nearby table before I fall flat on my face. That would be embarrassing to do in front of the Council. Sherry turns to me and concern pulls her brows down though she doesn't make a move to help me. I silently thank her for that.

I make it to the table where the three Council members sit, eyeing me like a bug under a microscope. I shiver at their stares but smile and hold out my hand to them, hoping I can display confidence rather than the nervousness I truly feel.

"Hello, I'm Jo Maski. Nice to meet you." My hand hangs in the air with no reciprocation from the Council. After another few seconds of silence, I clear my throat and slowly pull my hand back. "Ok, then."

Sherry and I sit across from them and I nervously fidget with my fingers while I wait for them to say something.

The Council continues to sit silently, and it starts to irritate me. They are the ones who summoned me here. I know Sherry said not to speak unless spoken to and I kind of already broke that rule but if they didn't say something soon then I would break it again. As if hearing my thoughts, Sherry places her hand on my arm and squeezes slightly. I calm my fidgeting fingers and press my lips together to force myself to stay quiet but when another minute of silence passes, I break.

"What do you guys want with me?" No one had ever called me patient, that was for sure.

The man on my left chuckles drawing my attention to him. He looks to be in his late thirties, maybe early forties. He is wearing a gray trench coat over a suit and has a short beard. His eyes are dark brown, but they shine with mirth. "I was wondering when you would ask."

"I was starting to think we would be here all morning," another Council member adds.

I turn my attention to her and take in her foreign beauty. She sounds Scandinavian and has straight light blonde hair and the prettiest blue eyes I have ever seen. Her skin is flawless, and I swear a golden light surrounds her, however, when I try to stare at the light directly it disappears, only to reappear when I look elsewhere.

"Wait, so you guys were waiting for me to start this?" I ask in disbelief and glance at Sherry wondering if I understood correctly.

She frowns at the man in the trench coat, just as confused as I am. She seems hesitant to speak but does so anyway. "Why did you call Jo here today? She hasn't chosen a House yet."

The man on my right, across from Sherry answers. "We were intrigued by the story of your Genesis." White hair looks like fluff around his head and the area around his dull colored eyes almost sag. Even his voice sounds old as he is slow to release the words from his mouth.

Sherry sits up straighter at his words, but I can't tell if it is out of respect for the old man or alarm that my Genesis was intriguing to them. She doesn't say anything, though I can tell she struggles between duty and curiosity.

"What was so interesting about it?" I ask warily.

The woman leans forward, and I see the glow around her body from the corner of my eye but once again when I look directly at it, the light disappears. "It is not every day someone comes into a power. Do you know how people obtain powers?"

I open my mouth to answer her but freeze. I do not know actually. I glance at Sherry wondering why she never told me, but she is frowning at the woman which tells me she doesn't know either.

"The House of Mystery discovered that powers come from the portals and whatever is on the Other side. They have a certain…energy. Energy that they were able to link to the Other dimension. I won't bore you with the details," the bearded man on my left informs us.

There is no way I could get bored with what they were saying. I have spent seven years of my life studying the monsters that roam our earth and the heroes that fight them. I have never been able to find out much about the portals or Geneses, so if they are sharing, I am listening. I want to know everything about the portals and powers.

The mystery surrounding them is too enticing. However, the Council continues, not picking up on my interest.

"When portals appear, they explode with energy, infecting those nearby. Some may develop gifts, which is the Genesis, and some may not in which they stay normal," the glowing woman explains.

I nod slowly, letting them know I understand but I am still processing it. If all those who had a Genesis were infected by energy from another dimension, then that means I have encountered that energy recently. The only time I remember seeing a portal was seven years ago right before the car accident. That was when Sherry developed her powers which means she had been infected with interdimensional energy. Yet, I expressed nothing until yesterday. Does that mean a portal was nearby? It makes sense because maybe that is where the wyvern came from.

Something still does not make sense though. If all powers stem from the same place yet no one else had been summoned to the Council when they had their Genesis, then why am I here?

"So…what does that all have to do with me?"

The older man nods as if approving of my question. "There was no portal occurrence yesterday."

Sherry forgoes her duty of staying quiet and blurts out, "Wait, then how did she get powers?"

"That is what we would like to know," the old man says calmly.

"Can you describe your power? And tell us what happened yesterday, but this time," the bearded man says pointing at me, "I want it from your point of view."

25

Chapter 3

I leave the meeting with more questions than answers. I summarized everything that happened yesterday including my Genesis and what it did to the monster, though I hesitated at that part, not wanting to seem even more abnormal than I already am. They still came up with nothing. Thankfully, they did not lock me up or hand me over to the House of Discovery to be tested.

"Well, that was…interesting," Sherry says as the driver drops us off in front of our condo.

I nod but I am still thinking over everything, so I don't respond.

Sherry sighs when we get inside and pulls out her phone. "I never got to finish my call with mom, so I am going to be in my room catching her up," Sherry informs me.

Again, I nod, and as soon as she is gone, I grab my notebook and rush to find a comfy spot on the couch so I can start writing. This notebook holds all my information about powers, portals, and monsters. I turn the lamp on the side table one then quickly find a blank page and jot everything down that the Council told us. I make sure to add a section about the Council since I do not know the next time I will see them again and now that I know what they look like. Only now do I realize they never told me their names, so I add in filler names until I can learn the real ones. I dub the trench coat wearing man Trenchy, the glowing woman as Glowworm, and the old man as Grandpa. Yes, I know, not the best names but they will do for now. I then add their descriptions next to their pseudonyms.

After I write down everything I can remember, I throw my notebook on the coffee table and sit back. I glance at Sherry's bedroom door and wonder how it is going with her mom. Is my adopted mom freaking out about having another daughter with powers? Irma Bennington is not thrilled about Sherry's line of work which she makes known every time she hears on the news about a hero getting hurt or monster attacks occurring again. I cringe at the conversation they must be having about me and I expect a call from Irma later.

Speaking of line of work…

I grin as I jump forward and snatch the brochures up from in front of me, ready to delve into what my future may hold. I really need to figure out a name. Maybe…Blue Lightning Girl. I immediately cringe and shake my head. That is a terrible name! Oh well, I will figure something out. I also need to start sketching outfits. I am a decent artist and tend to draw my own pictures of monsters for my cards, so I am sure I could draft a uniform.

One of the brochures fall as I bring the stack over to my lap. I bend over to grab it and notice it is a brochure for the House of Mystery. I never got a chance to look at it before I left earlier.

Curious about the House, I move it to the top of the pile and look through it. The design of an intricate, circular, green Celtic knot and the House name are the only things on the front. Inside, it is dark and the only line of text in elegant gold handwriting adds a splash of color to it.

"To uncover the darkness, you must shed light upon it," I read out loud. What is that supposed to mean? Is it a quote from one of their Agents? I turn over the brochure looking for more but there is nothing. Well, that is a waste of paper. I toss it on the side table then open the House of Heroes brochure, marveling at the famous heroes displayed on the inside. One day I hope my sister and I end up on their brochure.

Sherry walks out of her room and comes over to stand by me, grimacing as she holds up her phone. "Well, mom is pleased," she says sarcastically.

"She will call me soon?" I ask. Sherry nods and looks apologetic, but I shrug. "It was inevitable."

Sherry glances to the side then frowns. "What's this?" she asks and peers down at the paper on the side table. "To uncover the darkness, you must shed light upon it," she reads. I am about to tell her it is the brochure for the House of Mystery, but she continues, "but the true path will only be revealed under Violet's light." She frowns and looks up at me with confusion. "Who is Violet?"

I sit up quickly and lean over the couch arm to see the brochure. "Say what now?" I ask surprised. There is more in the brochure?

Right there under the lamplight is a dark brochure with two elegantly written lines of text instead of one.

I look up at my sister surprised. "I swear that second part was not there before."

Sherry glances at me curiously then picks up the brochure to study it better. She gasps and I pop up from the couch to stand at her side and examine the House of Mystery's brochure in her hand, wondering what made her react that way. I gasp as well when I see there is now only one line of text inside.

"How is that possible?" Sherry asks, flipping the brochure over to look at the front as if the cover would reveal the answers.

I snatch it from her hands and turn it back over to look inside again. "To uncover the darkness, you must shed light upon it," I reread softly. I glance at the side table and the lamp that sits there. "I wonder…" I mutter then place the brochure back on the side table.

This time Sherry and I both gasp at the same time when a line of text starts to appear on the paper. A second later, the second line about Violet's light lays before us as if it had always been there. The lamp shed light on the dark paper and revealed the hidden message! A jolt of excitement zips through me at the mysterious brochure.

"They really live up to their name, don't they?" Sherry asks in wonder then touches the message on the paper softly, as if it would disappear if she handled it wrong.

The second line of text runs endlessly through my mind as I try to decipher its meaning. Who is Violet and why would her light be the key? Is she a superhero? I sit on the couch and grab my notebook from the coffee table, then flip through it until I come across the list of Heroes I made.

Sherry stands in front of me and reads the notebook upside down as I scan the list. "Maybe she is not part of the House of Heroes," Sherry suggests after I find no match.

I let out a frustrated sigh. "I do not have the list of the members in the other Houses."

Sherry's mouth twists to the side and she holds up her hands looking apologetic. "Don't know what to tell ya."

I look away, feeling bummed that I cannot solve the mystery of the brochure. Sherry sits beside me and pulls out a different pamphlet from the stack on the table then places it in front of me. "It does not matter anyway. It is not like you're joining House of Mystery, you are joining House of Heroes, so cheer up."

I pick up the paper and stare at the upside-down yellow triangle but for some reason it does not bring me the same level of excitement as before.

Sherry's phone rings. She pulls it from her pocket and checks the screen then stands up urgently. Adrenaline makes sparks race down my arms and hover at my fingertips.

"What's wrong?" I ask.

Sherry shakes her head and smiles, trying to show me it is not a big deal. "Nothing much, just another attack. I am being called in."

I frown at the news. "Another attack? This close to the last one?" Two attacks in the same city and within days of each other is not necessarily unheard of, but it is not common either.

She shrugs then races to her room to change into her hero suit. When she comes back out, she grabs her keys but hesitates by the door. "Are you coming?" Her eyes flick down to the energy racing across my hands.

I would be a danger to the mission and the innocents if I went out there. I still do not know how to control my powers and if they went haywire, I could end up helping the monster instead of her. I would be more of a hindrance. She will never say it, but I know she is thinking it.

I shake my head and she nods, accepting my answer. She does not stay to convince me to go with her. Instead, she races out the door and I hear the engine start up almost right away.

Now that I am alone, I frown down at my hands.

Teacups. Bunnies. Pie.

The sparks disappear and I drop my hands to my lap. I wish I knew more about my power or knew who to talk to about it. I would have thought the Council would help but they did not know about it either. Something the older Councilman, Grandpa, said before I left IHOP repeats itself in my mind. *"Such a mystery you are."* Maybe what I need are experts on mystery.

I quickly lean over the arm of the couch and stare down at the double lines of elegant text on the paper under the light. "Violet's light, Violet's light," I repeat over and over, hoping the repetition will jog an idea from my mind.

I need to go to the House of Mystery and talk to someone there. The House of Heroes is in a tower downtown. The House of Glamour is in a giant mansion on a hill. The House of Discovery is at a research lab near the museum. The House of Mystery and House of Rogues are the only ones hidden which is highly inconvenient for me right now. The only clue I might get to the location of the House is from the brochure, yet I cannot figure it out. I slam my fist down on the arm of the couch and sparks shoot out, hitting the lamp and causing it to short circuit. The light dies and only one line of text is now on the paper. I growl at the lamp though it is not the appliance's fault.

"Violet's light, true path," I mutter crossing my arms. It sounds like a riddle and all riddles have more to it than one first suspects. I sit up straighter and smile, finally having an idea. Maybe Violet is not a person.

I jolt from the couch and race for the door. Because it is a condo I live in, it does not take me long to reach my neighbor's home. I pound on his door loudly, hoping he is inside so I do not have to wait until later. After another minute of pounding impatiently my neighbor yanks open the door and scowls at me.

"What do you want!" Then he realizes who I am, and his face smooths out. "Oh, Jo, I didn't know it was you." He looks behind me searching for something. "Everything alright?" He asks, brows knit with concern.

I smile at the older man's concern and nod. "Yup, I just need to borrow your blacklight."

George Cabal moved here from Arizona and brought his blacklight along with him. I remember finding him using it at night once along our walls and when I asked what he was looking for he said his blacklight would reveal scorpions. I tried telling him there weren't any desert scorpions on the east coast, but he waved me off. As far as I know, he still checks for scorpions every night.

He narrows his eyes at my request but when I do not reveal my plans he turns and disappears into his house to search for the light. I bounce on my feet, feeling surer every second that I am on the right track.

When George appears with the light stick that apparently revealed scorpions in Arizona, I grab it and race off, too excited to stay and chat.

"Thank you!" I shout over my shoulder. "I will return it tomorrow."

If he responded I don't hear it. I dart back into my own condo and head for the side table where the brochure and broken light still sit.

"Please work," I whisper as I turn on the blacklight and hold it over the mysterious paper.

My heart races as I wait for something to happen and blue energy zips up and down my arms. I just hope it will not break the light I hold.

My heart nearly stops when an image begins to appear on the inside of the paper. I have to stop myself from jumping in glee and hold the light still when a map forms under the light with a large X marking the location of the House. Well, I hope that is what it is marking. I squeal in delight at my accomplishment.

I pull out my phone and snap a picture of the map then turn off the blacklight. I will keep both close by just in case I need to reveal it again but for now I should be good. I pull up Sherry's number to text her and let her know I figured out the mystery of the second line but stop myself. She is fighting a monster right now. She cannot afford distractions. Instead, I swipe to the picture I took and stare at it.

I am quite familiar with the layout of the city and know just about where everything is located. I took a summer job as a tour guide once then another as an Uber driver. Both jobs helped me get a lay of the land as well as its history. However, looking at the map of the city and the X that marks a spot on it, I draw a blank. I have absolutely no idea where that X is marking. I have never seen anything other than trees in that area before.

Yet another mysterious thing about the House of Mystery. A zing of excitement travels through my body again. I love uncovering mysteries. I am tempted to find my Sherlock Holmes hat but quickly discard that idea. I do not want to show up to the House of Mystery looking like a loon.

I glance at my phone and notice it is late afternoon already. I should wait for Sherry so we can go to the House together but who knows if it will still be open by the time she gets back.

The Houses are not residential. They are mainly used as headquarters for the various branches of this mystical world and have opening and closing hours just like every other business.

I decide to find it on my own and just tell her about it later. I have too many questions and I am too intrigued to wait. Unfortunately, we only have one car and since Sherry took it for her mission, I am stuck with only two options to get there. Either ride public transportation which is barely reliable on the best of days or call an Uber. I will have to wait for either one to arrive, so I go with option number two. I pull out my phone and quickly request an Uber ride from the app. As I wait, I grab my tactical bag and make sure it has everything stocked then shove the brochure and blacklight into it. It is a tight fit, but I make it work.

Soon, I am in a blue Honda CR-V and a guy named John is asking where I need to go. I tell him I will give him directions and just to drive south for now. He gives me a look of suspicion in the rear-view mirror but does as I say. I use the picture of the map on my phone to direct John as close to the X as I can before asking him to pull over. We are just on the outskirts of town along a small stretch of road with only trees and more trees around.

"Are you sure this is where you want to be?" John asks, and glances at the time then compares it to the position of the sun.

I appreciate his concern, but my map shows I am on the right track and the rest is on foot. I nod and shut the door then wave until he pulls away, leaving me on the side of the road. I make sure to pay on the app and give him a great review before turning toward the woods to finish my journey.

The map on my phone says the X is straight ahead. Thankfully, there is still light out so I will not be traipsing through the woods in the dark. I look around for a path but unsurprisingly I cannot find one. I shrug and make my way into the forest. Unfortunately, the map does not give me any landmarks to go off of except the trees, so I have no idea when or if I will find the House's location.

I had John drop me off relatively close so all I had to do was go straight and try not to curve. A small part of me is afraid I will get lost and never find my way out, but I push that part down and keep going. I pull out a compass from my bag to help me stay steady.

After ten minutes I am beginning to lose hope. I know I should have lasted a little longer than ten minutes but again, no one ever called me patient. Growling in frustration I stop for a break and slip my backpack off my shoulders. I grab my water and take a swig from it then pull out the blacklight and brochure. Maybe there is something else on the map that will give me another clue.

I click on the light and hold it over the brochure, looking closely at each part of the paper for something that could point me in the direction of the House. Annoyingly, nothing else jumps out at me. It is still a map of the city with an X marking the spot I am standing in. The House should be right around here.

"Hello?" I call out, breaking the silence of the woods. "House of Mystery? Are you there?" As if I actually expect someone to answer, but it is worth a try.

Aaaand nothing.

I put the map and blacklight away then slip my backpack back over my shoulders, deciding to trudge ahead to try to find the mysterious House for a little longer. As I take the first step, a sound freezes me to the spot. Growling, and not from a frustrated person this time, sounds off to my right. This is the sound of an angry animal and I have just trespassed on its turf. I slowly turn to face the growling animal and see it is a large, white wolf with hackles raised and sharp teeth bared.

"Nice doggy?"

That only seems to make it angrier. The wolf crouches and I fearfully back up a step. Before I can decide whether to run or pull some beef jerky from my bag to give as a peace offering, the wolf launches itself at me and all I can do before it tears me apart is scream.

Chapter 4

"Lola! Here!"

The wolf's weight lifts off me and retreats. I continue laying on my back and wait for my heart to stop racing and limbs to unfreeze before I try to sit up. The wolf had me pinned to the ground, but I did not feel any teeth or claw marks, so I think I am ok. I pat myself down anyway and look over my body.

"Sorry about that. She is suspicious of strangers that shout out the House's name." The woman whose command had saved my life does not smile but mirth shines in her eyes, letting me know she is joking.

I stand up on shaky legs and retreat a step, even though Lola, the scary wolf, is safely hidden away behind the mysterious woman. "Do you have strangers shouting out the House's name often?"

Now the woman smiles. "Not at all." She steps forward and holds out a hand. "I'm Harmony." Harmony has curly, sandy blonde hair tied back and is wearing a blue tank top over black leggings. She looks like she just finished with a workout.

I hesitate, glancing at the wolf to make sure it stays away, then shake her hand. "I'm Jo."

"Well, Jo, what brings you out here?"

As if on cue, blue sparks race up both my arms and back down then around each of my fingers. I hold my hands up as my answer.

Harmony raises an eyebrow and tilts her head. "Hmm, interesting. How about we go inside and talk."

"Inside?" I look around but there is nothing but trees in sight. "Where?"

Harmony reaches into her shirt and brings out a tiny remote on a necklace. She pushes a button and looks up. I follow her gaze to the treetops and my mouth falls open.

The air shimmers and suddenly a large house in the trees pops into existence where there was nothing but leaves and branches before.

"The House of Mystery is in a treehouse?" I exclaim.

I would have walked right past it. That cloaking device was powerful.

She chuckles and leads me over to one of the five trees that is supporting the large house. She taps the tree and part of the bark slides away to reveal a panel. I gape at it as she places her hand on the panel and it scans her handprint. When it confirms her identity, the bark covers the panel again and a whirring noise sounds above us. I look up and watch a platform descend slowly until it is on the ground a few feet from where we are standing.

Harmony kneels beside the wolf and whispers in its ear. The wolf whines then trots off into the woods. Harmony straightens and smiles at my shocked expression. Honestly, she should probably just expect me to have this expression for the rest of the day because I am sure there is more I will be amazed by before I go home.

"Shall we?" Harmony leads me to the platform and makes sure I am securely in the middle before pressing a few buttons on a control bar and lifting us into the air.

"So, how did you find us?" Harmony asks casually as we wait for the platform to bring us to the top.

I snort. "Technically, I didn't find you. You found me."

"True," Harmony slows our ascent and looks at the approaching house as she responds, "but how did you get all the way out here for me to find you?"

I move my backpack to my front and reach in, pulling out the map and showing it to her. "I followed the clues."

"Excellent. You'll fit right in."

Before I can tell her I am only here to ask a few questions, not join the House, the platform jolts to a stop, causing me to stumble. Harmony holds the gate open and sweeps her hand toward the treehouse, grinning like she is showing me the best kept secret in the world. Which she probably is. Who knows? It is the House of Mystery afterall.

I step forward and place one foot on the wooden walkway that extends out over the forest floor and test my weight on it before leaving the platform completely. Not having the same reservations, Harmony steps onto the walkway with confidence and leads me around to the front of the house. I stay as close as I can to the house so I will not fall off the edge as I follow her.

The inside takes my breath away. The whole house is made of dark colored wood and rises high above my head. Throughout the house, as far as I can see, the trunks of the trees break through the floor and extend up out of the roof but somehow the house just exists around them seamlessly. I move to the center of the open living space and turn around, taking everything in. It reminds me of a cabin but a really nice one that people stay in for vacation. There is arts and craft style furniture throughout the room, and I think I see a kitchen down one of the halls. I wish I can explore but I do not think Harmony would appreciate a stranger snooping around her super-secret headquarters.

"Would you like to meet everyone?" Before I can respond, Harmony shouts, causing me to jump. "Come here and meet the new recruit!"

I hold up my hands and start to protest. "I am not here to j—"

Footsteps thunder down one of the halls and soon three people are circling me with different levels of curiosity and excitement.

"Jo, these are some Agents of the House of Mystery. We have fifty-three Agents right now but most of them are scattered throughout the United States," Harmony says. "There are other branches in other countries, but we will not get into that right now."

My eyebrows rise in disbelief. "Fifty-three? That's it?"

"Well, we have a very difficult entrance exam, so to say," one of the newcomers says, though it sounds sarcastic and all four of them laugh.

At my confused head tilt, Harmony points at the brochure I am still holding. "Not many people solve the clues or do not care to try."

I stare down at the paper in awe. I feel thrilled that I am one of the few who figured it out and followed the clues. The other Houses have hundreds of members. I think House of Heroes has the most at seven hundred across the whole United States and its territories. The fact that the House of Mystery only has fifty-three who could solve and follow the clues says something. It says Jo is a big smarty pants. I feel like doing a happy dance.

"That and some of the ones who figure it out and make it here decide to go join a different House in the end," a girl with blue and green hair says.

My happy dance urge fizzles and guilt makes my shoulders slump. That is exactly what I plan on doing. I wonder how many made it to this spot then decided to go somewhere else.

"Anyway, these three help me run this House," Harmony says and gestures to the three Agents, bringing us back to the introductions.

The blue-green haired girl holds out her hand. "You can call me Astra."

I shake her hand.

The guy next to her snorts. "More like Sleeping Beauty."

Astra frowns at him and punches him in the arm then turns back to me with an innocent smile. "I can astral project but unfortunately when I do, my physical body slips into a sleep-like state."

"Yeah, she even snores," the other guy near Harmony says laughingly.

Astra's cheeks redden and she looks like she is about to murder her colleagues. Harmony bites her lip to keep from laughing.

"That sounds…cool." I don't know what else to say. I am not too familiar with astral projecting, and I am afraid any questions will cause more jokes to be thrown around which may cause Astra to explode with anger.

The guy Astra punched steps forward and flings an arm around my shoulders. He is tall with messy, brown hair that flops across his eyebrows. He is cute and I can tell he is the flirty one of the group by the way he smiles down at me. "You can call me Bone Crusher."

Astra rolls her eyes and folds her arms across her chest. "That is not your alias." She looks at me with an expression that says *can you believe this guy?*

Alias? Oh! Sherry told me about this a few years ago. Members of the various Houses always introduce themselves with their aliases to keep their real identity secret. Though only the Heroes use masks, so I never understood why the other Houses follow the same introduction rule. So, Harmony and Astra are not their real names then.

I want to stick my bottom lip out and pout. They have an alias, but I don't yet. I should introduce myself as…Electrica.

I mentally shake my head. No, never mind. That name is bad. I will think of something else.

The other guy steps away from Harmony and shoves his colleague's arm off my shoulders. "Sorry about them. He is Dynamic Motion and I am Specter."

My eyes widen and now it's my turn to try not to laugh. I turn to look at Dynamic Motion. "Maybe you should stick with Bone Crusher."

He pouts. "No one will let me change it. I was under a lot of pressure and chose the first name that came to mind."

"And you chose Dynamic Motion?" I ask, holding back my giggles.

Harmony and Astra don't even try to hold their laughs. They start laughing so hard that tears pool in their eyes.

Dynamic Motion frowns and starts muttering, "Stupid kinetic energy, stupid name, they do this every time."

When Harmony catches her breath and calms down a bit, she waves in his direction. "We just call him by his real name, but that is up to him whether he wants you to know it yet."

I look at the tall, messy haired member questioningly. His frown disappears as he smiles and shrugs. "Anything is better than Dynamic Motion. Is there any chance you will call me Bone Crusher?" He asks hopefully, waggling his eyebrows.

I chuckle and shake my head. His shoulders deflate. "Oh, alright. I guess since I know your real identity it is only fair you know mine. Call me Jake."

"Now that you have met them do you want to follow me to my office to talk?" Harmony asks, hinting to the others that it is time for them to go away.

Specter, Astra, and Jake wave goodbye and tell me it is nice to meet me before going back to whatever they were doing before I came in. Once they are gone, I follow Harmony to the first door down the hall and step into her office.

The office mimics the feel of the living room with its arts and craft style furniture. The bookcase and desk look to be hand made from the same wood the house is made from. The only personal things that identify it as

Harmony's office is the picture of her and Lola on the desk and the green tie dye tapestry hanging over the window.

"How about you tell me more about why you came here," Harmony prompts as she sits behind her desk.

I take the chair across from her and put my backpack on the floor next to my seat. "I just got my powers yesterday, but something is wrong with them." Harmony stays quiet so I continue. "They came out of nowhere and it seemed to strengthen the monster rather than hurt it."

Harmony raises her eyebrow and leans forward. "Interesting."

"I am hoping the House of Mystery has some answers. The Council did not seem to know how I got this power or why it works this way."

"You spoke to the Council?"

She seems surprised. I don't blame her. Not many people meet the Council. I wonder if she has met them. How long has Harmony been in this business? "The three of them met me in an IHOP this morning."

Harmony blinks and tilts her head. "An IHOP?" Slowly she begins to smile, unable to hide her amusement.

I chuckle and shrug. I guess if I had to change the location of my meetings all the time, I would eventually choose an IHOP too.

Harmony's smile turns into a confused frown. "Wait. You said three?"

I nod slowly, not understanding the confusion.

"I wonder which one did not show up," she mutters to herself. Before I can ask what she means, she shakes her head and smiles brightly. "Well, you have come to the right place. We have many resources here and our Agents across the nation are always reporting new findings. You will fit right in."

Again, I try to tell her I do not want to become a member and that I am only here to get some answers then I am off to the House of Heroes, but she starts moving papers around on her desk and talking once more.

"Astra knows quite a bit about the interdimensional portals so you should start by asking her some questions." Harmony opens a planner in front of her and skims her finger down a page until she finds what she is looking for. "She has a mission tomorrow morning. You can accompany her if you'd like." She looks up, waiting for my answer.

I open my mouth then shut it. I do not know what to say. I am surprised that she is okay with me going on a mission. Isn't that dangerous? I am not even a full member of the House. What if I mess it up? What was the mission even about? Despite all my worries, I can't help the jolt of excitement that runs through me. Here I am, being handed a chance to find answers about my new power and help on a real mission. Even if it is not a Hero mission it still sounds intriguing. I have no idea what the

House of Mystery does, but I can see firsthand tomorrow if I accept.

I grin at Harmony and before I fully comprehend what I am doing, I nod. "Sure, sounds fun."

Harmony closes her planner and sits back in her seat. "Great. I will let her know."

Chapter 5

"Where have you been?"

I stumble back into the door I just came through as my sister tackles me in a hug. The sun had set, but thankfully Harmony drove me home so I would not have to walk out in the forest or along the highway in the dark.

Sherry pulls back and holds me at arm's length, inspecting me from head to toe for injuries. I roll my eyes and shrug her off.

"Stop being so dramatic. I was only gone for a few hours."

"You didn't tell me you were leaving, and you didn't answer your phone! Where have you been?" Sherry puts her hands on her hips. She is still wearing her hero uniform, so her pose makes her look like a stereotypical superhero. Except the frown. The frown kind of ruins it.

As an answer, I pull my backpack around to my front and take out the brochure and blacklight I stashed there after my meeting. I turn the blacklight on and hover it over the inside of the paper, making sure my sister can see the map with the X marking the spot.

Sherry's eyes widen and her hands fall from her hips in shock. "You figured it out?"

I smile smugly. "Yup, and I found where the House is located." I leave out the part about being attacked by a wolf and only finding the House by accident.

Sherry's eyes grow even wider. For a second, I think I am going to have to pick her eyeballs off the floor.

"How did it go? Did they know anything about your power?" Sherry's eyes go back to normal size as she moves toward her room to change.

I follow her, taking my backpack off and throwing it on a table near the door as I go. "The House leader did not know much but she directed me to someone who might. I have to meet with them tomorrow."

Sherry turns slightly to study me. "You aren't thinking of joining them, are you?"

I scoff. "No, of course not. I still want to be a hero."

I try to ignore the memories of the treehouse, the intriguing mysteries the House of Mystery solves, and the cool people I met today. I am not interested in joining them. I just need answers.

Sherry eyes me up and down once more then turns away and starts stripping out of her hero uniform. I turn so my back is to her and ask about her mission.

She sighs, though it sounds muffled. After a couple of seconds of movement and clothing being thrown around, she comes to stand in front of me. "It was only a ghoul."

Ghouls are only level two which means they are super easy to defeat. They are slow and only focus on one thing--consuming human flesh. However, they are green, oozing, and stinky, so they are not fun to go up against.

"Then why do you sound so down?" I ask. I do not think it was the lack of a challenge that caused her sigh.

Sherry shakes her head and looks off to the side with a thoughtful frown. "This has been two attacks in two days and a couple other heroes have been reporting the same in their cities. It could be nothing, but something feels off about it." Sherry shakes her head again, this time to clear it of her thoughts then smiles at me. She hooks an arm around my shoulders and guides me out of her room. "Enough of that. Why don't we eat some dinner then brainstorm superhero names."

I perk up and eagerly let her guide me to the kitchen, grabbing my notebook of all things monsters and superheroes on the way.

An unfamiliar number lights my phone screen. I stare at it, wondering if I should answer it or let it go to voicemail. After another couple of rings, I decide to answer it. If it is a spam caller I can just hang up.

"Hello?"

"Are you ready?"

I frown, not recognizing the voice. "Who is this?"

"It's Astra. I'm right outside your home. Are you ready to go?"

I get up from the couch, the phone pressed to my ear, and open my door. There, in the community parking lot in front of my condo, is a Mini Coupe. Astra waves from the driver's seat.

I hold up a finger. "Give me a minute. I will be right out."

I hang up and rush inside to get ready. I thought I had another couple of hours until I had to meet Astra for the mission. I also thought I would meet her at the treehouse.

"Who was that?" Sherry asks from the couch, a bowl of cereal in her pajama clad lap.

"Astra from the House of Mystery. She's here to pick me up."

Sherry sits up and places the bowl on the coffee table. "Really?" Sherry looks toward the door as if Astra will walk through any moment.

I don't respond. I am too busy trying to find a clean pair of pants and stuff things into my tactical backpack. When I come back into the living room, Sherry is nowhere to be seen. Oh well, she knows where I am going, I can text her that I am leaving once I am in the car. I throw my hair back into a ponytail and head out.

Then I stop short. Sherry has her arms crossed as she talks to Astra through the driver's side window.

So that is where my sister disappeared to.

Hoping that she is not saying anything embarrassing about me, I jog over to the passenger side and settle in.

Astra turns to me with a grin. "I didn't know your sister is Blast."

I glance at Sherry through Astra's window. She does not look like a superhero at the moment. She is still in her pajamas and hasn't brushed her hair yet. I smile at her and wave, signaling it is time for us to leave. Sherry gives a small wave back, but her face looks guarded. I do not know if that means she doesn't like Astra or if she is wary of the mission I am tagging along on.

I turn to Astra as I put on my seatbelt. "Yup, that's my sis. Ready to go?"

Astra waves at Sherry and backs out of the parking space. I wait until we are on the road before I ask Astra about the mission.

"So where are we going? What are we going to have to do? Did Harmony tell you why I was coming along?" Despite my decision to join the House of Heroes I am still interested in what the House of Mystery does. Something about the House keeps drawing me in and this mission is giving me little thrills of excitement. That or it's my newfound power coursing through my body.

Astra gives me an amused half smile then focuses back on the road. "Yes, Harmony told me a bit about why you are coming with me. You got a little problem with your powers? I do not know how I can help but go ahead and ask me anything. We have a two hour drive until we get there so I am at your mercy."

My mouth drops open. Two hours? What kind of mission would take us two hours away? I did not expect to be gone all day. I will have to let Sherry know at some point, but for now, I have a House of Mystery member sitting beside me who will answer any question I have. I decide to worry about the mission later and focus on why I am here to begin with.

"When I met the Council, they told me how people get powers. Can you tell me what you know?"

Astra beams, though she keeps her eyes on the road this time. "I was the one to discover the connection of our powers to the Other world."

My eyes widen. "What? really?"

Astra bobs her head side to side. "Well, me and a member of the House of Discovery. I astral projected and walked through a portal. I couldn't stay in long, but I did some quick tests and came back with the results. We discovered our powers and the Other world have the same energies. It was later that we learned those energies explode out of the portals and infect humans."

What she said lines up with what the Council told me, but that still does not explain how I got powers. "Is there another way to get powers?"

Astra laughs and shakes her head. "Do you mean like radioactive waste or genetic engineering?" she jokes.

"There was no portal nearby when I discovered my powers."

Astra glances at me curiously. "Interesting."

Really? Was that the House of Mystery slogan or something?

"I don't know of any other way to get powers. Can you tell me exactly what happened?"

Astra listened intently through my whole explanation, only interrupting a couple times to ask follow up questions. When I finish, she breathes out slowly. "That is strange." Her head spins around to me until her gaze locks with mine. There is an excited gleam in her eyes, and she pats the steering wheel with enthusiasm. "I do love it when strange things occur."

I grin at her, not at all put off by the childlike glee my strangeness has brought out in her.

"We will have to see if we can test out your abilities today so I can study them and find answers for you."

I slump a bit. I was hoping she would already have answers. Harmony seemed to think she might. I understand why Harmony pointed me in Astra's direction though. It sounds like Astra has experience with the energies of the Other world.

Assuming I will have to wait to get answers about my powers, I decide to learn a little about the House before I leave it to become a hero. "So, what does the House of Mystery do? I never heard much about them."

Astra snorts. "That's because the House of Discovery likes to take credit for our findings."

I tilt my head, wondering what she means.

"We do all the field work and investigations. We write all the findings and have extensive knowledge about how this strange world works. When monsters start terrorizing people, it is us they call to identify what it is."

"The heroes call you guys to identify monsters? How hard can it be? If it walks like a ghoul and acts like a ghoul, it is probably a ghoul."

Astra shakes her head. "They call when it is not obvious. That is where we are going today. Something odd has been happening in the city we are heading to, but no monster has been sighted. It could be normal humans but that is what I will find out. It is our job to investigate and uncover the mystery. Once we know what it is, we can either call in a hero or deal with it ourselves."

My mouth drops open. "You mean we can take out a monster? We don't have to call a hero to do it?"

Astra frowns and looks at me like I said something ridiculous. "We have powers too. The heroes may have the title, but we are just as capable of protecting people. We just don't focus on that. We focus on uncovering the truth."

I nod slowly, absorbing the information she just told me. The Mystery Agents do not hide away in their treehouse and research like I imagined. They actually get out in the world and seek out how our supernatural world works. They strive to understand it and, in this case, knowledge really is power. They look to understand the monsters more than attack them. The more we know about the monsters the better prepared we can be. Maybe one day, the House can help find a way to shut the portals for good.

"Each member of the House takes on a mystery to solve on top of their House work. It can be personal, or it can help the supernatural community as a whole."

That intrigues me. The House gives their Agents a chance to answer their own questions. No wonder Harmony was fine with me accompanying Astra. She considered this part of my training and a way for me to find answers for my own mystery. Too bad I am not sticking around.

"What is your mystery?" I ask.

Astra keeps her eyes focused on the road, but her shoulders slump a little. "I want to know what is on the Other side."

"Of the portals? You have gone through, right? What did you see?"

Astra sighs. "I have been through, but I cannot stay there for more than five minutes. The portals do not stay open long and if my astral projection gets caught there, I will be in a coma for who knows how long." She smiles as she remembers her time on the other side. "What I did see though were thick forests and twinkling lights. Lush grasses and beautiful flowers."

"Did you ever see any monsters or…people?"

Astra shakes her head. "I never saw anyone or anything but like I said, I could never stay there long. It is also impossible to determine where a portal will appear so finding one for me to go through has been difficult."

I laugh softly. "You couldn't have chosen an easy mystery?" I joke.

Astra laughs with me. "I like the challenge. Plus, I am the only one who can do it. We don't want to risk sending in a physical body."

That may be true, but if she got stuck there it would be almost the same as losing her. I wonder what the Other world looks like. She described it briefly, but I want to see it with my own eyes. Maybe I can see pictures or notes when we get back.

If she has any.

I am excited to learn more about her discoveries and research, about *all* their discoveries and research. Sherry had never been that interested in the interdimensional portals or the monsters. That is my hobby and why I am the one with the detailed notebook and trading cards.

Chapter 6

Astra gets out of the car after parking in a public parking garage and grabs a duffle bag from the back seat. I brush my bangs out of my eyes then put my sunglasses and tactical backpack on. I follow her out of the garage with nerves fluttering in my belly. Blue electricity dances down my arms and between each of my fingers. Astra stares at it with a raised eyebrow.

I shrug sheepishly then try to calm my power by thinking of random things.

Potato. Turkey. Apple pie.

Great, now I am hungry. At least the energy stopped.

"What now?" I ask, looking around to take in my surroundings.

There are no tall skyscrapers towering over the people like in my city. There are small shops along the street and fast-food restaurants at the corners. Cute lampposts dot the sidewalks, and the crosswalks are made of cobblestone. Traffic clogs the roads and political signs mark each intersection. It feels like an old-fashioned town within a modern city.

Astra thankfully ignores the show of energy I displayed. "Now we investigate. The reports state many of the odd occurrences originate at a local movie theater." Astra grabs a folder from within the duffle bag and hands it to me.

There are at least ten pictures of women, each one attached to a different statement detailing what they remembered. The youngest looks to be a teenager and the oldest no more than thirty. Each woman was different in size, ethnicity, hair or eye color. It seems the only thing linking them is the movie theater and that they are young.

"What happened to them?" I could read the statements, but it will be faster if Astra tells me a summary instead.

She looks both ways before jaywalking across the street. I rush to follow, keeping an eye on traffic to make sure I don't get hit by a car. Her strides are quick, and I almost have to jog to keep up with her as we walk down the sidewalk.

"Each one of those women were hospitalized with the same symptoms." She stops long enough to point to a line on the first sheet in the folder.

I look down at where she pointed and read the medical record. "High levels of estrogen and dopamine. Fatigue lasting days. Hazy thoughts. What do these mean?" I did not do too well in science in high school, but I do remember that dopamine is the happy chemical.

Astra stops, causing me to stumble into her. I right myself and catch the folder of papers before it flies out of my hands.

"Estrogen can cause lust and dopamine causes happy or positive feelings. The lack of energy and hazy thoughts when the patient is otherwise healthy suggests a monster that can effect people's brain chemicals."

I scrunch my face, not quite believing it is a monster. "A number of other things can cause those symptoms. Why do you think it is a monster?"

"Their statements." Astra looks up and I follow her gaze. The pink and white striped sign over our head says Cinema. The theater is small and only shows four movies at a time. I would have walked right past it if Astra had not stopped. She leads me inside and looks around, searching for an attendant.

I take my sunglasses off and put them in a side pocket of my bag. Lowering my voice so I don't bother the other customers, I ask, "What about the statements?"

Astra holds up a finger, pausing our conversation as she walks up to a manager. She pulls something out of her duffle bag and shows the manager whose eyes widen in recognition. The man nods and waves his hand for us to follow him.

Questions build in my mind, but I squeeze my mouth shut to keep from blurting them out. I am sure I will find out what is going on soon enough. *Patience,* I tell myself.

The manager stops in front of a door and steps aside to let us pass. Once I am in the room, I realize we are in a security office. The room is small, only big enough for a couple of people, so the manager leaves us to our business. Five screens fill one wall in front of me while two computers sit on a desk below them. Astra takes a seat at one of the chairs and starts fiddling with the keyboard. I take the other seat, watching the customers buy their popcorn on two of the screens.

I want popcorn.

Ignoring my hungry stomach, I watch Astra pull up security footage from a few nights ago. Before I can ask, Astra sits back and, pointing to the screen, explains what we are doing. "This is the footage from when the last victim was here, the teenager you see at the top of the pile in the folder."

I glance down at the folder in my hand, but it is not open. It does not matter though. I remember the girl's face.

"She was in critical condition, worse than the others. Her heart almost stopped. Luckily, someone found her in the park nearby."

I gasp. This is not just a case of lust and bone deep fatigue. Someone almost died.

"You asked about the statements. Each girl mentioned seeing a movie here where they met a guy who flirted with them and convinced them to leave with him. Then they don't remember anything else until they woke up in the hospital."

I shake my head slowly. "Were they…were they…" It is difficult to think about what could have happened to them and it is even harder to put it into words.

Astra pats my arm, her face softening as she realizes what I am struggling to say. "No, there were no signs of rape." She turns back to the screen with a frown. "But the one responsible nearly killed someone and who knows, just because there were no cases of deaths or rape does not mean it can't happen."

"You said this is a monster. What if it is just someone who is drugging women?"

Astra tilts her head at the screen. "That is what we are here to determine. But if I am right, we are dealing with an incubus."

My eyes widen and I search the screen for signs of an incubus though I have no idea what I am looking for. An incubus is the opposite of a succubus, less common but still dangerous. They feed off the sexual energy of women. In mythology, they had their way with sleeping women but if what happened to these women was caused by an incubus then it sounds like real incubi get their energy in a different way. I have never heard of a hero going against one or one ever being reported but that does not mean they do not exist. They are on my list of monsters as a level five.

"There." Astra pauses the video and points to a man with his arm around the girl from our file. She writes down a few notes on a notepad that I hadn't noticed was there until now then presses play on the video.

The girl is so smitten she never takes her eyes off him, not even to watch where she is going. He leads her out, no one giving them a second glance. The camera angle shifts with a few clicks and now we are watching them from the outside camera. He leans down and whispers in her ear then kisses her on her mouth. The kiss deepens and hands start roaming. I feel so uncomfortable watching it I have to look away. After another minute I peek through my lashes to see if it is over and notice they have disappeared. "Where did they go?"

Astra clicks a few more times and types something into the computer but sits back with a frustrated grunt. She rewinds the video to just before they left to look for clues. I lean closer and squint my eyes to see better though I doubt it really helps. Not only is the girl smitten but she looks completely dazed now. Not just he-kissed-her-brains-out dazed but more like she is in a confused daze. I notice she is sagging against him and point it out to Astra.

Astra lets out a resigned sigh. "Unfortunately, I was right. It looks to be the work of an incubus."

Since incubi have never been publicly reported and no heroes that I know of have fought one, I have no idea how to deal with this monster. Would silver weaken it? Would a bullet kill it?

"What do we do now?" I ask softly.

Astra jumps up with a grin. I tilt my head with a confused frown. She looks weirdly excited about this situation.

"Now? Now we find the incubus."

I jump to my feet and wave my hands in the air. "How do we do that?" I shout.

Is she crazy? We need to call in a hero to deal with this. We can't let the incubus continue absorbing women's energy.

"I thought our job was just to identify the monster."

Astra gives me a single nod and packs up her notebook. "Right. Now we have to find him, and if we are lucky, we can deal with him without having to involve the House of Heroes."

I gape at her, but she ignores my look and walks us out of the security room with her duffel bag slung over one shoulder. The manager spots us and hurries over, looking around to make sure no one has noticed us. I guess it would be bad for business if people knew a House of Mystery member was investigating a monster at the theater.

"Thanks, we have everything we need," Astra tells the manager when he is within hearing distance.

The manager glances around again then nods and heads to the security room. Probably to see what we were looking at in there. I wait until we are out of the theater to start my barrage of questions.

"We have everything we need? How are we going to find him? How do you kill an incubus?"

Astra leads us to an intersection where a group of people are waiting to cross. She does not answer my questions, but I don't push it. I know she doesn't want to talk about monsters when civilians could overhear us. The light finally turns green and the crowd starts forward. Astra hangs back a second to let them pass before crossing the road behind them.

She leans over and whispers while keeping her eyes on the path before her, "We are going to follow his trail. The last victim was found in the park nearby." She nods her head at something in front of us though the crowd blocks my view. "He should be out hunting today. The pattern is every three days and the teenager was hospitalized three days ago."

My eyes widen. Three days? Shivers race down my arms as I look at every face around me, wondering if the monster is near me. How do we know we will find him here though? His hunting ground is the theater and it is kind of early for anyone to be out right now. I swallow my worries. I have to trust Astra. She knows what she is doing.

We come up to a small park surrounded by trees. Signs display the entrances to hiking trails and a few of the civilians that crossed the street with us make their way to one of them. Over on the left of the park are shouting kids and a playground. Through the trees I can make out a fenced off area that I assume is the dog park.

"What are we hoping to find here?"

Astra leads us through the trees, away from the playground and hiking trails. There are not many people on this side of the park though I can see a couple of joggers taking advantage of the quiet to run in the area.

Astra drops down onto a bench and rifles through her duffle. I sit beside her, tapping my foot impatiently. We do not have time to sit. We must find the incubus. I exhale an amused puff of air through my nose when Astra pulls out a pillow.

She looks up at my laugh and fights a smile. "I know what this must look like, but no I am not just taking a nap in the middle of a park."

I shrug. "Could have fooled me."

Astra shakes her head then situates the pillow and lays back on it. "Astral projecting puts me to sleep."

I remember Jake calling her Sleeping Beauty and her explaining her power yesterday.

"Watch my body. I am going to scout around."

Before I can ask her about scouting and what I am supposed to do while she is gone, she closes her eyes and seemingly falls into a deep sleep. I poke her to make sure she is actually asleep then look around to see if I can see her projection. I see joggers in the distance and a couple of dogs in the nearby dog park but nothing that looks like a ghostly form of Astra. I stand up from the bench and pace, making sure not to wander too far from Astra's physical body. After a few minutes I throw my head back and groan. This waiting around business is boring. I have no idea how long it will take for her to scout around for an incubus, so I pull out my notebook and start writing about the Other world and incubi. I also create a new page to start making a list of Mystery Agents like I did for the Heroes and write down Astra's name and power.

Astra suddenly lets out a loud snore and I have to cover my mouth to stop from laughing. I go sit on the bench, bumping Astra's leg in the process which halts her snoring. I put my notebook away then pull out my trading cards and colored pencils. Time to add a new card. I could be reading the statements of the victims while I wait but what is the fun in that? At least this way I am studying about incubi. Ha! Yeah right.

I write in the stats I made up, except the danger level which is determined by the Council, then pull up a memory of the incubus' face from the surveillance footage and sketch it out on the top part of the card. My skill of sketching faces is not the best. Oh well, I can just use digital art when I get home.

"Is that supposed to be me?"

Startled, my hand jerks toward my body, marking a line across the drawing.

I glare up at the stranger, but my anger quickly turns to shock when I recognize who it is and I gasp. His words finally register, and I let out a little squeak. It's the incubus from the footage. I can't help but notice how gorgeous he is in person. Light brown hair, hazel eyes, a boyish smirk. I think I see a tattoo peeking out from under his shirt sleeve. His hands are in the pockets of his dark jeans and he casually leans against the back of the bench.

Despite the racing of my heart and the fear trying to lock my limbs in place, I glance down at the drawing and snort. "Well, not anymore."

Chapter 7

The incubus chuckles. His smile softens his face and my breath catches at how attractive it makes him. If I had not seen him with that teenager in the video, I would not have suspected him as an incubus. Then again, he is almost mesmerizing. It would be hard not to notice him. Is that part of his charm? Is he actually an average looking guy but his incubus allure is making me see an angel? Turning away from his face so I don't do something stupid like touch it reverently, I put my notebook and ruined trading card away. I briefly glance at my sleeping companion, making sure she is okay and hope the incubus doesn't focus on her.

I slide my hand in one of the side pockets of my backpack and slowly pull out a silver dagger, hiding the movement with my body so the monster does not notice. It is weird calling him a monster when he looks so human, but that's what he is. I have to remember that.

"Nuh, uh, uh," the incubus scolds, gently placing his hand on mine to prevent me from taking the dagger out the rest of the way.

Suddenly his face is right beside my ear. I feel his hot breath against my neck and can't stop the shiver of pleasure it elicits. That is not natural! I should be terrified. Yet, all I want to do is turn my head and see what his lips feel like.

As if hearing my thoughts, the incubus presses his lips against the shell of my ear and trails kisses down to my shoulder. "Stand up for me," the incubus says in a husky voice.

Tingles race down my neck to my chest then to the rest of my body. I do as he says, confused about why I am listening to him, but my body moves on its own.

"Good girl," the incubus says, still beside my ear. He nuzzles my neck and brings his hands up to rub my shoulders. I close my eyes and groan. It feels so good. My mind starts to get hazy. I shake my head to clear it and suddenly remember who is behind me. I quickly step away, dislodging his hands, and spin around to face him. I do my best to glare but he doesn't look concerned. Instead, he smirks and shakes a finger at me playfully.

"You are strong." He *tsks*, taking a step closer. "The ones with powers are always strong."

My mouth drops open and I forget to keep glaring. How does he know I have powers?

My surprise must amuse him because he chuckles again and takes another step.

I raise my hands defensively. "Don't come any closer. I will zap you with a thousand bolts of lightning." My power sparks at my fingertips, a show that hopefully seems like I will follow through on my threat.

The incubus pauses, eyeing my hands warily. His smile falters and a hard glint enters his eye. Feeling confident, I slowly make my way to my backpack to get my silver dagger, making sure to keep him in sight. When I have the dagger in hand, I whip it out and hold it in front of me, point aimed at the monster's chest.

The incubus raises his hands. "Now, now, you don't want to do that. We could have so much fun if you put it down."

I snort. "Fun like ending up in a hospital after you drain all my energy?"

The incubus shrugs like what I said is not a big deal.

I risk a glance at Astra to see if she has woken up yet. I do not know what to do with the monster and I will not be able to hold him here forever. I need Astra. My gaze flits to the emergency button hanging on the side of my backpack. I could call a hero and have them deal with the monster. I look at the incubus to make sure he did not get any closer and see his eyes narrowed on my backpack.

Darn it! He must have seen me look at the button. It is now or never then. Deciding to go for it, I lunge for the backpack.

The incubus springs into action and clasps his hand around my wrist before I can reach it. His other arm snakes around my waist and pulls me away from the bench. Unfortunately, he is holding the hand that has the dagger so I cannot swing the weapon at him. My body warms at his touch, making me want to drop the knife and lean my head against his chest while I sigh in contentment. Shaking my head of the feeling, I let the energy that has been pooling inside me since I fought the wyvern pour out. Blue sparks light up my whole body until I feel like an electrified fence. I push it away so the lightning arcs into the incubus behind me.

The arm drops from around my waist and his hand lets go of my wrist. I spin around with the dagger raised, ready to plunge it into his chest if he tries to grab me again.

I needn't have worried.

The incubus thrashes on the ground groaning in pain. Electricity zips up and down his body with blue light making each part it touches twitch. He starts panting and curls up in a ball. I feel a moment of regret until his pained noises turn into something else.

I frown at what appears to be a noise of enjoyment. His head tilts back, eyes closed, smile euphoric. I step closer to see if I heard it correctly. The incubus moans but it is not one of pain, it is one of pleasure. I step back startled.

"Are you…are you turned on by the electricity?"

The energy stops and the incubus unravels himself. He starts laughing deeply until it fills the whole area. I glance around, wondering if anyone will hear him but there is no one. I can't even see the joggers anymore. He stands up with a grin and stretches. "That was the best! I mean at first it hurt but then…" he closes his eyes and sighs with satisfaction. "I feel like I fed from three humans at once." The incubus looks down and I follow his gaze to the enormous bulge trying to punch its way out of his pants.

My face scrunches in disgust and I quickly look away.

The incubus lets out a throaty chuckle making my insides warm. How is it I can be attracted to and disgusted by him at the same time?

"Even more than that, I feel stronger."

He takes a step forward and runs a finger up my arm, tingles following in its wake, until he cups my face and forces me to look at him.

I hate that his laugh is attractive and that his touch still affects me. I hate even more that I made his allure stronger by zapping him with my lightning. I was able to pull myself away before but now I feel locked in place.

Stupid blue lightning power.

Luckily, my mouth isn't locked. "You're going to get fat if you feed anymore today."

I probably could have said something better to make him let go of me, but that was the first thing that came to mind. It's not like I could have threatened him with my lightning. He probably would have liked that.

The incubus nuzzles my neck then kisses the tip of my nose. Without conscious thought, my lightning zaps him.

My body feels it is in danger and is trying to protect me. Unfortunately, it just encourages the monster. He pushes me against a nearby tree and presses his body against mine.

"Do it again," he pleads.

I scrunch my nose up but he kisses me, making me forget why I was grossed out. The longer he kisses me, the more I forget why I was even trying to get away. When he pulls back my mind is hazy. I blink, vaguely remembering my friend on the bench and a monster I should be aware of, but I can't remember who the monster is. I tilt my head up at him. Man, this guy is gorgeous. I can't look away from his eyes. I want him to kiss me again. I lean forward, urging him to do it.

As if hearing my thoughts, he captures my lips with his and nips at my bottom lip. My mouth parts and his tongue darts out to run over the place he bit to soothe it. I moan and wrap my arms around his neck. My lightning sparks again, jumping between us. He groans and pushes against me harder. I'm going to have bark marks on my skin after this. His hand slides up my shirt to rest on my stomach.

My energy begins to wane. Even though I want to continue kissing and touching, my movements slow. He has to hold me up after a minute, but we don't stop.

Suddenly I am hit with cold air as the guy is ripped away from me. I whimper at the loss of contact and reach out wanting to pull him back. I blink rapidly but my mind is so hazy I can't process what is going on. Someone else is here, facing off against the guy I had been kissing.

"What are you doing here?" the kisser asks with a scathing look.

"You've had your fill," the newcomer growls.

I frown at him. My mind is foggy, but I am pretty sure I have never met him before. He is about the same height as my guy which puts him a few inches over me. He has blond hair in a low fade, stubble around his jaw, and startling blue eyes. The color is vaguely familiar, but I can't pinpoint what it reminds me of. The most interesting part about him is the purple vest. He looks classy and almost as gorgeous as my guy. Where did he come from? I look around as if the answer is hiding somewhere nearby.

"I don't take orders from you here."

That must have been the wrong thing to say, because the newcomer launches himself at my guy and they both fall to the ground in a tangle of limbs.

My guy? When did I start referring to him as that?

I step toward them, ready to stop the fight but vest-guy shouts at me to stay back. I'm not really into strangers telling me what to do but I feel weak and wouldn't be much help anyway. Why are they fighting though?

Vest-guy gets a hit in and I cringe at the crunch it makes. The sound doesn't clear my mind completely, but it helps me gain my senses a bit. After another hit by vest-guy, I suddenly remember why I am here and who he is fighting.

Eww, I kissed the incubus! He manipulated me with his monster voodoo and made me kiss him. I scrub vigorously at my mouth with the tips of my fingers. My skin crawls at the memory of his touch. I look to Astra on the bench, but she is still asleep. How long has it been since she astral projected?

Somehow in my brief look away, the incubus was able to turn the tides and now has vest-guy below him as he tries to pound in his face. I need to help the stranger! I stumble to the dagger I had dropped at some point and lift it with a shaky hand. I have to close my eyes against the wave of dizziness before I can move toward the fighters.

I raise my hand, ready to plunge my dagger into the monster's shoulder just enough to injure, but I don't get a chance. The two become a blur as if everything is sped up. I feel like I am watching a movie in fast forward. The vest guy pushes the incubus away then speeds out from under him and in the blink of an eye, he has the incubus on his knees and double taps his face with two incredibly fast punches. The incubus collapses, not even stirring when vest guy nudges him with a boot. The stranger looks up at me and smirks.

I drop my hand holding the dagger to my side and stare at the newcomer with wide eyes. "Are you a hero?" I don't think I pressed the button. The incubus had prevented me from calling for help.

The stranger snorts. "No."

"Then who are you?"

The stranger's smile drops, a serious and determined expression taking its place. He steps toward me with an outstretched hand. My heart beats faster. In fear? Anticipation? I can't tell.

Before he can reach me, a noise from the bench draws our attention. I look over and see Astra waking.

"Come on, you can tell both—" I stop when I see he is gone and spin around. Where did he go?

"Jo?" Astra asks, looking around and finding me by the tree a few feet away. Then she spots the incubus on the ground. Her brow rises. "What happened here?"

I take one more look around to see if the stranger is still nearby, but I can't find him. I sigh. I start to walk over to the bench but make a little detour to the incubus. Without another thought, I raise my foot and kick the monster between the legs in his manly bits. He doesn't move but that will definitely hurt when he wakes up.

I walk over to the bench and plop down, still feeling weak and exhausted. My head lolls and it takes every shred of energy I have left to stay awake now that adrenaline is not doing the job.

I wave my hand in the direction of the incubus. "He showed up after you fell asleep."

Astra silently studies me, taking in my half-closed eyes and droopy arms. I don't want her interrogation right now. I just want to get to the car and sleep until we get home. Honestly, I don't need a car, I am willing to grab Astra's pillow and simply take a nap on the bench.

"He got to you, didn't he?" Astra asks.

I don't try to disagree. She is too observant for that. I bob my head, the motion making me a bit dizzy.

"Try to stay conscious for a few more minutes, I will check your vitals after the incubus is dealt with." Astra pulls out her phone and dials a number. I watch her through half-lidded eyes talk to someone on the other end then hang up and dig through her duffle bag. She stuffs the pillow back in and I almost whine. In a few minutes it won't matter anyway, I will be passed out with or without that pillow.

A cloud of black vapors appears next to Astra. Startled, I squeak and almost fall off the bench. My lightning sparks across my body and the only thing that keeps it from jumping to the black cloud is Astra holding her arms out toward the vapors and smiling. She looks as if she is about to give the shadowy smoke a hug. The dark vapors disappear and in its place is a woman dressed all in black. Black skirt over black leggings, black boots, and even black lipstick. Around her neck is a feather of what I assume is a crow or a raven. The only color she expresses is her bright red hair.

"Raven! Long time no see!" Astra envelops the woman in a hug which is returned with the same level of enthusiasm, if not more.

When they pull back, they do not go far. Raven holds on to Astra's shoulders while Astra reaches up to hold Raven's hands. They stare at each other with soft smiles, getting lost in each other's eyes and shared memories. I would have left them to their moment if I wasn't about to pass out or if there was no incubus a few feet away. I clear my throat causing Astra to jump.

She turns to me, dislodging Raven's hold. Her cheeks begin to redden, and she tucks a blue strand of hair behind her ear. "Oh, right. Raven, this is Jo. Jo, this is Raven from House of Discovery. She discovered the energies in the Other world with me."

My brows rise in surprise. I remember Astra saying she worked with a Discovery member on the portals. However, I imagined all members of the Discovery House to be uptight, lab coat wearing, know-it-alls or mad scientists. Not a beautiful goth woman who may or may not be more than my mentor's research partner.

Raven leans around Astra and waves though once she sees me her smile is replaced with concern. Her eyes land on the monster, finally seeing him on the ground. With lips pursed, she pushes her shoulders back and marches to him, pulling out a pair of electrified monster cuffs.

"What are you going to do with him?" I ask, slurring my words. It took way too much energy to get them to pass my lips.

"I'm gonna take him back to the House of Discovery," Raven answers, surprising me once again with a southern accent.

I want to ask her what the House will do with him, but Raven gives one last longing look at Astra then disappears with the incubus in a cloud of black smoke.

My head lolls backward and I barely hear Astra talking to me. I can't keep my eyes open any longer now that I know the danger is gone. Astra will just have to carry me or call Raven back to teleport us home.

Chapter 8

"Why don't you just pour water on her face?"

I hear a loud *thwack* followed by a pained curse.

"What?" the voice shouts. "I thought you wanted to ask her questions."

"Her energy was sucked out by an incubus, I think I can wait for her to wake up on her own," another voice whispers angrily. It sounds like Astra.

Who is she talking to?

Where are we?

That question brings me fully awake, my heart beating faster and adrenaline readying me for a fight. My eyes pop open and I stare up at the two arguing people hovering over me. One is Astra and the other is Jake. They do not see me yet, too busy glaring at each other, so I take in my surroundings before my heart beats out of my chest and runs away. Wooden walls surround a tree trunk in the middle of the room. The furniture is made from various parts of a tree except the couch that I am laying on which is faux leather. My backpack rests in the chair across from me.

I guess I slept the whole way back. Did Astra carry me to the treehouse? That must have been awkward.

I try to sit up but flop back down when I lose my energy halfway there. Astra and Jake quit their glaring contest and look down at me with concern.

"You're awake!"

Jake snorts. "We can see that. No need to point out the obvious."

Astra raises her hand to slap Jake again, but he dances back to get out of reach.

"Yeah, I thought I should join the conversation before Jake pours water on me." My voice comes out slow and groggy.

Stupid incubus.

Jake shrugs and flashes me a flirty grin. "Wouldn't be the first time I've done it."

I blink at him, wondering if I should ask about his past experiences with pouring water on people or let it go for now. Astra makes the decision for me.

"How are you feeling?" she asks, leaning over the couch to give me a concerned once-over. She looks up and scowls at Jake. "Don't just stand there. Get her some water."

I lift my hand to tell Jake he doesn't have to, but I drop it before I say anything. My throat is parched, and I don't have the energy to get up yet to get it myself. Jake rushes from the room in the direction of the kitchen.

"Do you have something against your coworker?" I ask once Jake is gone.

"What do you mean?" Astra asks with a smile as if she had not just abused and scowled at Jake.

Ever since I met them, Jake has poked at Astra and Astra has responded with physical contact or harsh tones. Jake laughs it off, but I wonder if they have a rivalry or something. "Just that you seem to scold him a lot."

Astra shakes her head and waves away my words. "Jake and I have known each other a long time. We're fine."

I wasn't sure if that answered my question, but I let it go. I struggle to sit up, this time with slower movements and gripping the back of the couch for support. Astra puts her hand on my back to push me up. Once I am in a sitting position, Astra makes her way around the couch and sits at the end where my head used to be. Jake comes back with a water bottle and hands it over before plopping down on the other side of me. Now I am trapped in between the two Agents.

"Can you tell us what happened while I was, um…" Astra glances at Jake uncomfortably.

"Sleeping on the job again?" Jake jokes though a note of worry enters his voice and his smile does not quite reach his eyes.

I look at each of them wondering if Astra is going to smack him or if Jake is going to harass her about the way she uses her gift. Neither of them says anything. Jake's brows are furrowed, and Astra is looking down at her shirt to avoid our eyes. I take a sip of water to clear my throat then try to answer their question with a clear voice rather than a weak, groggy one.

"The incubus showed up and started talking to me. His voice drew me in, but I could resist him by reminding myself that he was a monster and keeping my distance. It wasn't until I blasted him with my lightning that his power grew, and I was a slave to his voodoo."

Jake pushes air through his nose in a snort of laughter at my use of the word voodoo but his amusement quickly fades.

"Your lightning made him stronger?" Jake asks in disbelief.

Guilt pierces my heart at what I did. A supercharged incubus who can seduce women with his monster voodoo would have been extremely dangerous. If he had gotten away, he would have been able to do anything and get away with it with just one heated look and one flirty whisper. And it would have been all my fault. I don't know what I would have done if that blond guy with the handsome vest didn't show up. Who is he? He scoffed when I suggested he was a hero. Is he in one of the other Houses? For some reason, I keep quiet about my savior.

Astra and Jake share a surprised look. Guilt worms further into my chest until I am hunched. "It did that with a wyvern a couple days ago too." I straighten and turn to Astra. "That's why I want to figure this power out. I can't become a hero until I know that I will help people rather than put them in danger."

This is the first time I admit to the Mystery Agents that I want to be a hero. It is also the first time I admit that I can't be a hero yet, implying I will be hanging around for a bit. Has anyone ever switched Houses? I hope it is possible because as of right now I am joining the House of Mystery. Only until I solve my personal mystery then I will join my sister in the House of Heroes. Despite knowing I will only be here a short while, a burst of excitement races through me, causing sparks to race over my skin.

Jake and Astra lean away. I quickly pull my hands to my chest and hunch my shoulders sheepishly. "Sorry." With just a few thoughts I calm my power and the energy disappears. I wait for them to kick me out or report me to the Council.

"Welcome to House of Mystery! You will definitely fit in here," Astra says after a moment, shocking me.

"We will help however we can," Jake adds. He slings an arm around my shoulders and pulls me in for a side hug. "It's not like any of us haven't had trouble with our powers before."

"You mean you have super charged a monster too?" I joke, feeling lighter now that I know they don't hate me.

Jake tilts his head. "Well, no, but Astra over there used to fall asleep in the middle of a task, and accidentally astral projected."

Astra smacks Jake's arm off my shoulders. "Yeah, well, Jake fell off the edge of the treehouse and almost destroyed the place. He absorbed the energy as he fell, and it blasted out of him when he hit the ground."

Jake sits forward to glare around me at Astra. "Well, it was that or become a pancake for Lola to eat off the ground."

Astra and Jake chuckle at the memories and I can't help but smile. They have an interesting dynamic. Almost like siblings.

Siblings! Sherry!

I lunge for my backpack on the chair, and nearly fall from dizziness. Astra and Jake both reach for me at the same time and help steady me. I flash them a grateful smile then rifle through my bag until I grasp my phone.

There are two messages from my sister. I open the conversation on the message app and read them. One is her asking how things are going. I check the time stamp on the message then the time at the top of my phone. She asked that four hours ago. The second text she sent was to let me know she was being called on another mission and would be back soon. That was an hour ago. I frown at the phone, rereading her last message. Another monster in our city? Why are there so many suddenly? And where are all the other heroes? Why is my sister the one being called for all of them?

"Everything alright?" Astra asks.

I look up and share my concern with them. "My sister has been getting summoned for missions a lot this week. It doesn't seem normal."

Jake shrugs. "She is a hero, isn't she?"

I nod but look back at my phone with concern still etched on my face. I shrug a shoulder. "Yeah, but it just seems like there are more monsters than usual." It feels like something is wrong or different.

Astra pats my shoulder. "It is not too abnormal. It happens. Depending on where portals show up."

I nod and shake off the feeling. "You're right." I send a quick text letting Sherry know I am back in town then tuck the phone into a side pocket of my pack. "Anyway," I put on a smile to hide my lingering worry, "want to show me the ropes?"

I should know what to do now that I have decided to work for the House of Mystery and worrying about monsters or my sister will not help me do my job. It will also not help me find out about these strange, unhelpful powers.

Astra grins and jumps up from the couch. "Great idea. It will be a day or two until your full energy returns so we can start you on research and case files."

"So, you're putting me on desk duty?" I ask, trying to hide my disappointment. I want to be out in the field.

Astra gives me a sympathetic look as she nods. "Yeah, sorry." Then she claps her hands and spins around, heading off toward Harmony's office. "Well, let's get your forms."

Jake jumps up to follow but takes a moment to help me stand. I lean against him as we head to Harmony's office. I expect to see the head of the House sitting at her desk but there is no one there when Astra throws open the door and marches in.

My confusion must be obvious because Jake chuckles as he waves a hand toward the desk and explains, "Harmony is almost never here. She is either with Lola, working a case, recruiting new members, or visiting the other Houses."

I must have been lucky then to run into Harmony when I was searching for this place. If I had never come looking that day or been attacked by Lola then I may never have joined the House. Fate or coincidence?

"Where are they? I know Harmony put some aside." Astra rifles through a desk drawer, taking papers out then stuffing them back in when she doesn't find what she is looking for. She looks up and smiles. "Harmony knew you would join."

I frown at her comment. How could Harmony have known? I decided only a few minutes ago. "Does she have a clairvoyant ability?"

Astra shakes her head but doesn't look at me, already busy rummaging through another drawer. "She communicates with animals and can sometimes use their senses as her own, but no clairvoyance."

That still does not explain how she knew but I just chalk it up to hopeful thinking rather than true knowledge.

"Yes! I found them!" Astra holds up two pieces of paper triumphantly.

Jakes guides me over to the chair and Astra places the papers in front of me with a pen. They stare at me expectantly, but I hesitate.

Is this really what I want to do? As soon as I sign these papers, I will be a member of the House of Mystery. Will it be difficult to transfer later? Sherry is going to be upset. We always dreamed of being heroes together, with uniforms and cool names. Well, I can at least have a cool name and my place here is only temporary so the uniform will come later.

I sign the papers before I change my mind. Astra takes them from me when I finish and hands me an ID card. I turn it over but other than a Celtic circle at the top, it is blank on both sides. I look up at her with a raised brow.

"We can add your picture to it later but carry it with you always. You will need it to get into certain places."

I remember her flashing a badge to the theater manager to get access to the security tapes. This badge could probably get me into the Mayor's office. Better make sure it stays hidden. If a Rogue got their hand on it, that could spell trouble. I nod and stuff it into my pocket, telling myself to find a better spot for it in my backpack later.

Astra places the signed papers in the drawer she found them in then moves around the desk until she is standing beside me. "Now, I would give you a tour and show you to the desk you will work at for the rest of this week, but you look like you are about to pass out again. Let me take you home and Jake will pick you up tomorrow for your first official day of work. Sound good?"

"I will?" Jake asks from behind my chair.

Astra ignores him.

I want to argue that I am fine and can work today, or that I will be ready for a real mission tomorrow, but she does not seem open to disagreement. Instead, I nod and use the chair arms to support me as I stand.

Astra and Jake hover near me ready to catch me if I fall but thankfully it is not needed. I hope Harmony is here tomorrow so I can try to convince her to give me a real mission. I also want to ask her about all the monster appearances. Is the House of Rogues behind it or are there more portals opening up nearby? I will not find out anything today though, so I walk back to the living room where my backpack sits on the chair and toss it over my shoulders, indicating I am ready to go home.

Astra whispers something to Jake who purses his lips and nods. I don't think I have ever seen him so serious, but I have only known him a day, so I do not have much to go off of. He gives me a wink and a wave goodbye then heads off down one of the halls, disappearing from view a minute later once he rounds a corner.

Astra grabs a jacket from a hook near the door and waves at me to follow her out of the treehouse. She doesn't say anything about what she was saying to Jake and I don't ask.

"Eat lots of food when you get home. Food is a great way to gain energy back. That and sleep," Astra suggests once we are descending on the platform.

She sounds like my sister and I resist an eye roll. I don't know what it is with them thinking food will fix everything. However, I can get behind the sleep suggestion. I am going to dive into my bed when I get home.

Astra leads me out of the forest to a small parking area near the road where her Mini Coupe sits beside a blue Jeep. At my look, Astra points to the Jeep with her key. "Jake's. He will pick you up tomorrow morning," she reminds me.

When I am in her car and all buckled up, I sigh and lean my head back against the headrest, ready to take a nap right here. Something moves in my peripheral vision, and I jerk my head around to see what it is. It better not be a bear. If there are bears *and* wolves out here, I will have to talk to Harmony about relocating our headquarters.

I see a flash of familiar blond hair then piercing blue eyes meet mine from behind a tree. I startle and sit forward until my face is pressed against the passenger window.

Is that…?

The driver side door opens, and I turn to see Astra settling into the car as she starts the engine. I turn back to the woods and open my mouth to tell Astra that someone is watching us, but the figure is gone. I am surprised even though I shouldn't be. He has super speed, so it is possible for him to disappear in a blink. Though I can't help but wonder if I imagined seeing my savior. We are two hours away from where the incubus attacked me, and this place is supposed to be secret. I shake my head. Great, now I am seeing things. Maybe I need food and sleep more than I thought.

"Ready?" Astra asks.

I nod, deciding not to tell her of the apparition. I look toward the trees one last time as she pulls out of the parking space, but he is not there.

Despite not seeing anyone, I feel like there are eyes watching me, making me shiver.

Chapter 9

After Astra dropped me off, I ate a Pop-tart then fell asleep on the couch while waiting for my sister to get home. Nearly three hours later, the slamming of the front door wakes me up in time to see her weariness.

My sister looks exhausted. Her shoulders are slumped, movement slow, and her uniform is covered in dirt. I assess her for injuries but thankfully I do not see any.

"What happened?" I ask, successfully sitting up without toppling backwards. Yay, energy! I would not be running around any time soon, but I feel stronger and more awake than earlier.

Sherry doesn't bother going to her room to change. She comes over and plops down at the end of the couch, forcing me to yank my feet back before she sits on them.

"Gnomes. Hundreds of gnomes." Sherry closes her eyes and shudders.

I bark out laugh. "Gnomes?"

Sherry shoots me a withering look and I bite my lip to keep from smiling.

"*Evil* gnomes," she says drawing out the first word to make sure I understood they were not normal gnomes.

"Aren't they, like…" I look up at the ceiling for the answer and once I remember I look back at my sister, "…a level one monster?" I can stop the smile, but I can't hide the humor in my voice.

Sherry frowns at my tone and huffs. "Not if hundreds of them team up and start destroying houses."

My eyes widen at the image in my head of hundreds of little, one foot tall, men with pointed hats and long beards hacking at the base of a house with their miniature tools. It seems impossible. I frown, wondering how they succeeded in destroying a house.

"I know what you're thinking but these are no garden gnomes. They are like little goblins. They are fishes of earth."

"Fishes of earth?"

"They swim through the earth and if hundreds do that underneath houses, they can knock a house off its foundation, or worse, cause a sinkhole." Sherry's voice rises with each word until the last of her sentence is said in a high-pitched voice projecting all the stress she had been feeling for hours.

I reach over and place my hands on her shoulders, pushing down until she calms. Sherry takes a deep breath and gives me a nod, letting me know she is okay now. I remove my hands slowly, waiting for her to freak out again so I can put them back on her shoulders. When she doesn't move or speak, I lay my hands in my lap and nudge my sister with my shoulder.

"So, how did you stop them? Didn't you have help?" I frown, annoyed she has been on three missions in just a week. "And why are you always the one being called for missions these days?"

Sherry bites her lip and looks away. I narrow my eyes, realizing she is hiding something.

"Spit it out."

Sherry's shoulders slump and she turns to me hesitantly. "Ok, don't freak out, but apparently heroes are disappearing."

My brows shoot up at the news. "What do you mean they are disappearing?"

"Some of the heroes have not reported to the House or local headquarters and their whereabouts are unknown. I have been getting called in more because the heroes are being stretched thin as they have to make up for the lost numbers in other cities. There used to be about ten of us in this city plus any heroes that were here to visit the House of Heroes but now there are only five."

I gasp and picture heroes turning up dead in a ditch or mauled by a monster in the woods. My protective instincts flare up and I would like to lock my sister in our house and refuse to let her put herself in danger.

However, I know she is one of the few heroes left in the city and it is her job to help innocents and fight monsters.

I shoot my sister a determined, no-nonsense frown. "You better let me know where you are at all times and always take a partner. Better yet, we will order a tracker and sew it into your uniform so I can track you."

Sherry raises a brow at that, giving me an *oh really?* look. I grab my phone and start researching trackers and the best place to get one. Sherry snorts out a laugh and grabs the phone from me.

"You're not going to put a tracker on me. Calm down."

I reach for my phone as I grumble, "Says the person who just admitted to heroes mysteriously disappearing. All the while monsters are attacking more frequently."

Sherry sighs and leans her head back against the couch. I manage to grab my phone back while she is distracted but I don't try to research trackers right now. My sister needs water and food. I slowly get up from the couch, testing my legs to make sure I have enough energy to wander around, then go to the kitchen. When I come back with a glass of water and leftover spaghetti from the fridge, my sister is gone. I place the food and drink on the coffee table then wander to her bedroom, assuming she went in there to change.

I knock softly on her door and she calls back that she will be just a moment. I go back to the couch to wait for her, trying to figure out the best way to tell her I joined the House of Mystery. She is not going to be happy about it. I manage to eat a couple bites of her spaghetti before she finally emerges from her room in her pajamas. I decide it would be best just to blurt it out and get it over with. The longer I delay the more likely I won't admit it tonight.

"So, about the Houses—" I start but am interrupted.

"I don't think you should join the House of Heroes."

I gape at my sister. A pang of hurt squeezes my chest. I was about to tell her I wasn't going to join the Heroes but to hear her say she doesn't want me to…

"You...what?"

Sherry frowns sadly and presses her lips into a thin line. She comes over and sits beside me on the couch, ignoring the food on the table. "I don't think it is safe right now."

The hurt eases as I realize she *does* want me to join but not right now because heroes are disappearing. She is trying to keep me safe. In a way, I joined the House of Mystery for the same reason…to keep others safe.

I chuckle. Sherry leans back startled and searches my face in confusion.

"I was actually just about to tell you that I joined the House of Mystery today."

Now it is her turn to look hurt.

I rush to explain. "I think it is a good idea to figure out these powers before I try fighting monsters as a hero." I describe my encounter with the incubus today and remind her of the wyvern.

In the end she nods with understanding though she seems reluctant to agree.

I hug my sister and whisper into her hair, "Don't worry, we will figure all this out, then we can be heroes together."

I feel her nod against me and we pull back, both of us trying to contain tears. Sherry sniffles and finally looks at the spaghetti. "Is that for me?"

"Yeah, I figure you need a refuel after those pesky gnomes," I say in a mocking tone.

"There were hundreds of them!" Sherry exclaims sending us both into fits of giggles.

Jake is at my door at 7:30am sharp. I am glad he texted me last night to let me know he would be this early, so I could be prepared this time, unlike when Astra showed up unexpectedly yesterday morning and I was forced to rush around. My sister opens the door, already dressed for the day and Jake immediately starts flirting. I roll my eyes and grab my backpack, making sure it has everything I could possibly need then push Jake out of our doorway, away from my sister.

"Hey, if you wanted to have your hands all over me all you had to do was ask."

I ignore his comment and turn to wave to Sherry. She gives me an amused smile and waves before shutting the door. I turn back with a glare aimed at Jake and point at him threateningly. "No flirting with Sherry."

"Aww, are you jealous?" Jake grins and leads me to his Jeep.

I snort. "You wish."

He chuckles but does not say more about it. Not even a promise to leave my sister alone. I will have to keep an eye on him when he is around Sherry.

"Thanks for giving me a ride," I say once we are on the road. "I probably could have taken my sister's car, but she needs it more than me right now. Especially now."

Jake glances at me briefly before focusing on the road again. "She was part of that mission yesterday with the gnomes, right?"

I gape at him. "Yes! How did you know about that?"

Jake grimaces and shakes his head. "Gnomes are nasty buggers." He shudders and I have to wonder if my imagination of gnomes really is too gentle compared to the real thing. "My mission for the House right now is to track the cases of monsters in the city and try to figure out where they are coming from, so I usually get a detailed report about each sighting and fight."

His words make relief flood my body causing my shoulders to sag as a weight of worry I hadn't realized was there disappears. I am happy to know that someone is trying to figure out the cause of the increase in monsters. I guess it makes sense that it would be the House of Mystery to solve it.

When Jake pulls into the hidden forest parking lot, I immediately look for the mysterious blond guy in a vest. Of course, I find no one.

"What are you looking at?" Jake asks next to my ear.

I scream and jump away causing the flirt to laugh. He steps forward and slings an arm around my shoulders, guiding me to the treehouse. I shrug him off but let him lead me. I have been here twice now. The first time I found it accidentally and the second time I was unconscious so I think I would get lost if left to find the place on my own. Hopefully, I will get used to the path soon.

I am too busy looking up trying to spot the house that I don't see the wolf until low growls catch my attention. I snap my head around and spot Lola only a couple feet away. My heart pounds, wanting me to run but my eyes stay locked on the wolf's. Bad idea I realize as my gaze only causes the wolf to growl deeper and step closer. Lola looks like she wants to tear my head off. Does her presence mean Harmony is nearby? I look around for the animal whisperer, but she is nowhere to be seen.

"Jake," I call out nervously taking a couple steps in his direction. Blue energy zips up and down my arms in anticipation of a fight. I wonder what it would do to a normal animal rather than a monster.

Jake glances at the wolf then me and shrugs. "What?"

I nod to the wolf and widen my eyes at Jake, silently telling him to do something. He chuckles but gives a soft whistle which must be a signal because Lola gives me one last growl then trots off into the woods.

"She's harmless, now c'mon, let's get you settled for your first day."

I huff at his nonchalance. "Yeah, harmless." Not.

The tree house is not much farther and soon we are riding up on the platform and sidling along the edge of the tree house until we are inside the beautiful, hidden structure. As soon as the door closes Harmony comes out of her office to greet us. She gives me a friendly smile and holds out her hand. "Welcome officially to the House of Mystery."

I shake her hand and look around wondering where the other Agents are. Harmony answers my unspoken question. "The others are out doing their work. But I hear you will be here for the rest of the week recuperating from an incubus attack."

I don't deny her claims since the others had already established I would be on desk duty for the first week doing research. However, after a long night of rest I feel completely fine. I remember Astra saying the other victims took weeks to recover their energy but maybe since he did not finish with me, I took less time to recover. That or it is some other unexplainable thing about my new powers.

"What would you like me to work on?" I ask politely, ready to start uncovering secrets and solving mysteries. I smile at my thoughts. I sound like a Scooby Doo character.

Harmony nods at Jake, dismissing him and tells me to follow her. We go down the opposite hallway from her office, sadly away from the kitchen, to the other side of the House that I have not seen yet.

She points to a door on our left as we pass saying it is the library and the other rooms are various workshops or studies that Agents have free access to.

"Astra said I could look through some of her journals," I say.

Harmony nods and points to the library. "The studies and mission reports are stored in there."

I nod, telling myself I will have to look through the reports sometime. But first, I have House missions I need to do. Harmony shows me into one of the studies and holds out her hand to the chair at one of the desks. "Get settled. I will have Specter bring you some files for you to start working on."

She leaves before I can ask her about Specter. She said everyone is out doing mission stuff so why is he here?

I look around at the tiny room, my new workspace for the next few days, as I make my way to the desk. There aren't any windows and the space is sparsely furnished with only a desk and a small filing cabinet. It is a bit chilly, but I don't think they would appreciate me bringing a space heater into a wooden treehouse. Does this place even have outlets? I bend over and search the bottom of the walls for outlets.

Someone clears their throat making me shriek and jump back. I crash into the filing cabinet nearly tipping it over. Luckily, my reflexes are not completely gone, and I catch it before it falls. When I have it settled back in place, I turn to the person who scared me.

Specter looks back at me with amusement and holds out a stack of files. "Welcome to the House of Mystery."

I take them, avoiding his eyes since I don't want to see his silent laughter at my screaming and stumbling around, and place them on my desk. "What do I need to do?"

Specter moves forward and meets me at the desk, then flips open one of the files. "Most of your job will be to research. Find as much information about each case and write reports to place in the files. When you are done, submit them to Harmony. She will let you know if you need anything else." He moves to the door. "I will be around for a bit today if you need any help. Just call out for me." Then he walks through the door.

I gasp and wait for him to appear again. I wave my hands in front of me, looking for him but make no contact with a body. Specter did not open the door, he literally walked into the door and disappeared. Whether his power is just to walk through walls or something more…spectral, I decide his power is neat but also creepy. No wonder I had been scared. I never heard the door open because it never did. After a few seconds of no reappearance I make my way behind the desk and open the first case file.

For the next few hours, I write notes and visit the library looking for information that could help me with the cases. In some of the cases I must identify monsters based on sightings and damage caused. In some I have to research interdimensional portals of which I make a note to show Astra so she can add my findings to her own case on the subject. In others I read about the origin of powers and investigate whether we can predict what power someone may get when they are infected with the Other energy. From what I have seen so far, a couple of the cases will need field missions for further investigation. I am hoping Harmony will let me do one.

I gather the files I have done so far and leave to give them to Harmony. I don't need to give them to her until I leave for the day, but I need to get up and move around. I feel restless.

Harmony looks up from her computer and a notebook when I knock on her open door. She smiles brightly and sits back, giving me her full attention. I love that about her. She is a busy woman, but makes me feel like I am just as important as her work and other colleagues.

"Hey, I was just thinking about you," she says.

I tilt my head and move forward to hand her the files. "Oh? What for?" Maybe she has more files she needs me to examine.

"I just received an invitation to the House of Glamour's annual Gala."

I do not understand what it has to do with me. My sister mentioned it last year claiming she would rather stay at home than parade in front of rich benefactors. Apparently, the House of Glamour puts on a Gala each year as a sort of meet and greet between the Houses and sponsors. Sponsors donate tons of money which is a big part of how we get paid for our work.

"Oh, neat. Are you planning on going?" I ask politely.

She chuckles and leans forward, grabbing something from her desk and holding it out to me. "Well, I don't have much of a choice, but I am allowed to bring two people from my House and was hoping you would be one. It would be a great way to introduce you to the other Houses."

I take the paper and realize it is an invitation. It is sturdier than I first thought and I can tell it is made of expensive paper. It has the House of Glamour's symbol of a purple and silver star trophy at the top. In the middle of the invitation are words in cursive script stating the date, time, and location of the event.

"You want me to go?" I ask astonished.

"Sure! Why not? It is this weekend so you should be recovered by then." Concern pulls her brows down. "Unless you don't think you will be feeling well by then."

I quickly shake my head. "I am already feeling much better. I will be fine." I hold up the invitation. "Thank you, Harmony, I will be there."

Chapter 10

"The Gala is tomorrow, and I still don't have a dress," I whine to my sister Friday night.

This week had been full of busy work leaving me drained each night. Tonight is no exception. Despite the House arrest I am currently on and the exhaustion I find myself feeling each night, a little part of me is thrilled at investigating and looking for clues even if it is only in case files for the time being. I feel like a true detective. However, all that investigating and tired nights made it so I had no time to search for a dress suitable for a Gala.

Specter is the other person attending which does not surprise me. Over the week I noticed Specter and Harmony were close, maybe even intimately close though they never showed any PDA in the treehouse. They both probably already have everything ready for tomorrow evening, but I am facing the possibility of attending in my prom dress from senior year of high school. Since that was only last year, I know it will still fit, but it is not elegant enough for a Gala.

"Why don't you just wear your—"

"I am not wearing my prom dress," I interrupt.

My sister chuckles then waves her hand toward the door. "Then just go pick something up from town tomorrow."

I grumble and flop back against my seat in the living room. My sister is reading a book in the armchair next to the couch which means her mind is barely comprehending my problem. I sigh long and loud until Sherry finally looks up from her book. She gives me an exasperated eye roll and makes a show of marking her page with a bookmark, closing the book, and laying it down on the coffee table then turning her body toward mine to show me I have her full attention now.

I grin and sit up with nervous excitement. "What should I wear? What should I do? Who do you think will be there?"

I hadn't fully processed I was going and that there would be important people at the Gala until today. Before, it just seemed like a dream.

Sherry tilts her head. "Well, I assume you will wear a dress, and that you will dance and eat food, and probably meet the head of the Houses," she answers all at once.

I gasp. "You think I will have to dance?" I glance down and flit my eyes over the carpet thinking about my new problem as panic begins to rise in my chest.

Sherry chuckles and shakes her head at me. "You will be fine. I am sure you won't have to dance if you don't want to. Just go and have a good time, stop worrying."

I am glad she didn't push the dancing. She knows I am a terrible dancer. That, and it is dangerous. Ever since her cousin's birthday party when I was twelve and almost electrocuted the birthday girl by tripping over a wire and destroying the entire DJ system, I have avoided dancing. Even at prom, I was a wallflower and only participated in the Cha-Cha Slide.

I stick my bottom lip out in a pout. "I wish you were going too."

Sherry snorts and shakes her head. "Even if I was invited, I wouldn't go. Plus, I have you to tell me all about it and it will be like I didn't miss a thing." Sherry reaches for her book, signaling the end of the conversation. "I will take you shopping tomorrow and we can find you a dress."

I nod, accepting the pause in this discussion for now, even though she cannot see it since she is already immersed in her book again. I smile thinking about how tomorrow will go. I have not gone shopping with my sister in a long time.

This is the first time Sherry has gone out without her hero uniform in some time. She is wearing jeans and a pink blouse and has her blonde hair down which frames her golden-brown eyes. She made sure to call off for the afternoon and, despite the hero shortage, the House agreed though they told her to be on call.

I wear jean shorts and a simple spaghetti strap shirt. I decided to wear something easy to change out of since I will probably be trying on dresses for a while. I keep my black hair in a ponytail, though my bangs still brush my face.

"Is there anywhere specific you want to go?" Sherry asks as she pulls into a parking space along the street.

I get out and pay the meter enough for two hours, hoping that is all we need. I itch to bring my backpack but today is supposed to be about shopping, so I leave it in the car. "Nope, I figure we can just wander until I find something suitable."

We walk down the street and enter each shop, even if it does not have any dresses. Window shopping is just as fun as actual shopping in my book. Sherry tries to convince me to wear a dark tie dye dress we find in a Bohemian clothing shop and while it is pretty, I don't feel as if it is me. Eventually, Sherry gets in on the dressing up and we each take turns in the dressing rooms of each shop we stop in. I find myself having fun and my worries are pushed to the back of my mind. No missing heroes. No unhelpful powers. No monster activity. Just two sisters trying on dresses and spending time together.

"Alright, Sherry, tell me what you think of this one. I think this might be the one." I step out of the dressing room and spin, the skirt of the dress twirling around me making me feel like a princess. I giggle and smooth down my skirt when I stop spinning and look up to see what my sister thinks of it.

My smile falls when I don't see anyone waiting for me. Where did she go? I step away from the dressing rooms and stand up on my toes to peer over the displays and racks. Maybe she is in one of the rooms. I turn back to the dressing area and whisper-yell, "Sherry!" but no one responds.

I start to head to my dressing room to get my phone that I stashed in my jeans pocket but a voice behind me makes me freeze.

"It's beautiful."

I whirl around at the unfamiliar male voice and instantly back up a step when I see it is the stranger from the incubus incident...and maybe the forest near the House of Mystery. What is he doing here?

"What?"

The man steps closer and smiles. "The dress. It's beautiful."

My heart skips. His smile totally lights up his face and makes him look gorgeous. Is he an incubus too? He has blond stubble around his jaw and once again his eyes are a familiar blue though I can't pinpoint where I have seen the color before. He is wearing a vest again but this time it is reddish-brown over a white shirt, the sleeves rolled up partway.

"What are you doing here?" I say harshly. My hands spark with blue energy as I ball them into fists. "Are you stalking me?" If he is here to finish what the incubus failed at then he would be in for a surprise. A deadly surprise.

His eyes narrow on my hands then he grins wider, seeming unfazed by the tone of my questions, and looks around at the store. "I didn't realize I wasn't allowed to shop here. It is a store for both men and women, right?"

His gaze lands on me again and his eyes travel the length of me. My body heats under his appraisal, but it isn't an unnatural pull due to monster voodoo. So maybe he isn't an incubus, but he is still a stranger and seems to be following me. The energy on my hands sparks and jumps away from me toward the stranger but does not quite reach him. His gaze comes up to rest on mine. I gasp at the intensity in his eyes. He does not look frightened, rather he seems intrigued and…hungry? The look quickly passes, and I almost believe I imagined it.

He holds up something. "I'm just here to try on some clothes, same as you."

I blink in confusion. I realize then that he has a stack of vests hung over an arm and my cheeks blaze at how I spoke to him. Of course, he can shop here. It isn't unheard of to run into people I know. We run into Sherry's colleagues and friends all the time when we are downtown. I don't know why I was being so harsh and defensive to someone who helped me fight off a monster.

I unclench my fists and will away the energy by thinking of random words.

Pinecone. Pretzel. Dress.

I shift, embarrassed, then wave my hand toward an open dressing room. "Well…carry on then."

He passes me, chuckling, which sends more heat coursing through me. His laugh is deep and makes my heart beat faster. Goodness, what is wrong with me? I barely know the guy.

He stops by my side and leans in. His breath tickles my ear as he whispers, "You should get the dress, Sapphire, it suits you."

My mind momentarily fritzes and I stand there for a moment, with my mouth hanging open and my heart trying to even itself out, before I finally whirl around to tell him that isn't my name, but he is gone.

Darn him and his super speed.

"Jo?"

I sigh with relief at the familiar voice and turn to see my sister with three dresses in her arms standing a few feet away.

"Everything ok? You look a little flushed."

I swallow hard and look down at my feet, trying to mask my confusion and red cheeks. I nod after a second and force a laugh. "Yup, just looking for you." I twirl and smile at my sister, hoping she doesn't read into my expression too much. "What do you think?"

Sherry grins and drops the dresses she was holding in a nearby return cart. "I think that dress is definitely the one. No need to try on more."

I giggle and swish the dress from side to side. She is right, it is definitely the one. My smile falters as the stranger's words come to mind. *You should get the dress, Sapphire, it suits you.* I shake my head. I am getting this dress because my sister and I like it not because he told me to.

"I think so too. Let me change and we can head out." I rush to the dressing room and stare at my reflection in the mirror. The dress is long, sleeveless, and has beaded ribbon around the middle. Strips of fabric hang off the skirt which makes it flowy when I walk or turn. The color is a gorgeous blue almost like…I gasp, realizing he called me Sapphire because of the color of my dress. I smile at my reflection. Sapphire suits it.

I change into my mundane clothes and carefully hang the dress on a hanger then meet my sister at the checkout counter. She has chosen a light pink evening gown with bright jewel-looking beads dotting the skirt making it shine.

"Who says you are the only one allowed to dress up," she says when I raise my brow at her purchase.

I hold up my hands. "I didn't say anything."

"Put them both on my card, please," Sherry tells the cashier.

I reach forward to stop her. "Sherry, no, you don't have to do that." Heroes get paid well but she doesn't need to be spending money on me. She already lets me live in the condo rent free. Sherry holds me back and nods at the cashier to proceed. "Think of it as a gift for joining a House," she tells me.

I purse my lips but stop struggling. She is too stubborn and will not let me stop her anyway and she will never allow me to pay her back. "Fine, but I get will dinner for the rest of the week."

Sherry rolls her eyes and hands me my bag. "You're having dinner at the Gala tonight."

Just like that, all my worries and nerves return.

"Right, I forgot." I fiddle with the bag in my hand.

My sister finishes paying then throws an arm across my shoulders and guides me out of the shop. "Let's go get you ready."

I still have a few hours until I have to be there, but Sherry makes it seem like we will need that much time to get me ready. How hard would it be to put on a dress?

"Food first?" I ask hopefully, eyeing a crepe shop across the street.

Sherry follows my gaze and chuckles. "Sure, I am always down for some crepes. Just don't fill up before you go to the Gala."

We make our way across the street and grab a table after we order. The tables are all outside and the crepe shop is more of a food cart that has taken up residence on a street corner. It has been there for as long as I can remember, and the owner always gives us a discount. He is a huge Blast fan. Sherry does not like to use her hero status to get discounts, but the owner of the crepe cart refuses to let us pay full price so eventually we just accepted it.

Sherry has been a hero for seven years, mostly an apprentice when she was younger, but still full of honor and loyalty. She saw it as her mission to save everyone since she was not able to save my parents. I never blamed her and still don't, but I think she still harbors regret. Hopefully soon, I can be the one to protect her. I just need to figure out this lightning and maybe the monster problem.

"Here you go ladies," the cart owner says as he lays two plates of delicious looking dessert crepes in front of us.

"Thank you!" We say simultaneously then dig into our food.

We eat in comfortable silence for a while. I know when we are done, she will go back to being a hero on duty rather than a sister off work. I will miss this. Thankfully, I have her to myself until the Gala and can enjoy our time together while it lasts.

Chapter 11

Sherry claps her hands over her mouth. "Oh my God! You are gorgeous!" She shouts, though her hands muffle the sound.

I grin and look down at my dress, twisting a bit from side to side so my dress twirls around my ankles. I curled my dark hair and Sherry twisted it up behind me into a stylish bun with a tiny braid on each side looping into the hair. With a touch of mascara, blue eye shadow, and some lip gloss, I was ready.

"I'm so nervous," I admit, rubbing my hands together to rid them of sweat.

Sherry waves at me. "Don't be. You don't have to dance or talk to anyone. Just be yourself and, uh, maybe don't zap anyone."

She turns away before I can figure out if she is referring to my incident at her cousin's birthday party or my unhelpful power.

"Say cheese!" She turns back to me with her phone held up in front of her. A quick click tells me she took a picture. "Alright now let's go before you're late."

I nod and give my backpack a longing look before following Sherry out to her car. I wanted to fit a few weapons and monster repelling items in my purse, but Sherry wouldn't let me. Probably for the best. There would be bag checks and security at the Gala.

I gaze out of the window on the way there as Sherry talks and I instantly know when we are close. Spotlights shine into the sky drawing attention to an event that is too far away to see yet. Traffic begins to back up and more than one limousine passes us. My goodness, they make it seem like this is the Grammys or Oscars. However, I should not expect anything less from the House of Glamour. Half of them are famous movie stars and singers.

"I think I should drop you off here. The traffic will only get worse and the hall where the Gala is being held is only a block away." Sherry pulls over in the first available spot on the side of the road and turns to me. "Will you be okay to get there on your own from here?"

I crane my neck to see over the cars hoping I can spot the hall but there are too many buildings and vehicles in the way. Why hadn't they chosen the mansion where the House is located for their Gala? That would have been easier to find. The spotlights are much closer though so I figure I can use them as a guiding light.

"I think I will be fine." I give my sister a quick hug then get out of the car, waiting until she safely merges back into traffic before making my way toward the lights.

She is right about how close the Gala is from where she drops me off. I don't have to walk long before I come across the large building displaying banners with the House of Glamour's symbol on them—a purple and silver star trophy. A group of photographers crowd one side of the walkway while the other side has valets and a line of cars waiting to drop off their passengers. I duck my head, hoping to get by unnoticed as I skirt along the line of photographers to the entrance. I see a few flashes aimed in my direction, but I ignore them and enter the hall where a security check is set up before guests can proceed to the Gala.

I always get nervous going through security checks. Even if I do not have anything illegal or prohibited in my bags I always imagine being tackled or eyed suspiciously by security.

I place my small purse into a bin and scoot it along the line. A security woman grabs my bin and I tense thinking she will ask me to step to the side even though there is only a phone, lip gloss, wallet, and invitation in the purse. The woman smiles after a quick search then asks me to step through a metal detector. I do as she says then retrieve my purse from the bin on the other side. I let out a breath I had not realized I was holding then make my way inside to the Gala.

I stop beside the door when I enter to take everything in. On the far right is a refreshment table. An orchestra, an actual live orchestra, plays in the corner at the front of the room next to a small stage. People mingle about but leave the middle of the floor open for anyone who wants to dance which no one seems inclined to do. Hanging chandeliers light the room nicely but string lights are also set up along each wall. I look at each of the well-dressed individuals for someone I recognize but I only see strangers.

Someone enters the room behind me, reminding me I am blocking the doorway. I head to the refreshment table and decide to hang there for a bit while I munch nervously on crackers and mini sausages. There is a dinner scheduled a bit later, so I try not to fill up on the appetizers.

"Jo?"

I spin around at my name and find Harmony and Specter. Harmony is wearing a short-sleeved forest green gown with a wolf brooch. Her hair is curled but loose and hanging around her face. Specter is wearing a white tuxedo and a forest green pocket square in his breast pocket. I smile at how adorable they look together.

Harmony returns my smile and steps forward to hug me. "I'm glad you made it! You look gorgeous!"

I blush and give my thanks. Specter nods a greeting to me, and I nod one in return.

"When did you two get here?" I ask them.

Harmony looks around the room as she answers. "A little while ago, we've been mingling." Then she turns back to me, grabs my hand, and starts dragging me away excitedly. I manage to place my plate of appetizers on the table before I am whisked away. Specter follows us at a slower, more relaxed pace. "C'mon, I want to introduce you to some people."

The first is an older man with salt and pepper hair and a thick beard. He has light green eyes that shine with joy when Harmony, Specter, and I approach.

"Ah, how is my favorite House doing?" the man asks with a bright smile.

"Great as always Mr. Hughes," Harmony replies politely. She gestures to me. "This is our newest member." She leans toward me and softly explains, "This is our biggest benefactor for our House."

I make sure to leave out my name just as Harmony did when I greet him. I know House members are supposed to use their pseudonyms when facing the public, but I do not yet have one. "Hello, nice to meet you, I am excited to be working with the House of Mystery."

Mr. Hughes does not seem bothered by my omission of a name and chuckles jovially. "I am excited to see what you and the others discover and solve this year." His smile falls a bit and he looks around to make sure no one can hear us. "Maybe you can figure out what is happening to the heroes and monsters."

I bite my lip, unsure what to say to that and glance at Harmony for guidance. She smiles at Mr. Hughes and nods. "We are already doing what we can. Have a good night, sir."

He waves as Harmony leads us away from him. I wonder how much benefactors are allowed to be involved in the Houses. By the way Harmony led us away and avoided the questions as much as she could, I would guess not much.

Harmony introduces me to more people including each of the other House leaders and some of the other benefactors. I smile, wave, and talk when necessary but I begin to feel exhausted and overwhelmed by all the new faces.

Specter steps in front of Harmony when she tries to lead me to another person. She stops surprised and he nods at the stage. Harmony and I follow his gesture to see someone standing there waiting for everyone to quiet down. The orchestra stops playing and the crowd turns to the woman. I gasp when I see the golden glow outlining the woman in red. It's Glowworm.

"I didn't realize the Council is here," I whisper to Harmony.

She leans closer and whispers, "Not many know who is in the Council. I would bet only a few people here know she is part of it."

My eyes widen at her words. So, most of the attendees don't realize the Council is here tonight? I look around at the other guests wondering who else knows. I assume the House leaders know the identity of the Council, but who else?

"That is Aphrodite to anyone else, a famous Star of the House of Glamour, who has the power to hypnotize people," Harmony continues. "She is the one who puts together the Gala every year."

Not Glowworm then.

This time Specter speaks though he does so without taking his eyes from the stage. "Each member of the Council is associated with one of the Houses, excluding the House of Rogues of course."

Harmony nods at Specter's words and glances around the room searchingly. When she finds what she is looking for she nods her head toward it. I follow her gesture and see Grandpa, the old Council member, standing near the doors that lead to the banquet hall.

"That is Father Time, he is the Agent in charge of our House, and can slow down time." Before I can ask her about him she flicks her wrist to a guy next to him. I almost don't recognize him. His hair is slicked back and instead of a trench coat he is in a form fitting black tuxedo. "And that is Revelation, Researcher of the House of Discovery. He can see the present in visions."

"The present?" I ask, unsure how that is a useful skill.

Specter finally takes his eyes from the stage and looks over at Revelation. "Seeing the present of anything or anyone can be a useful and dangerous power. It means there are no secrets that he cannot discover."

I shiver involuntarily at Specter's tone and the fact that Revelation can peer into my life at any moment should he choose to do so. I wonder if he saw me coming that day I was summoned to meet them. Aphrodite, Father Time, and Revelation. I frown as something occurs to me.

"Who is the fourth Council member?" I only met the three of them, but I remember Harmony saying something about there being four in the treehouse when I first met her. Specter also said each member is associated with a House, so who is the Council member for House of Heroes?

Harmony shifts and looks at the stage uncomfortably. Specter is silent even more so than usual. Their prolonged silence unnerves me.

"Who is it?"

Maybe they are not allowed to tell me?

"Mystico, but he is missing," Harmony finally reveals.

I frown at her and try to keep my voice low. "What do you mean he is missing?"

Harmony sighs and glances at me briefly before turning her gaze back to the glowing woman on stage. "He is one of the missing heroes."

I gasp. Not only are heroes missing but a member of the Council is too. That is serious! I wonder why I haven't heard about it before. Probably because the Council is trying to keep quiet about it. No one is supposed to be able to touch the Council and it could cause panic if people found out one of them is missing.

"Was it the monsters?"

Harmony shrugs. "Probably not, I would bet it is the House of Rogues."

That is all she gets to say before Aphrodite starts to speak. Suddenly everyone's attention is trained on the glowing woman, almost like they are transfixed. Even my own eyes refuse to waver from her and I hang on to her every word.

"Welcome to the tenth annual Gala with the House of Glamour!" Light applause breaks out then quiets again as she continues. "I hope you had time to meet with each other. We will now proceed to the dining area and have a three-course meal followed by dancing in the ballroom here." She pauses to let that sink in and dread settles in my stomach. I hope we are not required to dance. "Each of you have been assigned to a table so please find your name and we will bring out dinner shortly." She holds her hand out toward the doors where Father Time and Revelation open them. Aphrodite's glow dims which seems to break her hold on the crowd. Everyone shuffles to the doors and finds their seats.

"I will see you after dinner." Harmony waves at me while she and Specter go find their placements.

I wander around until I finally find my place card, but it takes me a while because instead of Jo, it says Agent New Member. I really need to think of an alias. People are going to start calling me TBD-To Be Determined-otherwise.

I sit and wait for the rest of the guests to find their places, wondering who will be seated at my table. I lean over and read the placard next to me. Shane. I don't recognize the name. I look at the other side of me. Raven. That name I do recognize, and I am relieved that I will know at least one person during dinner.

A couple of strangers sit down across from me and I give them a small wave and smile. They give one in return then begin talking to each other. I sigh, relieved they do not want to make small talk with me right now. The seat next to me is pulled out and I turn to see Raven with her red hair pulled up on one side and wearing a knee length black dress with lace. This time she wears red lipstick to match her hair rather than the dark color I saw her wearing last time. She sits down and immediately turns to me with a smile.

"Good to see you again," I greet.

"Jo, right?" she replies in a southern accent as she situates herself comfortably in the chair and places a cloth napkin in her lap. "How are you?" The look of concern she gives me tells me she is thinking of the incubus attack.

I glance at the other guests at the table, just now realizing everyone but one is here. When I see no one is paying us any attention I nod at Raven. "I am much better. Thank you. Um, I was wondering," I glance at the table guests again then lower my voice, "What did you do with the monster?"

She gives me a reassuring smile. "I took him to the House of Discovery. We will be able to learn much about incubi thanks to him."

Her words send shivers down my arms. I do not like monsters, but I also do not think treating them like lab rats is ethical. "You guys won't hurt him, will you?"

Raven eyes me curiously for a moment then smiles sadly. "We will try not to."

That was not very reassuring. I want to ask her questions about what they do to him and the other monsters they bring in and ask her if they have gleaned anything from them about why there are more monster sightings, but I don't get a chance. Waiters begin streaming out of a side door with carts full of plates. I figure that topic of discussion is not appropriate for dinner, so I put a pin in it for now.

The first course is a choice of soup or salad. Since I am not a big fan of salads, I choose the soup and am pleased when clam chowder is placed in front of me. I thank the waiter and wait until the other guests at the table have received their appetizers before I dig into mine.

I am surprised the person, Shane, who is supposed to sit on my other side is not here yet.

Once I swallow the bite of chowder I took, I ask Raven, "Do you know who this Shane person is supposed to be?" I wave my spoon at the empty seat next to me.

Raven dabs her mouth of salad dressing after her bite then glances over to where I am pointing. She shakes her head and leans into whisper, "I have been with the House of Discovery for years and have traveled all over the place, but I still don't know half these people." She chuckles and goes back to her salad.

I laugh with her and continue eating my soup. The room is buzzing with quiet chatter and the other guests at our table introduce themselves to us. There are three benefactors and one Star from House of Glamour in addition to Raven and me. I tell them which House I am a part of but none of them seem bothered with my lack of name. After everyone is finished with their appetizers the waiters come in and clear away the dishes and replace them with our main meal. We get a choice of steak or fish and I go for the steak. The clam chowder is enough seafood for me today. When all the main dishes have been given and the table chatter picks up again, I turn to Raven.

"So, have you and Astra found any more portals to investigate?"

Raven freezes, fork halfway to her mouth. Her cheeks redden a bit but after a second, she clears her throat and shakes her head. "No, the portals disappear too quickly, or we are not informed in time."

I bite my lip to keep from smiling. It is cute to see how even the mention of my colleague makes Raven blush. I read through Astra's reports of the portals and found her findings very informative. Even though she is only able to stay in for a short amount of time, her accounts are extremely detailed and makes me feel as if I was there with her. From what she wrote, the Other world sounds like more than a barren land with vicious monsters roaming around like I previously thought. Astra wrote about seeing paths and signs of civilized life. It makes me wonder if there are humans that live there or if the monsters actually have a form of society.

The seat next to me moves and I startle, dropping my fork onto my plate and causing a loud clatter. The other dinner guests at our table look up at the noise and we all stare at the newcomer. My eyes widen with recognition and my mouth gapes open. Shane has finally arrived but to me he is the blond savior with a fondness for vests.

"Hello, Sapphire," he says with a wink, his lips pulling up into a smirk.

Chapter 12

"You're Shane?" I ask accusingly.

His smirk turns into a full-blown grin and he drops down into his seat. "That I am. Is that a problem, Sapphire?"

My energy sparks at my hands but thankfully disappears just as fast before anyone other than Shane and Raven notice.

A waiter arrives and asks what meal he would like for his main course but Shane waves him away, declining the offer, and asks only for some wine. I continue to stare at him in disbelief but that only amuses him.

Raven nudges me and nods to Shane with a questioning frown. I must look like a crazy person staring at Shane and accusing him of something as simple as a name. I clear my throat and shake my head at her letting her know it is nothing to worry about then swipe my palms on my cloth napkin in my lap to calm myself. I barely know the guy but every time I see him, I feel flustered.

"No, it's not a problem. I just didn't expect to see you here." It makes sense now why he is in town and why I saw him at the store.

I let my eyes trail over him. He is wearing a royal blue suit, the jacket of the suit unbuttoned to show the vest underneath. His tie is a lighter blue with white polka dots. He still has a stubbly beard and low fade hairstyle which combined with his suit makes him look mouth wateringly handsome. My heart beats a little faster. I am tempted to do a drool check. Instead, I rip my eyes away from him so I do not get drawn in any more than I already have. He chuckles softly letting me know he noticed my perusal. My cheeks warm in response and I look down at my plate to avoid his gaze. Thankfully, the others at the table have already gone back to their own conversations, though I can see Raven out of the corner of my eye studying us.

Raven waves at Shane. "Hello, I'm Raven, a friend of Jo's."

Shane leans forward to see her better since I am in the middle of them and smiles at her. "Nice to meet you Raven, you can call me Shane."

I frown at that. He has super speed so he must belong to one of the Houses, yet he uses his real name. I throw a confused frown at him. "What is your pseudonym?"

He gives me a slow smile and leans forward until we are only a few inches apart. My breath catches at his proximity. "You can call me Prince of Lightning if you'd like," he whispers. He holds my gaze waiting for a response.

Prince of Lightning? Probably named so because he is as fast as lightning. But the Prince part, insinuating no one is as fast or good as him, is a little cocky if you ask me.

I nod at him. "I think I will stick with Shane."

Jake also goes by his real name, so it isn't completely out of place.

He chuckles and leans back against his seat, giving us more space. I release the breath I was holding and turn back to my steak to take a couple of bites. I feel his gaze on me, but I don't look back.

"So, Shane. Are you a benefactor?" Raven asks.

"No." Shane and I both answer.

Raven glances between us. "Oh, um, so you're with a House then?"

I stay quiet, waiting for his reply. He never told me which House he belonged to, only that it wasn't the Heroes. I doubt he is part of the House of Glamour either. He doesn't seem like the kind of guy who enjoys the spotlight.

He looks away and stares at the wine glass in his hand. "You can say that."

He is so mysterious, and I don't know whether to find it intriguing or worrying. The waiters come out to clear our plates and hand us dessert before we can question him further. We get a choice of molten chocolate cake or a cup of chocolate mousse. I choose the cake and clap my hands together in delight when it is placed in front of me. Ice cream is piled on top of the small cake and when I dig into it, chocolate sauce pours out melting the ice cream a bit. Strawberry flavoring is drizzled on to the plate around the dessert and little sparklers are stuck into the cake giving the whole thing a volcano look. I can't help a tiny happy dance in my seat at the pretty presentation of it and the taste of the first bite.

Raven chooses the cake as well and we share a pleased smile as we eat it. I look over to see what Shane has chosen but he has nothing but his wine in front of him. However, he is staring at me with an intense blue gaze that makes my breathing falter. I shift uncomfortably and look down at my cake. I take a forkful and hold it out to Shane.

"Would you like some?"

Oh my God, what am I doing?! Am I really hand feeding this man I barely know?

He seems surprised as well because his intense gaze turns into a wide-eyed look at my fork then at me. His mouth opens and closes multiple times, but I don't know if it is because he is struggling with what to say or if he is actually going to bite the cake off my fork. After a few uncomfortable seconds, I bring the fork to my own mouth and eat the cake, saving us both from the awkward moment.

I laugh nervously and cover my mouth as I say through the bite of food, "Sorry about that, I guess you would have gotten one for yourself if you really wanted it."

Shane visibly swallows and turns away to take a long drink of his wine. I turn to Raven who is staring at me with wide eyes and biting her lip to keep from laughing. I shake my head slightly and give her a *what was that* look.

Aphrodite stands up from one of the tables at the front of the room, near the doors, and gets everyone's attention by tapping the side of her glass with a spoon. I never knew that trick worked in real life. I always thought it was just a movie thing. Aphrodite's glow intensifies and suddenly everyone is transfixed by her. I guess that comes in handy often in the House of Glamour.

"Feel free to dance and socialize in the next room when you finish your dessert. Snacks and drinks are also available there." She smiles and dims her light as she sits down, releasing everyone from her power.

Shane immediately stands and walks out. I frown after him then turn to Raven with a questioning look. She shrugs and continues eating.

Slowly, more people head to the other room including Raven when she is finished with her dessert. No matter how slowly I eat my cake, I eventually finish and have no choice but to follow the others.

I sidle along the wall when I enter the ballroom trying to hide behind people and tables, so I don't get pulled on to the dance floor. I have no idea where Raven disappeared to and haven't seen Harmony or Specter since before dinner. The orchestra starts playing making the music fill the room and capture the guest's attention. Some of the guests don't hesitate to grab a partner and begin dancing for all to see. It is one of those songs where the man leads the lady and it looks as if most of the dancers are using up the entire floor to move around rather than swaying in one place. I can't help watching them in fascination as they spin around with expert movements, making the women's dresses swish around their ankles.

I used to imagine going to a ball and dancing with handsome gentlemen. That is until my mishap with dancing shoved that dream out the window.

I find the snack table, ignoring the food since my belly cannot handle more, and take a drink to occupy my hands. I hold it in front of me only taking short sips when people glance at me to show them I am busy and not available to dance. I search the crowd once more and grin when I see Specter leading Harmony to the middle of the floor. They are totally cute together. I follow them with my eyes as Specter moves them around, his hand clasped at the small of her back, his eyes only for her. I am surprised at how amazing they are at dancing. They probably go to this thing every year so it makes sense they would know how.

"Would you like to dance?" a voice says from beside me.

I jump and drop my glass of cider. I didn't realize someone was beside me, too caught up in watching the dancers.

With lightning quick reflexes, Shane grabs the glass in midair without spilling a drop of the liquid inside then hands it back to me with a smirk.

I want to glare at him for scaring me, but I refrain. It isn't his fault I wasn't paying attention to my surroundings. And it wasn't like he crept up and yelled boo. He asked a simple question.

His question registers in my mind and I shake my head vehemently. "No, no thank you. I can't dance."

I chuckle nervously and look back at the dancers to avoid his gaze. I don't want to see what he thinks of that. He is probably laughing at me or staring at me in shock. I take a sip from my saved drink.

Shane plucks the drink from my hands and sets it on the table I am hiding behind. "That's ok, I can." Then he grabs my hand and tugs me toward the middle of the room.

I try to dig in my heels, but he is annoyingly strong. I think about shocking him but that is a little extreme plus I don't want to hurt him. I just want him to let go.

We make it to the edge of the dance floor before I successfully rip my hand away. He turns to me with one brow raised. I shake my head and back up a few steps. I feel people staring but I avoid their gazes as my cheeks heat.

"Seriously, I can't dance. I will embarrass you."

Shane smiles which is not the reaction I was expecting. He comes up to me until he is only a breath away and leans down to whisper in my ear. "Trust me." His breath tickles my skin sending shivers down my back. He holds his hand out and stares into my eyes, nodding once for me to take it.

I purse my lips and stare at his hand. I look up to tell him no for the final time, but his gaze makes the words freeze. That intense look is back, and it makes my breath falter. He mouths the words *trust me* again, keeping his smile in place. The next thing I know, my hand is in his and he is pulling me to the middle of the room.

I squeak as I am suddenly spun around and run into his chest. His arm comes around my waist to keep me in place which I am thankful for because I would have fallen backwards otherwise. His other hand clasps mine to lead us. I raise my free hand and hesitantly place it on his shoulder. He nods his approval then begins to move us.

My heart beats frantically both from the movement and the eyes on us. I glance around the room and down at my feet to make sure I don't run into anything or step on Shane. He moves us expertly and I have no control as he whisks me away to the next spot. Shane lets go of my hand but keeps his arm around my waist. He tilts my chin up until I am looking at him only.

"You're doing great. Keep your eyes on me, don't worry about anything else." He speaks so calmly that I find myself relaxing and agreeing to his order.

I stare into his electric blue eyes then startle when I realize where I have seen the color before. His eyes are the exact shade of my lightning. I smile at the connection. Even though there are probably other things that are the same shade, I like that it is my lightning that his eyes remind me of. It almost makes me feel like I am not alone in this power.

Crazy, I know, he doesn't even know me or my power.

We come to a stop as the music ends and, for a second, I think I did something wrong. Did I destroy the orchestra somehow? Did I hurt him and now everyone paused to see the disaster?

My fear abates when he smiles down at me with pride. "See? You did it. That was not so bad, was it?"

I let out an awkward chuckle and remove myself from his hold. "I guess not. You are a great dancer." I blush and look away.

"Would you like to dance with me again?"

I look up at him uncertainly. One dance was good enough, right? I shouldn't push my luck. However, my hand is already clasped in his again and we are back on the floor as the orchestra strikes up the next song before I can say no.

We are quiet for a minute, enjoying the movement and the music. His arms are strong and have no problem leading me where he wants us to go. I find myself enjoying our closeness and wonder if he is as affected as I am.

"Sapphire, I have something to ask of you."

"My name is Jo, you know that, right?"

He stares at me a moment then smiles and shakes his head softly. "I think I will stick with Sapphire. It suits you and your sparks."

As if my power knew he spoke of it the energy sparks at my fingertips, brushing against Shane. I gasp and pull my hands away from him. "I'm so sorry, I don't quite have a handle on it yet."

Shane shakes his head and waves away my worry. "It's ok, it didn't hurt."

My eyes widen at that. It didn't hurt? How did it not hurt him? Whenever I accidentally shock Sherry she yelps in pain.

Shane takes me back in his arms and moves us again since we are blocking the other dancers.

"Now, as I was saying before you interrupted me..."

My head snaps up to look at him, but he is smiling, letting me know he is joking. I laugh and mumble an apology then let him continue.

"I have something to ask of you." I nod for him to go on. "I have a lead on the occurrence of monsters in the city and the disappearance of the heroes."

I gasp and nearly stop again but he keeps us moving, making me stumble back. His arm tightens around me to keep me standing, making it look like I dipped backward on purpose.

"You what?"

I heard him the first time, but I want to hear it again.

"I have a lead on the monster and hero mystery," he says, glancing around to make sure we are not being overheard. When he sees no one is listening in he brings his gaze back to me. "I need you to help me."

So, Shane is the Agent on the trail of this mystery then. I thought Jake was doing it but maybe they have separate missions. It makes sense now why he was nearby when the incubus attacked. He must have been following a lead. And now he wants my help?

I frown. "What can I do? There are others who would be more helpful." My face falls and I try not to pout. "Harmony hasn't let me do field work yet."

"You are the perfect person to help me. Just talk to her. Tell her you have a lead and want to follow it."

The music stops and we are left alone as the orchestra takes a quick break and the other guests shuffle off to find refreshments. He still has not let go of me and my face heats as I realize how close we are.

It takes me a moment to answer as his eyes are almost hypnotizing which combined with the heat of his touch on my lower back has me speechless. I clear my throat before speaking. "Um, where is the lead?"

"Meet me at the train station tomorrow at noon. Bring a bag, as this will take a couple of days."

I open my mouth then close it, not sure what to say. He wants me to spend not just one but multiple days with him. Overnight. Away from home and HQ.

I am a newbie. It doesn't make sense that he would single me out to help him. I think of the others at the treehouse. Astra is always busy. Specter probably has his own missions to worry about. Jake is trying to investigate the monster appearances so he would be a better choice than me but maybe he has his own part in this mystery to solve. Without calling other Agents to HQ I guess I am the only one available right now. Would Harmony be ok with me going on this mission? I would have to tell her what the lead is, but he hasn't told me where we will be going. And why the train? There must be a better way to get to our destination.

"Will you do this with me, Sapphire?" His eyes are pleading and that is what does me in. He must really need someone which means this must be a serious and possibly dangerous lead. Good thing I am prepared for just about anything.

I take a deep breath, then as I let it out slowly, I answer him. "Sure, tomorrow at noon."

Chapter 13

"Seriously? Just like that?" I stare at my new boss with raised eyebrows and upturned hands.

Harmony glances up from her desk to pierce me with amused green eyes. "Yup, just like that." She glances at the door and smiles softly then looks back at me. "Make sure to bring your House badge."

I turn to see what she was looking at and see Specter standing there. I jump with a squeak and place a hand over my heart to calm its racing. I recently learned he could become intangible and even invisible just like a ghost, hence the name, Specter. It unnerves me every time I see him walk through walls or disappear from view right in front of me. It is also frightening to be snuck up on since his appearance is always silent.

"She is finally going on her first mission?" Specter asks, smirking at my tense posture as he walks by to stand next to Harmony at her desk.

"Yup, she has a lead on the monster and hero mystery and will be leaving for a couple days."

Again, I am shocked at how okay she is with my departure. "You don't need to know how I got my information or if the mission will be dangerous?" I probably should have just accepted her blessing and left. However, Sherry asked more questions than my boss and I don't know if that makes me happy or concerned.

Harmony chuckles and shakes her head. Specter huffs a breath through his nose which is the only indication he is amused.

"I don't ask people where they get their information. Informants are private and we are not the cops who will need witnesses to corroborate your story or anything. However, I am assuming it has something to do with that man you were dancing with last night." It wasn't a question but the slight lilt at the end of her sentence had a questioning note to it.

I stay quiet and she nods with a smile at my reaction. I don't know if she is proud that I did not rat out my informant or if I just confirmed what she is thinking. She probably knew it was him as she is the head of the House and sent him on that mission.

"And as for the danger, if I didn't think you were ready then I wouldn't let you go."

That makes my chest inflate a bit with pride. Harmony has been the only one to believe in me this much. Even

Sherry is hesitant when it comes to me being involved in all this.

I grin and head to the door, waving at Specter and Harmony on the way out. "Thanks, Harmony. I will keep you updated."

"I'm sure you will. Be careful!" Harmony calls to me before I am fully out of the office.

When I am outside, I check my phone for the time and see that I have an hour to get to the train station. I wish I could have said goodbye to Astra and Jake, but they had not been there, so I settle for a quick text letting them know I am going on my first mission.

Astra sends back an immediate reply with two thumbs up emojis and a be careful warning. Jake sends a lightning bolt and a smiley face a few seconds after.

I smile at my screen and tuck my phone away when I reach the car that Sherry is letting me borrow. I will be leaving the car in the train station parking lot for Sherry to pick up later. She would have dropped me off, but I told her I had to stop at the House of Mystery first and she isn't supposed to know where it is.

The drive to the station is not long and I find myself arriving twenty minutes early. I sit in my car gripping the steering wheel, suddenly unsure if I should be doing this. I glance at my tactical backpack next to me. I have been training to be a hero since Sherry joined the House of Heroes. And that was when I didn't have any powers. Now I have lightning, unpredictable and unhelpful lightning, but it is a power all the same. I also have my backpack that I spent years stuffing things in that could come in handy against monsters and help me survive in just about any situation. I can handle a simple mission for the House with a handsome stranger.

With that in mind, I place my sunglasses over my eyes, grab my bag and exit my vehicle. I don't need to leave my key behind since Sherry has her own set. It is only when I reach the ticket office that I realize I do not know where to meet Shane. He never gave me his number, so I have no idea how to contact him. I check the time on the clock near the exit. Fifteen minutes until noon. I spin in a slow circle, looking for a handsome blond guy in a vest.

"Sapphire."

I squeak and jump a foot in the air. Jeez! How did he sneak up on me? Must have been his super speed. I turn and glare at him for scaring me but he only smirks. He is wearing an emerald vest with a paisley design and has a duffle slung over one shoulder.

"Are you ready?" He glances at my backpack then tilts his head in the direction we need to go.

I nod and follow him to the train we need to board. It is only when we are on the train in our seats that I say, "So you never told me where we are going." I am sitting across from him, a little table being the only thing that separates us, so I am able to see his face lose its usual playfulness.

For once, Shane does not smirk or avoid the question. He leans forward and folds his hands on the table. I lean forward as well waiting for his answer. The direction we are going means it is somewhere in the west but how far west? He opens his mouth to say something then closes it. Shane looks to the side to stare out of the window. I wonder why he is hesitating. I am already on board with him, it is not like his answer will change my decision. His eyes darken and a frown pulls his brows down. He seems to be struggling with something. I lay a hand on his arm and he turns his head back to me surprised. He seems to shake himself of his troubling thoughts and gives me a small smile that doesn't reach his eyes.

"Pittsburgh," he finally says then sits back with crossed arms.

I fight the disappointment building inside me at his one-word answer and his distance.

"Ok," I say drawing out the word. "What's in Pittsburgh?"

"A lead." He looks past me down the lane at whatever is behind me.

I hold in a grumble at his refusal to tell me anything of importance. I thought we were partners in this. I push my sunglasses to the top of my head and pierce him with an impatient glare. "Look, you asked me here to help you. I need you to tell me what you know so I know what to expect."

Shane studies me, seeming unaffected by my glare or words. Was I not threatening enough? I conjure my energy to spark along my hands. His eyes move to the electricity and his eyes crinkle in amusement. Finally, I get something other than aloofness from him. However, I didn't expect him to find it amusing like my display was that of a child rather than an Agent of the House of Mystery.

He leans on the table again, so he is only a few inches from me. My sparks jump for him, but I pull my hands back before they can connect. What is it about him that causes my power to go crazy? His gaze traps me in place and heat pools in his eyes. My heart rate quickens, and I am suddenly grateful for the table between us. I look down at his lips but quickly avert my gaze when I watch them form a smirk.

He noticed my glance. That's embarrassing.

"Ok, Sapphire, I will tell you some of it."

Some of it. Fine, I will take what I can get.

"The House of Rogues have been working with the supernatural for some time," he starts.

Supernatural? Odd way of saying monsters. I knew the House of Rogues often used monsters in their schemes. To cause havoc. To cause a distraction. Whatever worked for them in the moment. A thought strikes me causing my eyes to widen. Are we going to the House of Rogues? No one knows where they gather though. I study Shane, looking for evidence that he knows where they are and that is where we are headed.

"I have a lead on their next attack. We are going to Pittsburgh to capture one of the supernatural or, if we are lucky, a Rogue to find out what is happening to the heroes."

I gasp. We are going to try and capture a Rogue? That is both terrifying and exciting. "You think it is the Rogues behind the disappearances?" Of course, it is. The Rogues are usually behind everything except the Otherworld portals, but I wouldn't put it past them to be behind those too.

Shane shrugs. "Yes and no."

What is that supposed to mean? I wish he would just tell me everything. However, it is his mystery assignment to solve and I am only here to help in this one mission. Maybe if I prove myself useful, he will trust me enough to tell me everything he knows. I doubt my power will work against the monsters, but it may be useful against a Rogue.

I sit back and cross my arms, staring out the window at the passing scenery.

Shane sighs. "Sapphire…"

"My name is Jo," I say with a bit more force than is necessary.

He is silent for a moment then surprises me by asking, "What is Jo short for? Josephine?"

That is not what I expected him to say. I thought he would shrug off my comment and continue with the Sapphire thing or give in and tell me more about what he knows of this mystery. Yet, he went for something personal.

I blush and look down at the table to avoid his gaze. I don't want to see him laughing at me when I tell him. "Uh, no, it's short for Jolene."

"Jolene?" he asks curiously, no hint of laughter in his voice…yet.

I chuckle nervously. "Yeah, from the song by Dolly Parton. My mother's favorite singer."

"Ah, I see." I glance up and see his teasing grin. "And how does your mother feel about you shortening your name to Jo?"

"I don't know, she…she died seven years ago. Along with my dad."

Shane's smile falls and he places a hand on mine. I had been scratching at the edge of the table but his touch stills my movements.

"I am truly sorry," he says softly. "I wish I could fix it and erase your pain."

Tears prick at the edges of my eyes. I take my hand out from under his and wipe them away. "Thanks. It was an accident caused by a portal. There is nothing anyone could have done."

He swallows thickly and looks away. I almost think he is going to join me with the tears. That's sweet. I reach over and place my hand on his and smile at him to let him know I am ok.

I need to move on from this topic though. "So, what is your family like?"

Shane nods, taking the hint to move away from the topic of my parents' death. He swallows once more and takes a breath before he speaks. "I've got an older brother who practically raised me. I haven't seen him in almost seven years though. Growing up with him was both enjoyable and frustrating. He believed he was always right." He says it with love and a tinge of sadness.

I chuckle. "I know how that goes."

One side of his mouth quirks up. "You have siblings?"

"I have a sister, her parents adopted me right after…you know." Shane purses his lips and nods. "You might know her as Blast."

Shane's eyes widen. "Blast is your sister?"

I nod.

"Well, that must be fun."

"It is, mostly." I laugh. "So why don't you see your family? Do you miss your brother?" I can't imagine not seeing Sherry for years.

"I do miss him, but it's…complicated."

I make an understanding sound but really, I don't understand. If you miss your family then talk to them or go see them. No matter the issues that may arise among them, family is family. I keep my opinions to myself though. I don't know his family or situation so I will just take his word for it.

"So, Sapphire, tell me about your Genesis."

I sigh, not really annoyed by the nickname but resigned. I will never admit it to him but I kind of like it.

I tell him the story about the banshee and wyvern and how there was no portal around, so it was odd that it manifested. When I reach the part about the power malfunctioning I hesitate. If he realizes my powers are not reliable, will he think he made a mistake inviting me on this mission? Will he send me back?

"And?" Shane presses, oblivious to my indecision.

"Um, well, somehow the wyvern got bigger and stronger. Thankfully, it flew away," I rush to say, hoping I glossed over the ending enough he wouldn't realize I was a liability rather than a help.

He studies me a moment with his finger tapping his lips in thought. My eyes dip to his lips that he is unknowingly drawing attention to. Before I can get carried away in a daydream, I avert my gaze.

"Interesting," he says.

I frown and bite my lip, but he does not say anything more about the topic. I am about to turn the tables and ask him about his Genesis, but he sits up straighter and smiles at someone over my shoulder. I turn and see the train conductor making his way toward us. We pull out our tickets and the conductor stamps them before moving on.

"I must make a call. We have about three hours until we are there so feel free to visit the refreshment bar or look out at the scenery. I will be right back." Shane stands and moves to a different car before I get a reply in.

I ignore his suggestion to visit the bar and pull out my monster book with its handmade trading cards instead to refresh myself on all the baddies out there. Maybe I will be able to help fight whatever the Rogues are planning by knowing about the monsters they might work with.

Once we capture a Rogue, I might even be able to add a new page in my notebook. Heroes, monsters, Council, and now Rogues. I will be the first one to have info written down about them. I am learning about so much more than I thought I could have. Secrets that the public are not privy to and uncovering the truths of our weird world. I grin down at my monster book and trace over the ruined incubus card.

I am starting to think joining the House of Mystery was the best choice I could have made.

Chapter 14

I stare up at the tall building with my mouth gaping open. I am wearing my sunglasses, but I still squint from the sun shining bright at the top of the building. The air is nice out and there are tons of people hanging out on the quad in front. I wish I could join them and act like my biggest worries are about passing classes or what clubs to join. Sherry and my adopted mother, Irma, tried getting me to go to college but it never appealed to me. I love learning but I didn't think spending thousands of dollars for a piece of paper was the way to do it. Plus, I don't feel right using their money, even though they never gave me reason to worry about that.

Being here makes me wonder what it would have been like.

The University of Pittsburgh is gorgeous and even more so is the Cathedral of Learning rising into the sky right in front of me. Sparks begin racing up and down my arms, reacting to the anger burning inside, at the thought of the Rogues attacking this place.

Shane places a hand on my arm. I turn to him startled he would touch me while my blue energy is covering my skin. He doesn't flinch or look pained which confuses me even more. He takes a deep breath, and his hand tightens fractionally but otherwise no reaction.

"Not here," he whispers, looking around at the college students.

None have noticed my display yet but if I reveal myself now, someone will surely record it and the Rogues may get tipped off. I close my eyes and breathe in deeply.

Grass. Chocolate. Jingle bells.

I feel the sparks disappear and open my eyes with a grateful smile. Shane is still holding on to me sending tingles across my skin. I quirk my brow at his hand on my arm and he immediately releases me and clears his throat.

"Let's go."

I follow Shane into the Cathedral of Learning. I have to stop when I am inside to avoid running into something while I look up and around the magnificent structure. Vaulted ceilings give the place a medieval European feeling and the stained glass makes the floors and walls light up with color. There are halls that branch off in all directions making me wish I was here for pleasure rather than business so I can explore.

Shane grabs my arm again and gently directs me away from the room. I stop looking up and pay attention to where we are going long enough to see that Shane seems to know his way around. On the way, we pass some classrooms from what I can tell and I have to stop myself from peering into them with wonder. Finally, Shane stops in front of a nondescript door and lets go of me. I peer down the hallway and realize I have no idea how to get back.

"What's in here?" I whisper. I don't know what the other doors hold but I don't want to disturb anyone or bring attention to us.

He pulls out a set of lock picks and goes to work on the lock. My eyes widen at his actions. Are we really breaking into this room?

"Why don't we just ask whoever is in charge here to let us in? That is why we have badges." I pat my pocket as if he could see the badge with its Celtic knot within.

He ignores my question, staying focused on his task, until the lock clicks and the door swings open. He stands up, pocketing the lock picks and grins.

"Where is the fun in that?" He gestures for me to follow then quickly closes and locks the door when we are inside. "And as for your previous question, books are in here."

I look around the room with my brows knit. It is a small library with only five bookcases in the middle of the room. Along one wall are gleaming filing cabinets. Portraits are placed in the open spaces on the walls around the room. I recognize three of them as the Council members I recently met. I study an unfamiliar portrait of a masked man hanging near the door. The name plate at the bottom of the frame says the man is Mystico. I study it closer now that I know the man in the portrait is the missing Council member for the Heroes. Mystico had—*has* I should say since I have to hope he is not dead—a purple, gray, and black hero suit with a black mask. His green eyes hold mirth and mischievousness can be seen in the way the corner of one side of his mouth pulls up into a hidden smirk.

What are pictures of the Council doing in this small library in the Cathedral of Learning?

I turn to Shane and put my hands on my hips, done with his aloofness. "Shane, what are we doing here? What is this place?"

"This," he spins in a slow circle with arms outstretched, "is the Other library."

He grins at me, arms still outstretched, waiting for a reaction. From the way he is looking at me I guess I am supposed to be impressed. I take another look around the room, but the bookcases are still there holding tons of books and journals and the filing cabinets are still metal and boring looking. Honestly, the room looks like the one at the treehouse except ours is more interesting.

"The other library from what?" Was he saying there are two? I am not surprised since we are in a place of learning.

He shakes his head and steps forward, placing his hands on my shoulders as he stares at me with barely suppressed excitement. "No, this the *Other* library," he says, adding emphasis on the word other. "The place where all the names of all the Houses' members are kept along with their real identities. The place where all the supernatural and information about the Other world are stored." He tilts his head. "Well, I assume the House of Mystery has most of this information too, but that place is hard to find. However, this place also holds the location of every House and branch in every part of the world."

He lets go of me and starts wandering around the room while I am frozen to the spot. All the names of every member of the Houses are here? All the locations of every House in the world? With that kind of information, the Houses could be wiped out. No wonder the Rogues are targeting this place. But how did they even know about it? I doubted many knew of it. The Council for sure, and maybe the heads of the Houses.

For the first time, a seed of suspicion enters my mind as I stare at Shane while he skims his fingers along the spines of books on a nearby shelf. Who is Shane? He must be pretty important among the Houses to know about this place. Or maybe he is part of the Rogues. The look in his eyes right before he let go of me to start searching the room flashes in my mind. He looked gleeful but there was something else there, almost greedy. A flash of panic hits me hard. Shane never confirmed to be part of the House of Mystery or any House for that matter. His response to Raven at the Gala comes to mind.

"Oh, um, so you're with a House then?"

"You can say that."

What if he is part of the House of Rogues? And I just helped him get in here, though I didn't do much. He picked the lock instead of asking someone to give us entrance. He always showed up wherever I was after I joined the House of Mystery. Now he has access to every House secret and claims the Rogues will be targeting here. What if the Rogue is already here? Alarm bells ring in my mind.

I take a step toward Shane and ball my hands into fists. "Shane."

The way I say his name must sound off because Shane freezes at my tone and turns to me, eyes widening slightly at my stance and the sparks racing up and down my arms. He straightens and gives me his full attention.

Slowly he steps forward. "Sapphire? Is something wrong?"

"Who are you? What House do you belong to?"

He frowns. "What do you mean? You know who I am."

"How do you know of this place? How do you know about the Rogues' plans?"

His eyebrows shoot up as understanding dawns. "Whoa, I am not a Rogue, Sapphire." Shane scrunches his nose, and he looks off to the side with disgust. "I would never work with them."

My anger falters at his expression and tone of voice.

Shane takes a step forward and reaches out but doesn't touch me. "Trust me, I am not here to do the Rogue's bidding. I don't believe in their methods of getting things done."

"Well, then, what House are you part of? How do you know of this place and their plans?" I am doubting his involvement with the Rogues, but I still can't let go of the fact I know nothing about him or how he knows of this important, secret place.

Shane's face flashes with conflicting emotions. He opens then closes his mouth then growls in frustration. "It's complicated," he finally says, balling his hands into fists and looking away from me.

"What is so complicated? Just tell me." I reach for the button on the side of my bag and hold my thumb over it. "Tell me or I will bring the Heroes here."

Shane eyes the button and purses his lips. "If you do that then we will both be brought in front of the Council."

I don't waver. I am not worried about the Council. I am confident I can tell them the story and they will find no fault with me, especially if I protect the Houses' secrets.

Shane stares at me for a moment longer but something in my expression must tell him I am not backing down because his shoulders slump and he rubs a hand over his face as he heaves out a sigh.

"I have…informants you could say, who are of the, uh, supernatural variety." He winces and looks up at me cautiously.

I frown. Supernatural variety? Then I remember that is what he calls the monsters, and my brows shoot up in surprise.

"You work with monsters?" Energy spreads to my shoulders until I have sleeves of blue sparks. "Rogues work with monsters."

Shane scowls. "I am not a Rogue. And in most instances the Rogues are the monsters not the supernatural. The supernatural are divided just as much as the humans with powers. Most of them just want to go home. Have you ever thought of that?"

I hadn't thought of that actually. Why would I have? All the reports that come in are of monsters attacking people or helping the Rogues. I always assumed they came over on purpose from the Other world to cause havoc. They are all evil. However…maybe not all? It is possible some monsters hide away, and we only see the ones willing to come out. I wonder how Shane convinced monsters to be his informants. The idea makes the Mystery member part of me want to record everything and ask him about his dealings with them. The idea that they want to go home is also intriguing. But then why don't they just go home then? Instead, they attack us.

I shake my head. No. Monsters are monsters and we do not work with them. The House of Mystery is not totally against monsters, more fascinated by them than anything, but they still know not to partner with them or give them free reign of our world.

I stay silent, musing over his words, which must give him encouragement to continue.

"However, you are right in the sense that some supernatural and Rogues work together. My informants have told me of their plans, and this place," he gestures around us, "is the first step in them completing their mission."

I eye him, looking for clues as to what his motivations and loyalties are. He didn't need to invite me on this mission. If he truly works for the Rogues, then he could have come here alone. With his speed, he could have easily searched the room and taken what he needed before anyone knew he was here. He also saved me from the incubus and attended the Gala as a guest. Maybe he isn't a Rogue, but he is hiding something. More than just having monster informants.

"What is their mission?" I ask, letting my sparks die down. I do not completely trust him, but I am willing to hear him out. For now.

He doesn't get a chance to respond. An alarm starts blaring and I can tell it is not just this room that is sounding because I hear the echoes of it down the halls and doors crashing open as people scramble about.

Shane suddenly disappears in a rush of wind and reappears by my side. He grasps my arms and tugs me further into the room, around the bookcases to the back near the filing cabinets. He tugs me once more, making me crouch next to him so we can both be hidden but still see the door. Shane places his lips near my ear sending tingles down my neck and back.

With a soft exhalation of breath, he whispers, "Wait for my signal."

I don't understand why we are hiding until I hear the door handle rattle as someone attempts to unlock it. With how long it is taking them to open the door, I assume they are getting in the same way we did. Which means it must be a Rogue, here to steal House secrets. Shane said the Rogues may be behind the disappearance of heroes. If they get their hands on the information in this room then all heroes will soon be gone. Including my sister.

I glance at Shane who is eyeing the door with narrowed eyes. His fist is clenched as it rests on his knee and the other hand is gripping the filing cabinet next to us. Maybe I was wrong about him. He doesn't look like someone who would help the Rogues. He looks like he is angry and ready to take this villain down.

The door opens and I quickly look away from Shane to see who is entering. A man clad in all black makes his way silently into the room. My pulse jumps and energy sparks at my fingertips. My hand involuntarily moves to the emergency button on the side of my backpack, but I freeze before pressing it. Not because of what Shane said about us being brought before the Council. I pause because this is a moment to prove to myself that I can be useful in a dangerous situation. I don't need backup. Shane and I are plenty capable of incapacitating a Rogue. Instead of pressing the button I reach a little further back and grab my silver dagger from the side pocket.

Shane looks at me and nods. In the next instant he zooms to the door to stand in front of it, blocking any escape the Rogue can make. I launch forward down the aisle of bookcases to prevent the Rogue from moving further into the room. The Rogue freezes, eyes going wide. He spins around to make a retreat but sees Shane blocking the doorway.

The Rogue positions himself so he is facing both of us and unsheathes two katanas from behind his back. I gape at the blades as he spins them around then points one at each of us.

Chapter 15

I take in the Rogue's appearance and threatening stance. When I first saw him come in, I noticed he wore all black but only now do I see the suit is tight so it clings to the man's body and he is wearing a mask that covers everything but his dark eyes. An insignia of a black mask outlined in silver is emblazoned on each arm. If I had any doubts before, that insignia confirms he is from the House of Rogues. I didn't notice the sheaths behind his back until he pulled two swords from them. I stare at the katanas then him, back and forth, then raise my brows in realization. Excitement and fear battle for dominance. I am about to fight a ninja! A freaking ninja! I look down at my dagger and hold in a groan. There is no way this little thing will be able to defeat a ninja.

I look up, past the ninja Rogue, and see Shane frowning at the man with clenched fists. He isn't deterred by this man's appearance. Somehow that gives me strength and I grip the handle of my dagger tighter. I am a decent fighter and I have lightning. With Shane's speed added to the fight we could subdue this guy.

"Who are you?" I ask with a note of awe in my tone.

Shane is the one to answer. "The Shadow Ninja. I've heard about him before."

The Shadow Ninja sharply turns his head to Shane but says nothing. Somehow finding me as the weaker opponent, the ninja launches toward me and attacks with a swift spin of his blades preventing any more discussion. I manage to back up fast enough to avoid getting my head chopped off by one of the blades and somehow deflect the other with my dagger. Shane, using his speed, comes flying in behind the ninja and knocks him away from me. The ninja Rogue comes back undeterred, but we are ready for him. Shane blocks the first few attacks and launches a few of his own. I swing out with fist and dagger looking for an opening. Our opponent does not have super speed, but he is quick to block both of us over and over.

The ninja suddenly jumps into the air and disappears. I halt just in time to avoid slicing Shane open with my dagger and he stares at me wide eyed and breathing heavily.

"Where did he go?" I ask as I lower my blade and look up to where the man vanished. It is too dark for me to see anything near the ceiling, even with the lamps on throughout the room.

"He is using the shadows," Shane says quietly as he turns in a slow circle, squinting at the room.

"The shadows?" I follow his line of sight to the shadows at the edges of the room and gasp when I realize what he means. "Is that his power?" The name Shadow Ninja makes more sense now.

Shane nods, still squinting at the parts of the room that are hidden by darkness.

Blending into the shadows must be a useful skill for a ninja Rogue. However, that means we are fighting an invisible foe. I look for movement, making sure to stay in the lighted areas so the Rogue cannot sneak up on me. I hold the dagger in one hand and form a small ball of energy in my other. It crackles with bright blue light and sends tingles along my arm. Out of the corner of my eye I see movement. Reacting on instinct I spin toward the movement and throw my ball of power. It whizzes through the air, creating a loud zapping sound as it soars.

I only see shadows, but my instinct was right because a second later, my ball of electricity makes contact with a body and the Rogue shouts in pain. Blue energy races across the man's body, allowing us to see his form in the shadows. Shane speeds to him and pulls him out to the middle of the room where we can see him better. I wince, when Shane makes contact with the energy on the Rogue's arm, but he is not fazed by it.

The Rogue contorts then rolls into a ball, the energy causing him pain. I expect him to be pleased by it and to grow stronger after the pain passes like the others I have zapped before the man continues to writhe. Maybe it only makes monsters stronger and brings pain to humans.

"Stop the energy," Shane commands, startling me from the display before me.

I blink at the Rogue on the floor and think of random words like I usually do when I want to dispel it from my own body. I never needed to consciously stop it from zapping someone else because it usually disappeared on its own.

Coconut. Roses. Teacup.

The energy stops and the Rogue sags, breathing raggedly. I only see his eyes through his mask but that is all I need to see for me to know he is scared.

Is he scared of me?

I look to Shane and raise my eyebrows, silently asking him what we should do now. Shane glances around the room but frowns when he doesn't find what he is looking for. Then his eyes land on my backpack still near the filing cabinets and he grins at me. "Any chance you have some rope in that bag?"

I share his grin and rush to my bag, digging inside until I come out with rope. I knew this would come in handy someday. I never thought it would be for tying up a Rogue though. Shane takes the rope from me and uses his super speed to quickly tie the Rogue's arms to his sides. I know better than to underestimate the ninja though. I have seen movies where ninjas can fight well with their feet. I take a couple steps away from the kicking zone then cross my arms, trying to look intimidating.

I look to Shane, wondering what he is going to ask the Rogue. The whole point of this mission is for us to interrogate a Rogue about the missing heroes and abundance of monsters. I want to jump in and demand answers, but I hold back, remembering this is Shane's mission and he asked me to tag along not lead it.

Shane crosses his arms and glares at the Rogue. "What were your plans here today?"

The ninja avoids our eyes, fixing his stare on a point on the far wall and keeping it there while he ignores Shane's question.

The ninja, unsurprisingly, is going to be difficult. I fidget with the dagger I am holding, wondering if we will have to torture the man. I am not sure I am okay with that. Maybe we will have to notify the Council after all and they can deal with him.

Shane kicks the man's foot lightly. "What are the Rogue's plans for the heroes?"

Again, nothing.

Shane frowns and crouches until he is in the Rogue's line of sight. "Why have you employed so many monsters? What are your plans?"

At that, the ninja finally meets Shane's gaze, crinkle lines appearing around the Rogue's dark eyes while light dances within. He found Shane's question humorous, but why?

Shane looks at me with pursed lips and a small crease between his brows. "Can you check the hall? Let me talk to him alone for a minute."

I open my mouth to protest but Shane nods his head to the door. I look to the ninja then back to Shane. I let out a breath of annoyance but do as he says and march to the door, glancing behind me a few times wondering what he is going to do that he doesn't want me to see.

I open the door and poke my head out into the hall, looking both ways to see if anyone is nearby. Curiosity pulls me back into the room though and I creep behind a bookshelf, pushing a couple books aside to peer through at what Shane is doing with the ninja.

Shane is still crouched in front of the Rogue but the captive kicks out at him with his feet. Shane places a hand on top of one foot and leans forward until the ninja meets his eyes. Shane says something too quiet for me to hear. The Rogue goes slack and stares at Shane with a dazed look.

What the heck?

Is there a pressure point in the leg that Shane is pressing? Did he drug the ninja without me seeing?

I lean forward to hear them better, holding my breath so I do not miss a single word.

"Let's try this again." Shane speaks with a dangerous note in his tone. "What were your plans here?"

I hold in a gasp when the Rogue answers with no hesitation.

"I need the list of people in service to the House of Heroes."

"Why?" Shane asks, with a slight growl.

The ninja bites his lips and his body shakes. He seems to be struggling against whatever Shane did to him but loses the fight and the words burst from him in a rush.

"There is a war coming."

"Between the Heroes and Rogues? What does that have to do with the supernatural?"

The Rogue frowns and tilts his head questioningly. Shane sighs and waves his hand in a circle of impatience. "The monsters."

The Rogue nods slowly, still dazed by Shane's mysterious spell over him, and answers readily. "There is a war coming…"

Shane growls again, and this time shivers race down my arms at how threatening he sounds. Like he is about to rip the head off the Rogue. "You already said that." He shakes the Rogue's foot, but the ninja is not bothered.

"…from the Other side," the Shadow Ninja finishes.

Shane visibly pales and falls back as if the words knocked into him physically.

The Other side? Does the Rogue mean more monsters are going to come through the portals soon? The Heroes are already at their limit, they cannot handle much more.

I can't stay hidden anymore, my curiosity too much to contain.

"What do you mean from the Other side?" I ask stepping out from my hiding place.

Shane startles, letting go of the Rogue, and turns to me with wide eyes. The Shadow Ninja shakes his head as if coming out of a sleep and his eyes are no longer glazed. The man wastes no time and kicks out connecting with Shane's head, sending him sprawling. The ninja then flips up from the floor onto his feet with no effort, despite his arms being tied to his sides. He then runs for the nearest shadow. I don't know exactly how his shadow power works but I know it won't be good for us if he reaches one.

I raise my hand toward the fleeing Rogue and push out all the bottled up energy inside me.

Blue energy bursts forth in a crackle of light hitting the Rogue squarely in the back. It is so bright that I see stars, and the sound is so loud that my ears feel as if they will burst. Sparks spray in all directions but fizzle out before they reach the bookcases. To my horror, Shane is not so lucky. He is in the blast zone and the sparks rain down on him causing him to twitch. When the energy disappears, the Rogue lays still and silence reigns.

I ignore the Rogue, feeling confident I dealt with him long enough that I don't need to worry about him escaping, and fall to my knees next to Shane. The sparks did not leave any marks but that doesn't reassure me. I shake his shoulder, panic working its way into my heart making it pound harder.

"Shane? Hey, wake up." I say it softly despite the urge to shout.

I shake him again and this time his eyes fly open. They are dark, pupils taking over the whole of his irises. I gasp and sit back. My hands spark involuntarily, and his dark eyes follow the energy across my hands. He blinks and his eyes are back to their original blue. It was so quick that I almost think I imagined it, but no, I definitely saw the eerie darkness.

He looks at me and frowns slightly. "Where…?" His eyes widen when he remembers. He looks around the room frantically then sighs when he sees the unconscious Rogue a few feet away. When he looks at me again, it is with a sheepish glance.

He clears his throat. "So, uh, is there a chance you will forget that I was knocked out by a Rogue?"

I stare at him, waiting for his eyes to turn black again. Maybe it was an effect from the sparks that touched him. When his eyes stay the striking blue they always were, I force myself to answer his question.

"Oh, definitely not."

Shane chuckles and shakes his head. I smile as I stand and hold my hand out to help him up. He takes it and when he is standing, we turn to the Shadow Ninja.

"Do you think I killed him?" I ask nervously.

Shane kneels next to the Rogue and checks the man's pulse. I wait with bated breath hoping I didn't kill him. Once the Council hears of our news, they will need to talk to him. Aphrodite may even be able to get more out of him than we could.

"He's alive, just barely."

I let out a sigh of relief. "We need to send him to the Council with our news." The Rogue's words come back to me and I shiver. A war is coming, from the Other side.

Shane pulls out his phone from his pocket and starts typing out a message. When he puts it away, he bends down and grabs the Rogue, throwing him over his shoulder with no problem then starts walking toward the door. "I have someone who will come get him and take him to where he needs to be. We need to leave before the Heroes check the room."

"Why?" I ask as I follow him. "Isn't that who we need?" Before I leave the room, I remember my backpack and run back inside to grab it. When I reach the hall, Shane is already turning a corner. I quickly lock the door and run down the hall to catch up. He is moving so fast!

"Shane!" I hiss loudly.

He pauses and looks back, waving his arm at me to hurry up, then continues on. I huff and run faster until I am finally walking next to him. He leads us around a few more turns then outside to what looks like the back of the building. I can hear sirens and commotion coming from the direction of the quad in the front, leaving the back of the Cathedral of Learning empty and quiet.

We find some shade near a tree and Shane drops the Rogue at our feet. He pulls out his phone and sends another message. When he puts it away, he looks at me and moves closer until we are only a couple inches apart. He cups my cheek and stares intently into my eyes. My heart beats a little faster and I will my breath to stay even though his nearness sends awareness throughout my body.

"Sapphire, are you ok?"

I swallow, finding that I can't speak when he is this close and touching me. I nod.

A small frown causes lines to appear between his brows and his eyes grow a little darker reminding me of when he woke up.

"I told you to check the hall," he scolds softly.

I blush and try to look away, but he tugs my chin until I am looking into his eyes again.

"Technically, I did check the hall." He continues to frown so I deflate. "I didn't mean to interrupt."

He shakes his head a little and sighs. "I guess you heard everything then?"

I remember the Rogue's words and the weird, entranced daze he was in when answering Shane's questions. I pull back and his hand drops to his side though he doesn't step away, keeping only inches between our bodies.

"How did you do that? With the Rogue? It looked like you hypnotized him."

This time it is Shane who avoids eye contact. "It's just a skill I picked up."

I know there is more that he is not saying but figure there are more important matters to discuss. I huff an annoyed sigh but let his non-answer go for now.

"We need to contact the Council. The House of Heroes. Somebody." I start pacing and throw my hands in the air, getting more worked up. "What did he mean a war is coming from the Other side?" Oh no, we never asked him where the missing heroes are! How are we going to fight a war with Rogues *and* monsters without our full force?"

Shane steps in front of me and puts his hands on my shoulders to prevent me from moving. His lips are tilted up in amusement. "Don't worry, we will figure it out." The way he sounds makes it seem like he means just the two of us.

He starts rubbing my arms up and down, sending warmth and calm through my body. I relax. He isn't freaking out so I shouldn't either.

Something catches my attention out of the corner of my eye sending adrenaline spiking through me.

"Watch out!" I shout, shoving Shane behind me and flinging out my hand to let my lightning fly.

Chapter 16

The monster halts while the blue energy from my blast crackles over the surface of its body. I expect the monster to collapse, writhe in pain, to shout out, but it only stands there like a statue frozen mid-step.

It is a bulky monster and human shaped but its skin is dry, gray, and cracked. It looks like someone fell in a bog of cement then came out of it and let it dry. Where its eyes should be are just two black holes.

"Jo," Shane places his hand on my shoulder from behind and moves to stand next to me. "It's ok, that's my contact, well, sort of."

"You…your contact?" I gape at him then the electrified monster.

The energy on the monster disappears and, like all the others, it seems to grow stronger. The monster's skin cracks, fissures running down its arms and across its face. I stare in horror as parts of its skin falls off and *thunks* on the ground. I take a closer look and notice the skin falling off are pieces of clay. In its place, new clay forms on the monster and doubles in thickness like a layer of armor over the body. When the skin stops falling off and growing back, the being flexes its fingers and turns in a circle, admiring its new skin. Suddenly it stops and reaches into its mouth, taking a piece of paper out then holding it out to me.

I take a step forward, fascinated with the monster in front of me. Once it finished its growth, I realized I was in front of a golem, level one on the monster scale. Now that it has stopped moving, I can't help but want to take a closer look.

"How do you know a golem?" I ask in awe, as I walk around the being to check it out.

The golem stays still, continuing to hold out the piece of paper it pulled from its mouth.

Golems are clay servants to whoever builds it and brings it to life. Usually, the name of the master is written on a piece of paper and put in the mouth of the creation which somehow animates it to do their bidding. I don't know what kind of magic or monster voodoo goes into it, but I do know that golems are pretty harmless unless told by its master to attack.

"I know a guy," Shane answers mysteriously.

I shoot him an annoyed look making Shane sigh. "Alright, I know a supernatural that can animate golems. This one has been sent to retrieve the Rogue and take him to the House of Heroes."

My eyes shoot up in surprise. "A…supernatural," I try out the word Shane uses, "is helping you bring a Rogue to justice?" It sounds unbelievable.

"Not all supernaturals are evil just like not all humans are good." He gives a pointed look at the Rogue.

He has a point about the humans, so…why can't it be true about mons— supernaturals?

I eye the golem again. "Why is it holding out a piece of paper?"

Shane frowns. "I'm not sure, I have never seen a golem do that before."

We both move closer and look down at the paper.

I gasp.

"It has my name on it!"

Shane reaches for it, but the golem pulls it back. Shane frowns and drops his hand, eyeing the golem warily. The golem holds it out again.

"I think it's for you," Shane says, keeping his eyes on the golem.

"Um, ok," I say, confusion marking my tone.

I reach out and this time the golem does not pull it back. I take the paper and the golem turns its body until it is facing me, hands by its side, face blank.

"What now?" I ask, holding the paper in front of me.

Shane tilts his head at the paper then the golem. "I think…I think it is waiting for you to give it an order."

"What!" I screech and drop the paper.

It is one thing to start to understand that not all supernaturals are evil but another to partake in the magic that is the Other world.

"I think it has something to do with your lightning," he surmises.

My cheeks redden. Just another thing to add to the list of what happens when I electrocute supernaturals. My power is totally helpful. Not.

Or maybe in this case it is. I now have an animated clay being to follow my commands.

"What do I do?"

"Put the paper in its mouth and give it an order." Shane leans in and whispers like it's a secret, "I suggest having it take the Rogue to the proper authorities."

I twist my mouth to the side in response to his sarcasm, causing him to chuckle.

I pick up the paper off the ground, gripping it tight between two fingers. "Alright then, here it goes."

I reach up and the golem automatically opens its mouth, continuing to stare straight ahead. I glance at Shane who nods encouragingly then place the paper in its mouth, quickly removing my hand once the paper is in and rubbing it on my pants.

"Ok, um, Golem, take this Rogue to the House of Heroes' nearest office with this message." I reach into my backpack and find some sticky notes and a pen, then quickly write out a note explaining who the Rogue is and what he told us. I sign it as House of Mystery rather than my name for validity and hope they take it seriously. The golem takes the note in one hand and picks up the Rogue in the other with zero effort then trots away from us without a backward glance.

"What will happen to the golem after its mission is done?" I ask, staring after the level one mons— I mean supernatural.

"It should dissolve into a pile of dust."

Fascinating. I need to add that to my notebook of information.

"So, I guess we should head back to The House of Mystery now?" I phrase my suggestion as a question, unsure if Shane has any need for me anymore. He brought me along for help, and now that we caught the Rogue and got our info, I feel like we are needed more at HQ than here in Pennsylvania. But I leave it up to him since he is the lead on this case.

I'm not ready to part from him yet. I have had more adventure and mystery with him than in my whole life. I also feel flustered, excited, and…heart pounding when he is near.

Shane bites his bottom lip and for a second I think he has somehow read my mind. My cheeks flush and I look down, pulling my backpack in front of me to search through it though I only want to hide my face.

"Well…" I see him from the corner of my eye rub the back of his neck and frown, struggling with something.

I look up and tilt my head. At my questioning look he seems to come to a decision and straightens. "Do you trust me?"

"Yes," I say without hesitation, surprising us both.

I should consider that I have only known him a couple of days which is not enough time to trust somebody. However, something in me trusts him despite the obvious secrets he is keeping. He saved my life, fought against the Rogue to protect the room of hero knowledge, and helped get vital information about the Rogues' plans.

He shoots me a dazzling smile and nods his head in the direction of town. "Shall we then?"

"Sure…Where are we going?"

"I thought you trusted me?"

I narrow my eyes at his evasiveness, making him chuckle but he gives in.

"We are going to meet a friend."

"Do we have time for…" The way he said friend makes me pause. "Wait, by friend, do you mean human or supernatural?"

The look he gives me doesn't put me at ease. If anything, I want to hyperventilate. Am I really following this mystery man to meet an unknown supernatural?

As I continue following him, I come to the realization that I am nervous and interested, but surprisingly not scared by the prospect.

In town, Shane moves confidently down the street. A couple of people wave to him, and after each one my brows pinch together a bit more. How many times has he been to Pittsburgh? Obviously enough for people to know him. Unless people of Pittsburgh are just that friendly, in which case why aren't they waving to me?

We turn a corner and I almost run into Shane's back when he stops suddenly and points across the street to a building with a simple sign stating it is a florist's shop. "Here we are."

I study the one-story, nondescript building with surprise. Without the sign, I would have assumed it was a random office building. There are bars on the windows and a few potted plants outside. A sign hanging on the door says it's open, but I don't see anyone going in or out.

"Your supernatural friend is a…florist?"

He smiles secretly and dips his head to my ear, whispering, "Actually, she is a wood nymph."

My jaw drops. I have read books that had the mythical creatures called wood nymphs, beings that inhabit trees and take on the characteristics of their woodlands. Is it true that inside that shop is real life wood nymph? Is she from the Other world?

I look at Shane out of the corner of my eye to see if he is joking but there is no sign that he is messing with me. Either not seeing my astonishment or choosing to ignore it, Shane looks both ways down the street then puts his hand on the small of my back and gently pushes me toward the shop.

A bell jingles as we enter, but there is no one here to greet us. I look around and inhale the aroma of the vibrant, fresh flowers. They are so bright and plump that I touch a petal of the nearest flower, a pink tulip, to make sure it is real. Vines creep up the walls and purple wisteria hang from the ceiling. Everywhere I look is some kind of greenery or flower. The most remarkable part of the shop though is the large tree in the middle of the room. It reaches up through the ceiling, though I don't remember seeing a tree sticking out of the roof from outside. It doesn't seem possible but there it is. Sunlight shines through the cracks around the trunk near the ceiling throwing a beam on the floor which creates a spotlight on the tree. I don't understand how the inside of this shop can be so beautiful, while the outside looks so dull.

"Follow me," Shane says, grabbing my hand and tugging me toward the back of the shop.

He stops in front of a door with an 'employees only' sign and turns to me. "There is something I should tell you before we go back there."

I chuckle. "More than the surprising fact that you know wood nymphs?"

He flashes me a brief smile. "Yes." He opens his mouth to tell me but the door behind him is suddenly flung open.

"My Lord," a female voice gasps.

Shane purses his lips and pinches the bridge of his nose as he closes his eyes for a moment.

"My Lord?" I whisper to him. "Are you some kind of King to the wood nymphs or something?" I laugh, thinking he will join in at my joke.

He opens his eyes and slowly drops his hand, giving me a weak smile.

My laughter dies and I stare at him with my mouth gaping. "Wait, what?" I shout. "You really are their King? How is that possible?"

Shane shakes his head. "Well, no, actually that is my brother."

I point at him. "You…You're…brother is a King?" Ok, I am obviously missing something huge here.

Shane sighs. "Let's go inside, I will explain everything." Shane looks around the store behind me nervously then takes my hand and leads me through the back door.

I really hope I am not making a big mistake by following him, but my curiosity is too much to ignore, and I trust Shane.

We pass by the woman who interrupted us, and I do a double take at her appearance. Her brown skin is layered with bark of a tree and vines twist around her arms and into her hair. Her hair is done up in a thousand little braids with flowers dotted throughout and her eyes are unnaturally large and mossy green. She smiles warmly at me though I can tell she is curious about my presence as she keeps shooting questioning glances at Shane. The wood nymph closes the door behind us while Shane leads me to a couch in an apartment of sorts.

"Can I get you anything?" The wood nymph asks us, mostly focusing on Shane— Lord Shane.

"Tea, please."

The wood nymph bows at Shane's request and enters a side room that I assume is the kitchen, leaving Shane and I alone.

I turn to him and raise my brows.

Shane clears his throat and shifts so he is facing me as well. "Alright, I guess I will just jump right in." He clears his throat and gives me a serious look. "Jo…I am not human."

My eyes widen. If he is not human, then what is he? And how is that possible? I thought he is part of the House of Mystery. However, now that I think about it he never confirmed that. I have been traveling with a supernatural! Oh my Gosh. I could have died or been kidnapped like the other Heroes.

No, Shane wouldn't do that. He had plenty of opportunities to hurt me and all he has done is save me and help me find information. But why? What is his gain?

"Jo? Say something."

"Um…" I am at a loss for words.

"Let me start at the beginning." He settles into the couch signaling that this will be a long story. "In Alstoria, or what the humans here call the Other world, there are three kingdoms." He ticks off the three on his fingers as he explains, "The Fae who mostly keep to themselves, the Besondere or 'Specials', and the Bestia or 'the Beasts'."

I nod to let him know I am listening, but my head is still trying to process the fact that my partner is not human. However, the more he speaks the more my chest fills with excitement and wonder at learning of this Other world, or Alstoria, and I want to urge him to speak faster so I can learn more. I pull out my notebook from my backpack and open it to a new page, ready to record everything he tells me.

"About sixty years ago, your time—"

"Your time?" I interrupt.

Shane nods patiently. "The time in this world is faster than Alstoria. To us it has only been twenty years or so but to you it has been six decades. So, about sixty years ago, your time, the king of the Bestia declared war on the Besondere, that's my people, by killing the King and Queen, my parents."

I gasp and cover my mouth. His parents were murdered? That's awful!

I place a comforting hand on his arm, and he shoots me a grateful smile before continuing.

"I wasn't much older than two years old, so I don't remember them very well. My brother immediately inherited a kingdom at war and a toddler to raise."

I blink. "Wait, wouldn't that make you, like, sixty-two years old then?"

Shane chuckles. "Time is different, remember? Here, I am about twenty-two. In Alstoria, I have only been gone for a little over two years so if I never left, I would only be seventeen. But since I came here, my body has adjusted to Earth time and seven years have passed."

I nod, but my mind is splitting from trying to keep up with the time difference. I can't help but picture him with an old man beard despite what he said.

The wood nymph comes back into the room with two steaming cups of tea, making Shane pause the story for a moment. She places them down in front of us on the table then bows to Shane and takes a seat in an armchair on the other side of the room.

"Thank you, Nessa," Shane says, nodding at the wood nymph.

I nod my thanks to her, then take the teacup into my hands. The warmth seeps into my skin and the aroma fills the space around me. I take a sip letting the liquid fill me with rosy sweetness.

"Ok, so this Bestia King declared war on the Besondere, your people…" I glance at Nessa wondering if she is part of the same kingdom then decide she must be if she called him 'my Lord.' "…and, what? Chased you out of your kingdom? Brought the war to this world? Why are you here and not there?"

That part is still confusing me. Why is he, a Prince, here if the war is in Alstoria? Are they refugees? Are they here to fight the Bestia on this side? So many questions!

Shane makes an uncomfortable cough and takes a swig of his tea. He flashes a glance at Nessa then looks back at me.

I look back and forth between them but when neither of them speaks I wave my hands in the air impatiently. "Well?"

Shane pushes his shoulders back and tugs at the bottom of his vest to straighten it. He tilts his chin up slightly, giving him an air of authority. "The Besondere have always been the protectors of the portals. However, when King Jerran of the Bestia started this war he found a way to tear the fabric of our world, causing random portals to appear all over the kingdoms and our people kept finding themselves randomly sucked through to this world, the portal stripping them of some of their energy as they go through making them weaker and unable to get back." Shane clears his throat and looks away. "I am one of those people."

Once again, I find myself gasping. One of these times I am going to be swallowing a fly with how much my mouth keeps hanging open.

"We think King Jerran has found a way to gather enough energy to open his own portals and will be sending his forces here soon," Nessa adds.

Shane nods at Nessa's words. "Yes, that is why heroes have been going missing, they have been drained of Alstoria energy to fuel his portals."

My mind spins at this information. *Drained of Alstoria energy.* He must mean the energy that the portals infect people with giving them superpowers.

"We need to tell the Council," I say, jumping from the couch.

Shane stands with a firm, "No."

I frown and turn to him. "Why not? The Council will know what to do about this impending threat. They are the logical next step."

"Jo," Shane points to Nessa and himself. "We are not exactly human. They don't like our kind and will never believe us."

I flinch at his comment. I want to deny it, but he is right. No one knows about the supernatural enough to see them as anything but a threat. But we must tell the Council something and who better to do it then a member of the House of Mystery? It is our job to uncover the mysteries of this unique Other world and report them to the Houses. They would have to believe me and accept my sources. Doubt niggles at my mind. I am new to the House of Mystery though and I don't even have an alias yet.

I grin as an idea forms. I pull my phone out and send a quick message then tuck it away once I get a response.

"What are you doing?" Shane asks warily.

"I know how we can get the Council to listen to us. We need to go home though and meet with a couple of people."

Shane sighs. "Fine. But if they try to kill me, I want you to know that I will not hesitate to say I told you so."

"Noted."

Nessa stands and collects our teacups. "Stay here for the night and leave in the morning."

I check the time on my phone and notice it is getting late in the day. I look nervously around the room. Stay in the same place as supernaturals? I ball my hands into fists, tired of my back and forth on how I feel about the supernatural. From now on, I am team Shane and whoever he says is an ally.

Shane nods and Nessa leaves the room.

We look nervously at each other and the moment grows awkward.

"So…you're not human, hmm?"

A look of fear crosses over his features but disappears just as fast. His shoulders tense and he avoids my eyes.

I reach out and touch his shoulder. "Hey, it's ok. It's not like I am going to call the Heroes here to detain you all."

Shane snorts. "As if they could catch me." He doesn't look as confident as he is trying to pull off.

It tugs at some protective part of me. "Seriously, I'm cool with it."

He gives me a small smile. "Thanks."

I open my mouth to ask what he is but close it thinking that seems kind of rude. It's rude, right?

"Well…" Shane points to a door on the other side of the living room. "You can take that room. I will sleep on the couch."

"What about Nessa?"

"I sleep in the tree," Nessa answers, coming out of the kitchen.

"Right, of course you do." I play it off but inside my mind is trying to comprehend how a person sleeps in a tree. Magic, that's how.

Nessa leaves, presumably to go sleep in her tree, and I head for the bedroom, needing to be alone to process everything.

"Jo," Shane calls out.

I turn, waiting expectantly.

"About your powers…"

I raise my brows waiting for him to finish. Does he know something about them?

He deflates and turns to the couch. "Never mind."

I narrow my eyes at his back but decide not to push it…yet. We have both had a long day.

Chapter 17

Nessa sees us off by handing me a pink carnation and some food for the trip back home. Shane nods at her and she bows in return.

When she stands straight, Nessa shoots me a hesitant glance. She leans in closer to Shane and whispers something. I feel a bit annoyed that she would hide something from me, but it quickly disappears. I am a random human to her. I don't blame her for not trusting me.

Shane shakes his head and pats her on the shoulder, reassuring her of something.

When Nessa goes back through the 'employees only' door, I sidle up to Shane, ready to ask what that was all about when we hear an explosion from outside. It is faint telling me it is maybe a block or two over. We rush out of the shop to see smoke billowing into the air over a few buildings in front of us. Immediately we hear the screams of people and the screeching of tires as drivers try to prevent crashing. With one look at each other we decide to investigate and race toward the screaming.

Shane is obviously much faster than I and once he notices my lag he stops and scoops me up into his arms. I let out a surprised squeak and grip his vest as he starts running at super speed, the wind whipping my hair around, lashing my cheeks. Everything is a blur, so I duck my head to rest against his chest to keep myself from dizziness.

In what seems like only a couple seconds, we are in the midst of chaos.

The first thing I notice is the two-story building on fire across the street with screaming people running in all directions away from it. The second thing I notice is the giant, swirling, blue-black portal about twenty feet away from the inferno.

I gasp and wiggle in Shane's arms until he puts me down. I immediately reach for my phone and dial Raven's number. Thank goodness I got her contact info at the Gala.

"Who are you calling?" Shane asks next to my ear.

Shivers race down my neck from his breath and my mind spins from his nearness. I shake my head to rid myself of the silly feelings. I need to get Raven and Astra here ASAP. I hold up my finger as a response and Shane backs off, turning back to the mayhem in front of us.

"Hello?" I hear a southern accent say from the other line.

"Raven? It's me, Jo. I am in Pittsburgh right now and a portal just opened up," I shout to be heard over the screaming people and crackling blaze.

"Send me the address, we will be right there." She hangs up before I can say more.

I smile and send her a quick text explaining where we are as best as I can without knowing the address. I am glad I didn't need to explain the situation more and that she knew exactly what I meant by calling her.

I put the phone away and look around. The portal couldn't have started the fire on its own which means something must have come through.

I turn to Shane who is eyeing the portal warily, seeming to be on the same track.

"We need to check for injured and see if anything came out of that portal," I say.

I start to run toward the fire to check around the building in case someone is stuck inside or fallen nearby but Shane reaches out and grabs my arm.

"You can't go over there!" He shouts urgently, almost panicked. His eyes are wide, fearful, as he glances at the flames.

"Why not?"

He stares at me incredulously and gestures wildly to the fire.

I smile at him, feeling touched that he would worry about me, then pat his hand which is still gripping my arm. "I will be fine, come with me if you're worried or check the portal's surroundings."

I don't wait to see if he follows. I pull away and run toward the fire until I cannot get any closer without burning my eyebrows off or searing my skin from the heat. I know shouting for anyone nearby would be useless. They wouldn't be able to hear me over the noise of the fire and screaming people. I search around the building and squint through the flames for any bodies, but I don't see anyone.

The building supports start to crack and fall, making the heat intensify. I back up with a hand over my face to block the heat and smoke and notice movement in my peripheral vision. I turn just in time to see a small, red, demon-like creature slip between two other buildings. It had little horns on its head, wings on its back, and a scorpion tail. Its arms and legs were long and gangly yet that didn't stop it from being quick.

I glance toward the portal to see if it is still there. My eyes widen and I take a step toward the portal when I see Raven holding an unconscious Astra near the blue-black void. Then I take a deep breath of relief when I realize Astra is resting on a pillow. She must be projecting her astral form. I look around for Shane but don't see him. I'm sure he is around somewhere but I don't have time to look for him.

I turn back to where I last saw the supernatural and run in between the buildings, my silver dagger at the ready. I know better than to blast it with lightning.

I am in an alley with a dead end, but everything seems quiet and still. Where are you, little monster? I walk slowly, carefully running my eyes over every little thing. From the one glimpse I saw of it, the creature is small so it could be hiding anywhere.

I check behind a dumpster and under a few boxes but still nothing. I make it all the way to the end without seeing anything. I can't spend my whole time looking for it. I will have to tell the Heroes and let them know about it running around. For now, I need to get back to the portal and help Astra.

Before I can take a step, a fireball shoots from the dumpster near the mouth of the alley heading straight for me. I dive to the right and crouch, letting the fireball hit the wall behind me then I spring up and race toward the dumpster. Another spout of fire is flung at me and I dodge it. This time I see the little red demon as it shoots out from its hiding place, into the street.

Oh no you don't.

Thankfully there are not as many people around, only those who are risking their lives to get a two-minute video that may or may not get them a million hits on YouTube. The cars have all stopped and been abandoned due to the fire and portal, so it is easy to follow the supernatural as it makes its way to…oh no. It's heading for the portal. Astra is still in there!

I fling my backpack around and replace my dagger with a gun. I figure regular bullets will do so I don't bother pulling out my short supply of silver bullets. I pause a second, aim, and fire.

A hiss from the little beast and a *thump* tell me I hit my mark.

I walk slower, gun at the ready, as I approach it. It hisses when I come into view and tries to move toward the portal again. I glance toward the unnatural blue-black circle and see Astra still lying down on the pillow in Raven's lap. A quick search around the area and still no Shane. Sirens blare in the distance.

Finally.

The response times for emergencies are terrible.

I put my gun away when I see the creature is not going to get away. The beast is small, only reaching my thigh. It is red with a wide mouth full of razor-sharp teeth. It's fingers and ears are pointed, and its eyes stare at me full of hatred. I don't know what it is but I know it is the one that caused the fire and probably would have done more damage if I hadn't stopped it.

I reach into my backpack for some monster cuffs, but the little demon suddenly shoots fire at me again causing me to drop my backpack as I dive to the side. Even wounded, the creature is fast and almost reaches the portal before I can stand up.

"Raven!" I shout, hoping she will hear me over the other noises.

Her head whips around and she spots the creature immediately. She gently lays Astra down and disappears in a cloud of black smoke. I start running toward the portal and Raven reappears in front of it, blocking the creature from escape.

The injured supernatural halts and veers to the side. Raven and I lunge for it but it slips out of our grasp.

"What is that?" Raven asks.

"I have no idea, but it shoots fire so be careful."

She nods and we go after it again.

Where is Shane? He could have this bagged and tagged in the blink of an eye.

If only I had a net in my backpack. Maybe I should add one the next time I get supplies. I startle, realizing the familiar weight on my back is missing. I look back to where I had fallen and see my black tactical pack lying near an abandoned Subaru.

"Jo!" I spin at the sound of Raven's panicked voice and see her pointing at the portal.

The portal is shrinking. Astra is still in there and there is no way we can get her out. Raven teleports over to Astra and starts tapping her cheek, trying to get her to wake up.

Without anyone chasing it anymore, the red supernatural veers toward the disappearing portal and flies at it. No! I shoot out a hand crackling with energy I don't remember summoning and shoot a bolt of blue lightning at the creature.

"Jo, no! Let it go!"

Shane? Where has he been? And why does he want me to let it get away?

Too late now.

The red demon makes it through a second before my blast reaches it. The bolt of blinding energy hits the portal instead and a loud *boom* followed by a *fizzle* reverberates, reminding me of a firework without the pretty colors. The portal halts its shrinking and starts to grow bigger. The light around it brightens and spins faster.

Shane appears at my side, gawking at the portal with dread. He has soot marks on his cheeks and his hair is disheveled.

His reaction makes an uneasy feeling settle in my stomach. "What? What is it?"

"You just locked the portal in place. Anything can come through now."

I locked the portal in place? What does that mean?

He doesn't get to explain.

A screeching noise, as if something is being dragged along metal, sounds behind us making Shane and I spin to face whatever new threat arrived.

Five individuals approach, forming a semi-circle around us, the front man grinning as he scrapes long metal…nails? talons?...along the side of a car.

Shane tenses, standing straighter with clenched fists, and angles his body to attack.

I don't need to ask anyone who these people are. By the menacing look in their eyes and the insignia of a black mask outlined in silver on their chests, they are Rogues.

Good. I know my lightning at least works against Rogues.

"Looky what we got here," The lead Rogue tells the one on his left. His hair is shaved on the sides leaving only a line of it on top and he has piercings on his left eyebrow.

The Rogue on the left grins, his long dark hair shading the sides of his face and raises his right hand to point at me—no not a hand, a hook. This guy has a hook for a hand! Please tell me his alias is Captain Hook. It doesn't matter either way, that is what I am calling him now.

"They will be happy about this catch, especially when we tell them what she can do," Captain Hook replies.

Shivers go down my arms at his words and my power responds by sending blue sparks racing across my skin. They want to kidnap us like the other missing Heroes. Well, I am not going down without a fight.

My eyes scan over the other three then I do a double take. The one on the far right of the lead Rogue is wearing a black cape and mask with pointed ears at the top. He has a utility belt filled with various items that I am both wary of and excited about. Maybe I should trade in my tactical backpack for a utility belt. I quickly trash that idea since

I have too many things and I would not get away with wearing it out in public, if not by Sherry then by the police.

"Holy costume, Batman," I giggle.

The knockoff Batman understands my reference but doesn't seem to appreciate it. He takes an item from his belt and throws it at me. I jump to the side just in time for the item to whiz past my legs. I risk a glance backward to see it wrapped around a light pole.

So, he has a bolas. Not as cool as a batarang, but whatever.

That must be the signal they needed to attack because suddenly the other four jump forward and we are in battle.

"You take Captain Hook and Wolverine. I've got Knockoff Batman and the other two."

"What, no name for the other two?" Shane asks jokingly.

"I'm working on it."

He grins at me then launches toward the Rogues in a blur of movement. I face the others and let my sparks intensify as I beat my fist into the palm of my other hand. My opponents pause, staring at my skin warily.

The three Rogues share a glance. Somehow reading each other's minds, all three split up to try to circle me.

I don't let them get far, knowing if they surround me I will be attacked from all sides which I cannot defend against.

I leap toward the one on my right, a woman in a skintight, reptilian-printed suit. Her auburn hair is pulled back into a ponytail and her eyes, which were once green, flash to yellow and slit like a reptile. I dub her Reptilia.

I toss out a bolt of energy, but she dodges by leaping onto the side of a vehicle and sticking there like a gecko. I don't have time to process this power as she leaps from the car at me. At the same time, I see Knockoff Batman from the corner of my eye pull something from his belt and twist it before tossing it at me. I duck and roll to avoid both attacks and watch in satisfaction as the item hits Reptilia instead. A blast of smoke is released against her body, billowing up to cover her face causing her to collapse in a coughing fit.

I spin toward Knockoff Batman and risk a glance around for the third Rogue. Where did he go?

My question is answered in the form of a kick to my back. I fly forward and manage to catch myself on a nearby vehicle before I fall to the ground. I whip around and raise my electrified hands. Darn it, where is my gun when I needed it.

Two of the three Rogues advance on me. Knockoff Batman with a device in his hand that looks similar to the smoke bomb and the other guy who I have yet to see use a power. I look past them, but I don't see Reptilia. With the car to my back, I am not worried about being snuck up on, so I look around for the missing Rogue.

I suck in a breath when I spot her heading toward Raven and Astra. Astra is now sitting up— thankfully she came back from the Other side— but they are both facing the portal and do not see the approaching threat.

"Raven!" I shout.

I toss a flurry of energy at the two Rogues in front of me making them step back and groan in pain, then race to my friends.

"Raven! Astra!"

Reptilia hisses like a snake and leaps toward them, realizing her element of surprise is gone. Thankfully, Raven heard me and turns to see Reptilia advancing on them. Her eyes widen and she says something to Astra that I am too far away to hear before they disappear in a cloud of black vapors. Reptilia flies through the smoke left behind by Raven's disappearance and turns to me with fists clenched.

I hear footsteps behind me and whirl around to face the two approaching Rogues. I form a ball of blue energy then fling it at Knockoff Batman with one hand while my other hand sends a bolt of lightning at the Rogue next to him. The lightning is loud and bright, nearly blinding me as it flies forward. Stars dot my vision, but I am still able to see I was successful in hitting the Rogue with lightning. He lies prone on the ground with a charred circle on his chest.

Knockoff Batman must have avoided my shot because he throws his smoke bomb without a hint of pain. It aims true and I have the brilliant idea to swat it out of the air like a baseball. Except my genius idea backfires when the bomb explodes against my hand sending debilitating smoke around me, into my face and lungs. I cough and double over, unable to pull in a decent breath.

"Get her!" Reptilia shouts behind me.

Something hits my legs and wraps around them. I fall to my knees, no longer able to move without tripping.

Darn bolas!

When a hand grabs my arm after the smoke dissipates, I send out a spark of energy. The owner of the hand, Knockoff Batman, yelps and pulls his hand away.

"You're going to have to prick her," Knockoff Batman says to Reptilia.

I am still coughing but I am finally able to get fresh breaths. "Don't…touch…me," I say through a fit of coughs.

I conjure my energy and have it spread up my arms to my shoulders. If they want to touch me, they will get a shock. Just then, a crackling sound comes from the portal. We turn our heads to see a little red demon come through.

"The imp is back," Reptilia grimaces.

So that's what the creature is. An imp. Reptilia doesn't sound like she is pleased to see it. I stay quiet and still, hoping they will forget about me.

"It's one of King Jerran's, we can probably use it to send a message to the Other side," Knockoff Batman says, continuing to ignore me.

I use their distraction to reach out and grip their ankles, sending electricity up their leg and across their bodies. They scream, spasm, then collapse to the ground on either side of me. I stare at them, looking for the rise and fall of their chests. When I see their chests move, I breathe out a sigh of relief.

A hissing noise makes my head jerk up to where the imp is standing near the portal. It is staring at me with its sharp teeth bared. It must have been alerted to my presence by the Rogue's screams.

I freeze. There is no way I can run with the bolas still around my legs. I can't electrocute it because I will only strengthen it. Fear pools in my gut.

It seems to know I am trapped because it slowly advances on me as it forms a fireball in its tiny hand.

I yank at the bolas, but it is annoyingly tight. I search for the balls on it so I can untangle it, but the imp is almost here. It raises its hand, ready to toss the fireball. I give up on the bolas for now and ready myself to roll away from the flames.

Suddenly the imp is tackled from the side by a blur causing the fire in its hand to be knocked off course. The fire hits a vehicle ten feet away from me. The car windows explode with the force of the blast and the metal body is immediately engulfed in flames.

I cover my head until I feel the raining glass cease then quickly look to the portal to see what happened with the imp.

Shane.

He is wrestling with the small demon, drawing too close to the portal for comfort. I hiss when the imp slashes Shane's face with its sharp nails and touch my cheek, feeling the sympathy pains on my own face. Shane jumps away before the imp can do it again.

I need to help him.

Instead of yanking ineffectually at the bolas, I take the time to untangle the balls and rope from around my legs. A grunt makes me look up to see another person has entered the fight. I growl at the situation and work faster.

Shane turns so he is facing both Wolverine and the imp. Blood runs down his cheek from the cut the imp gave him and his vest is torn on the side, probably from the same claws.

I finally get the bolas untied from around my legs, toss it aside, then jump up with sparks at the ready. I shoot out an arm at Wolverine, letting a stream of lightning fly, but he sees it and jumps out of the way. He isn't fast enough to avoid it completely and grabs his right arm where my blast hit him. He glares at me but turns back to Shane who is occupied with the imp.

I watch in horror as Wolverine rakes his metal nails down Shane's back using the arm that wasn't burned by my electricity. Shane's back arches in agony as his face contorts in pain. I sprint toward Shane and shoot a blast at Wolverine, but I am not paying too much attention to my aim and it misses him by a foot.

The imp takes this opportunity to flee the fight, disappearing among the abandoned cars and deserted buildings.

Uncaring about the imp's escape, Wolverine gives me a vicious grin before he raises his foot and kicks Shane in the back where the claw marks are oozing blood. Shane shouts in pain and falls toward the blue-black void.

I scream and wish with all my being I had Shane's speed. But my wish is unanswered, and I watch with tears in my eyes as Shane falls through the portal and disappears from this world.

I stop in my tracks and my knees wobble, almost sending me to the ground. This can't be happening. I stare at the portal hoping to see Shane come back through. A few seconds tick by and the portal is the same unchanging blue-black vortex.

I know he is a supernatural, born in Alstoria, and his travel through the portal should be safe but there is no way for me to know that for sure. I have no idea if he has enough energy for the trip or where he will land on the Other side or if I will ever see him again.

I turn a hate filled gaze on Wolverine.

He raises a hand to his mouth and widens his eyes innocently. "Oops." He cackles at his fake act.

Rage fills me and I scream as I launch myself at him, blue energy skating across my arms and hands. I form a ball of electricity and throw it at him. He dodges but I can tell the movement hurts his injured arm. His focus on my ball of energy gives me the chance to get close to him and I swing out with all the anger and sorrow I have and hit him in his injured arm. Not only does my punch cause him to have a dead arm for a moment, but the electricity I send out with it makes his whole body jerk and convulse. He never even had a chance to rake me with his metal talons before he collapses a couple feet from the portal.

I have an urge to roll him into the Other world but decide I will not stoop to his level of evil. Instead, I pull my phone out of my pocket— miraculously it is not broken— and dial Raven's number.

She picks up on the first ring.

"Jo?"

I swallow a lump of emotion. "I have five Rogue's here that need to be taken into custody," I say in a monotone voice.

"O-ok. Is…everything alright?"

I sigh audibly but before I can answer she speaks. "That bad? Ok, I will contact the Heroes and be right there."

I feel a sting in my neck. I swat at my neck hoping to get rid of the feeling and my fingers brush against a feather. Panic starts to flood my body. I yank at the feather in my neck and bring it around, realizing it is a dart. "Raven?" I say, panic in my tone.

"Yes?"

I don't answer. My body is going numb and holding the phone is becoming difficult. I can't open my mouth to speak as my jaw is now screwed shut.

"Jo? What's going on?"

The phone is plucked from my fingers and Reptilia steps into my line of sight, smiling smugly. I try to conjure my lightning, but nothing happens, and I can't move as my whole body is now paralyzed. She hangs up and tosses my phone away then pulls another dart from somewhere beyond my sight. She smirks at me as she licks the tip of the dart, her eyes flashing yellow and slitting like a reptile's, then pricks me in the neck with the coated dart. Everything goes fuzzy around the edges and my mind settles into a haze.

It feels like when I go to the dentist and they give me that gas to numb my mouth and it kind of gives my mind the feeling of being there but also not being there. That's how I feel now. I am here, awake, aware, but also in a daze where I can do nothing and don't really comprehend my surroundings. I am both unconscious and conscious.

Reptilia goes behind me and pulls my shoulders back until I start falling. She catches me and lifts me into her arms with strength that doesn't seem possible with her figure. Without a backward glance, she walks away from all the destruction, the portal, and her comrades.

I can do nothing but go along with the ride.

Chapter 18

Reptilia sets me down after what seems like forever. The surface beneath me is hard but flexible making me wonder what I was placed on. I still cannot move a muscle so I cannot look around to see where we are but straight above me is a tall ceiling with crisscrossing beams and long fluorescent lights. I have only seen these kinds of ceilings in warehouses such as Costco and in movies. What are we doing in a warehouse?

Reptilia leaves my line of sight but does not go far. She is close enough for me to hear her when she announces her arrival to whoever else is here. Three others welcome her, meaning there are at least four people I will have to get through to get out of here. Probably more, depending on where 'here' is.

"Where are the others?" One of the strangers asks her in a gravelly male voice.

"They will be along eventually…maybe."

Wow, some partner she is. Note: never trust a Rogue to have your back.

"Who's that? Do we need to put her in a cage?" A different voice, also male, asks.

If my muscles were not paralyzed, my body would have stiffened. As it is, my mind floods with terrible images of being thrown in a dirty cage like an animal among rows of other cages. Is this where they keep the other Heroes?

"Nah, she is good for now. Where is he?" Reptilia asks, ignoring his first question.

"What's it to you?" A female voice sneers.

Silence stretches. I imagine the two Rogues glaring at each other but cannot confirm my suspicions. I don't know this other Rogue, but I wouldn't antagonize Reptilia if I was her. Reptilia is a cold-blooded Rogue—probably in the literal sense as well—and may not hesitate to stick a poison dart into the other Rogue's neck.

While they are distracted, I focus on my fingers. My whole body is still but if I can just move one finger then I will know if the paralysis is wearing off. Only then can I figure out an escape plan.

"Hey, hey, c'mon, we're all on the same side," one of the men says. "He's upstairs."

"Did somebody ask for me?"

My focus strays to the newcomer. For some reason, his voice sends chills down my back. He speaks with an air of authority that suggests he is the head honcho and holds enough danger in his tone that sets my alarm bells ringing. I struggle harder to move, knowing if I don't do something soon I will either be dead or wish I was.

Reptilia snorts softly and mutters, "With your power, you know full well who was asking for you."

The boss man either doesn't hear her or chooses to ignore her comment. I hear footsteps move closer. A moment later, the boss man's voice is only a few away but I still cannot see him. "A hero? Why haven't you put her in a cage yet?"

Reptilia comes closer until her tight lizard-print suit is in my peripheral vision. "She is not going anywhere. She is under a heavy dose of my paralyzing venom." She makes a hesitant noise but cuts off.

"Well? What is it?" The boss man says impatiently.

The other three Rogues snicker quietly. Reptilia hisses at them before answering.

"This one's different. I thought you might like to know. She…she did something to the portal. She opened it again and, like, locked it in place or something. It is the longest I have ever seen a portal stay open before."

"Hmm, intriguing." The way he says it sends another round of chills down my back. It promises pain and experimentation. It promises terror and a loss of freedom more than a cage would. I don't know what my power can do but I know if they find a way to use it to open portals, the Rogue's will be unstoppable.

No, no, no. No way am I sticking around for that. I urge my power to rise up, my fear and desperation fueling it. I feel the smallest of sparks at my fingertips and move one, relief and hope flooding me when it twitches. The venom is wearing off!

"Does the portal still give off energy?"

I see Reptilia shrug out of the corner of my eye. While they are busy discussing the portal, I try to move more of my body and am pleased when all of my fingers move. I send more of my power out, hoping to burn away the venom some more.

The man's voice grows closer. "Imagine the soldiers we can create if we have unlimited energy from the Other world. Imagine King Jerran's glee when he finds out his army—" His words cut off and I quit trying to move, wondering what caused him to stop.

Now I see two people in my peripheral vision. I can only see them up to their elbows without hurting my eyeballs. Reptilia is crossing her arms, facing me and the man. The man is wearing a brown trench coat, the kind that reminds me of forties-era detectives in movies.

"Her?" He puffs out a breath of air through his nose, barely audible from where I lay. "I should have known," he mutters, only Reptilia and I able to hear him. He is facing me but abruptly spins around and stalks away. "Move her to a cage and make sure she is in a pair of power cuffs."

This is it. As soon as they put those cuffs on me, I will not be able to use my powers. And if Reptilia touches me while I am using my power to rid myself of the paralyzing venom, she will dose me again. I have one last chance.

I send as much electric energy as I can handle through my body as a last attempt at freeing myself. Blue light flashes around me as my body becomes a light show. All the Rogues gasp which quickly turns to shouts.

"Shoot her!" someone yells.

I don't know if they mean with real bullets or with Reptilia's venom darts, but I don't wait to find out which. My nerves tingle with feeling again and I jolt up into a sitting position, frantic to escape them. However, my movement is too quick and my body, still trying to get its muscles back into working condition, sends me tumbling off the makeshift bed which I now see are bags of fertilizer. I groan in pain when my head smacks against the side of some of the bags and my arm gets bent awkwardly beneath me.

"How did it wear off so quickly?" a Rogue asks.

"I don't know," Reptilia hisses. Her footsteps approach quickly.

I manage to raise my hand that isn't pinned beneath me and shoot a weak bolt of lightning at her, causing her to halt her progress. I use the hesitation to roll to the side, freeing my arm, and sit up. The room spins and I hold my head until the feeling passes.

Hands grip me and haul me up to a standing position. The rough movement makes my stomach twist with nausea. I conjure up my sparks and zap the person holding me. The Rogue man yelps and releases me, muttering a curse as he shakes his hands to rid them of the sting. I take the opportunity to run.

I only get a few feet away when an alarm blares and suddenly the room is filled with at least twenty Rogues. Some in costumes, some in jeans and a T-shirt. More than a few display powers while others hold weapons such as guns and knives. One guy even has a set of nunchucks. I spin in a circle and notice all my exits are blocked.

I curse and form a ball of lightning in my hand and glare at the few Rogues standing in front of the nearest door. I will not be able to defeat all these people, especially if some have powers, but I *can* fight until the end.

I throw the blue ball of crackling energy at the closest Rogue, a woman holding a gun, then dart forward to fight off the other two who are not holding any obvious weapons. My legs wobble, the muscles still weak from the venom, but I make do. I hear the others behind me rush forward and I know it is only a matter of time before I am subdued. I spin around and throw out more lightning to the people in front of me then fling my elbow backward, connecting with the gut of some guy who got too close.

I last only a couple minutes before the crowd becomes too much and I am at the pointed end of three blades and staring down the barrels of five guns. More Rogues crowd behind them shooting me glares, daring me to try to move against them.

Just then the doors behind me slam open and daylight spills in. I don't move to see the newcomer, my eyes trained on the weapons in front of me. With the way my luck is going, it is probably the boss man coming back to see what all the ruckus is about.

Pained screams erupt from behind me then abruptly cut off. I duck as a gunshot goes off and cover my head as if that will help against a bullet. Some Rogues in front of me surge forward and I roll away to avoid getting caught in the middle of them and whatever is behind me.

Bodies start dropping and the screams and battle cries get louder. Terror fills me at the sounds. I jump to my feet and spin around with a ball of energy in both hands, ready to face whatever threat has the Rogues falling left and right.

I gasp when I see what it is. *Who* it is.

The balls of energy in my hands die out.

It's Shane! He is alive and back on this world.

But his eyes are as dark as night, just like they were in the secret room in the Cathedral of Learning, and he has blood dripping from his mouth where two *fangs* protrude. Freaking fangs!

Shane zips about the room with his speed and snarls at his enemies as he disposes of their weapons and sends the Rogues flying across the room with a strength I have never seen him use before. One Rogue gets a slice in with his blade and Shane freezes. I shiver at the glare he shoots the man while a line of blood pools under his shirt from the attack. In the blink of an eye, Shane has the man held by the throat in one hand. He moves forward and sinks his fangs into the man's neck causing him to scream.

I place a hand over my gaping mouth to cover my gasp. Shane is a vampire.

Soon all the Rogues have either fled or lay about the warehouse unconscious or dead. I don't see Reptilia among the bodies, so I assume she escaped. Shane turns to me, the dark pools of his eyes seeming to peer into my soul and calling to my power. Blue sparks jump from my skin, reaching for him but we are too far away for them to touch him.

Shane slowly stalks toward me, keeping his intense eyes on mine, almost daring me to run. I stay still. I am not scared of him despite what I had just seen and the fact that his fangs are still peeking out. I know he won't hurt me. Three days ago, my first instinct would be to find a wooden stake to ram through his heart, but now, the very thought makes me sick. This is Shane. My savior. My partner. Dare I say, my friend.

He stops a foot in front of me and my sparks leap for him. This time they reach him and he inhales deeply when they make contact. A moment later the fangs disappear, and his black eyes fade away to reveal his natural deep blue color.

I gasp with realization. "That's why you never get hurt when my power touches you. You are not human."

Shane flinches and looks away.

"Wait, that doesn't make sense. Even supernaturals are in pain at first before it makes them stronger. You don't even flinch when the sparks touch you."

He says nothing.

I reach out a hand and lightly touch his arm, wanting him to look at me.

He tenses and backs away until my hand drops. "You must think I am a monster now. Go ahead. Call the Heroes." Resignation and sadness flicker over his face.

"Shane," I say softly. When he doesn't look at me, I say his name a bit more demanding. "Shane."

Finally, he looks up and my heart aches when I see the pain in his eyes. That look tells me everything I need to know. He doesn't want me to think of him as a monster which is probably why he didn't tell me what he is yesterday. He wants me to know him for *who* he is and not *what* he is. Now he thinks I will hate him. But I can never hate him. He could have easily let me be sucked dry from the incubus or killed by the Shadow Ninja. He didn't have to show up and help me now either. He also could have left me after the ball never to see me again, but he asked me to help him solve a mystery. He wouldn't have done all of that if he was evil. It's like he said to me at the Cathedral of Learning. Not all supernaturals are evil just like not all humans are good. That comment combined with his explanation from last night makes it so there is no way I could think any less of him.

I throw myself at him and wrap my arms around his neck, squeezing him to me in a tight hug. "I thought you were dead," I whisper into his neck.

His body tenses under mine but the longer I hold on the more his body relaxes until finally I feel his arms wrap around my middle, returning my embrace.

"When I came back through and you were missing, I flipped out. I thought they were going to drain your powers and kill you, or worse," he whispers back with a small growl at the end of his words. His hold on me tightens.

Or worse. The thought of being thrown into a cage and something worse than death happening sends shivers down my back. I pull back enough to look up at him.

"They said they were going to put me in a cage."

He frowns and his fangs appear, peeking out from below his lip. The sight doesn't frighten me, but it does make me curious to know more about his supernatural side.

I point at his fangs and quirk a brow. "You are going to have to tell me more about this, but for now we need to check this warehouse. I didn't mention the cage to upset you, just to suggest there may be others here." I raise both eyebrows waiting for him to catch on.

His eyes widen and his fangs slowly disappear back into his mouth. "The missing heroes."

Chapter 19

To my dismay, we don't find anyone. There is a total of five cages in the back of the warehouse, each with chains and a single blanket inside, but no Heroes. I don't know what that means but it doesn't bode well. A quick search around upstairs doesn't give us any leads either. Before we leave, I report the Rogues and hideout to Harmony using one of the Rogue's phones, thinking the House of Mystery would want to look around for any leads for their cases. I assume Harmony is going to send Discovery members and Heroes to help the House of Mystery do a more thorough investigation and clean up, but Shane and I don't stick around to wait for them.

We have a train to reschedule then catch, but first…a shower.

We make a quick stop at the Floral shop where a wide-eyed Nessa answers the door. Without questions, she ushers us into the apartment in the back. We are able to take a shower and change out of our ripped, bloody, dirty clothing while she makes us tea. I have a brief longing for my lost backpack and supplies but there is no use crying over it right now. I will do that later when I am alone.

Nessa gives me a loner outfit and a cup of tea before asking us about the attack. Shane gives her a quick recap and as the story progresses, Nessa's eyes get wider.

"Oh dear, that was quite an ordeal. What are you going to do now?"

Shane stands and holds out a hand to me. I take it, though I don't need help standing from the couch, and let him pull me up. "We must be going. Thank you for your help, I will contact you later." Once again, they share a meaningful look and I feel as if I am missing something.

Nessa nods and sees us out.

Luckily, we are able to get a train leaving within the hour. I spend the train ride grilling Shane about being a vampire and his life in Alstoria. At one point I remember the terrifying feeling of seeing him pushed through the portal. At the time I thought he would die and was happy when I saw him on this side of the void alive. However, that was his chance to go home.

"Earlier, when you were thrown back into Alstoria, why didn't you stay? You could have seen your brother again. Could have replenished your energy and gotten back to your life."

His blue eyes soften and seem to trap me within their depths. He does not say anything, but his gaze tells all.

Me. He came back for me.

My heart starts to race. My cheeks heat and I am sure they are turning red, but I can't look away. Shane's hand inches over and grips mine sending heat racing up my arms.

"I couldn't lose you," he finally says and leans forward.

I stop breathing in anticipation. It is not like the last time we were on the train. There is no table in between us. No immeasurable distance to overcome. In no time his lips are pressed to mine and the world fades until there is only us. This moment.

I open my mouth and kiss him back, turning my hand under his to grasp and pull so he moves closer. He lets go and moves his hand into my hair, ruining the carefully made ponytail.

Suddenly the train's whistle blows, making me jump, and the conductor announces our arrival in twenty minutes.

Shane blinks and leans back, releasing my hair. I smile softly when I see red appear in his cheeks letting me know he is as affected as I am. It is intriguing that a vampire can blush. Every story since ever has said vampires are like the living dead with no blood in their body. However, I can attest to the heat he exudes and the fire in his eyes. I guess that is one more thing mythology has wrong.

"Jo, you're ok!"

All I see is a flash of blue-green hair before I am tackled in a hug by Astra. I catch her and stumble back into Shane who braces us, preventing us from tumbling out through the door into the night. Astra pulls back and looks me over.

Suddenly I am grateful for the shower I took before leaving Nessa's home. Beforehand I looked like a crazy person who was dragged across a dirty street then tossed into a whirlwind. Now I had my clean, brushed, black hair tied back in a ponytail and a new, gray peasant blouse that Nessa thought would look cute on me. Shane already had clothes stashed there so after his shower he put on a fresh vest, dark blue this time, and his hair, once it was dried, looked soft to the touch which I can confirm after the kiss we shared. His scratches had long since healed thanks to his vampire healing, but I still sported a few along my arms and back.

"I'm fine," I tell my friend and colleague.

Seeming satisfied by my appearance and words, Astra moves aside to let me come farther in. Sitting on the living room couch is Harmony, Specter, and Jake. Specter gives me a respectful nod. Harmony smiles warmly and waves though I see her eyes flick curiously to Shane behind me.

Jake stands and wraps me in a tight hug. "Hey there! First mission went a little south did it? I can't wait to hear what you have to tell us. I heard it is quite the story."

Astra swats at Jake's arm. "Let her go. Can't you see she is all scratched up?"

I feel fine but I don't argue. Jake lets me go with a smile and I turn to search for my sister.

Hearing the commotion, Sherry comes rushing out of the kitchen followed closely by Raven. Both give me relieved looks before Sherry comes over and gives me a hug.

When she pulls back we stare at each other, multiple words and emotions passing between us with just a look. She gives me a nod and I relax. I know she wants to scold me for getting into danger, but she knows it is part of my job. She accepts it and supports me as I do her.

She leans closer and whispers, "Care to tell me why all these people are in our house tonight?"

I take a deep breath and let it out slowly. "You might want to sit down. It's a long story."

Sherry eyes Shane behind me sensing it has something to do with him but does as I say. Our home is not suited for many guests, so Sherry has to bring in our lawn chairs for her and Raven leaving me and Shane to either sit on the floor or stand.

"Well, to start with, this is Shane." I step aside so everyone can see him better. "He's a vampire."

Sherry jumps from her chair and her eyes turn pink telling me she is about to blast Shane right out of our house. I jump in front of him and hold up my hands.

"No, don't! He is not a monster."

I hear a gasp come from behind me and glance over my shoulder to see Shane's eyes filled with emotion. "You really think so?" he whispers.

I turn to him fully and place my hand on his chest. "I know so."

He leans in a bit and for a moment I think he is going to kiss me again. Anticipation fills me and I find myself leaning closer too.

"You better explain what you mean," Sherry demands, interrupting our moment.

I tell them of my adventures from getting on the train at noon, to the Rogue in the Cathedral of Learning, to the blast on a random Pittsburgh street. I tell them of the Rogues we encountered, my kidnapping and Shane's disappearance into the Other world, and finally about my visit with a wood nymph.

I pause there and glance at Shane. Understanding my hesitation, he steps forward to tell the rest of the story. This involves him more than me and it would be better coming from him, the original source.

As soon as he begins, Astra and Jake pull out a notepad and pencil and start scribbling furiously as Shane tells his story. I don't think I have seen Jake this serious before.

Shane tells them of the three kingdoms of Alstoria and how the Bestia declared war on the Besondere in turn leading to the random portals and supernatural occurrences on our world. I notice he leaves out his identity as Prince of one of those kingdoms and I keep quiet as well. As far as I see, it is unimportant to the overall story and if he wishes to keep a piece of him secret then I will respect that.

When he finishes, Sherry is gaping and Raven stares thoughtfully at the coffee table.

The Mystery Agents are smiling at each other probably feeling like they just hit the jackpot. "Interesting," the four of them say at once.

Classic House of Mystery motto.

"We need to alert the Council and find a way to stop these Bestia," I say to Harmony, seeing as she may know how to contact them since she is the head of a House.

"How can we tell the difference between the Bestia and Besondere?" Jake asks.

I blink at him. Oh, my goodness. How did I not think to ask such an obvious question!? I have been attacked by and seen all sorts of supernatural, but what Kingdom are they part of? I know Nessa is part of the Besondere because of her association with Shane, but what about the incubus or wyvern?

"Well, in short, the Besondere are more...humanlike. The Bestia are more animalistic."

"Humanlike?" Astra asks, still scribbling in her notepad.

It makes me itch to be writing in my own. A pang of loss shoots through my chest. All my equipment and research…lost.

Shane nods and gestures to himself. "The Besondere resemble humans more than the Bestia."

"What about the Fae?" Astra asks.

A couple others nod at her question wondering the same thing.

Shane makes a disgusted snort. "Those are fairies and elves. Too high and mighty to be bothering with the likes of us."

Astra nods as if she knows exactly what he means, though I don't see how.

"I have seen a banshee and a wyvern fight together but they are different kingdoms, right? A banshee looks human but a wyvern is more animal," Sherry remarks, flicking her gaze to mine before moving back to Shane. She is referencing the day I got my powers.

"When we cross over to this world, the portals strip us of some of our energy. Many supernatural who attack are trying to replenish their energy and the people infected from the portals store it in their bodies. It kind of drives the supernatural mad, you could say, to sense the Alstoria energy so close yet have it still be so far away. In other cases, supernaturals are hired by Rogues in exchange for energy."

"And you?" Harmony asks, speaking for the first time. "Are you mad?"

Harmony and Shane stare at each other for a long moment. They seem to be having a silent conversation, one I don't have the patience for to wait to the end.

"Of course, he's not mad. There are plenty of supernatural who aren't crazy."

Sherry's eyes widen at my conviction. It has only been a day or so and I have already changed my whole perspective. Now our views differ, and I can only hope she comes to see it my way. It is difficult though since Heroes keep going missing and some of the supernatural have their hands in the disappearances.

"Now, what are we going to do about this war?" I put my hands on my hips to show my authority even though my boss is sitting on my couch and there are plenty of people in the room who outrank me.

"I think I know where we can find Revelation," Raven says in her southern accent. "He should be at the House of Discovery."

"I don't know. The Council is on lockdown right now..." Harmony hesitates but Specter places a hand on her leg and nods for her to continue. She sighs. "Aphrodite is missing."

Raven, Sherry, and I gasp.

"Two Council members are missing?" I ask softly.

Harmony gives me a nod.

"Even more of a reason to find Revelation," Raven says. "Harmony, you must speak with the other Heads and we will go to the House of Discovery tomorrow." She gestures to Shane and me.

Harmony nods once. "Agreed. Report here tomorrow evening." She looks to Sherry with a soft smile. "If that is ok with you that is. It is your house after all."

Sherry waves away her concern. "Here is fine. I will see about getting the Heroes prepared."

"It's settled then," Shane says ending our meeting.

Jake, Astra, Specter and Harmony leave together, the latter stopping by me on her way out to whisper, "He's the one from the ball."

It isn't a question, but I nod my answer anyway.

She gives me a secretive smile before leaving but I have no idea how to interpret it.

Raven gives me a hug on her way out and whispers, "I'm glad you're ok. You gave me a scare there for a bit."

She gives Shane and Sherry a nod and a promise to be here at ten in the morning before disappearing in a cloud of black smoke.

Oh how I envy her power.

Sherry appears next and when I see what she is holding I place a hand over my mouth to hide my gasp. Tears brim in my eyes but I hold them back.

"Raven found it and told me to give it to you when she is gone."

I reach out and grasp the backpack. I open it and peer inside then give a gleeful shout when I see everything is still there, including my notebook of all things Other worldly. I hug the backpack to me tightly and whisper, "I will never let you out of my sight again." I nuzzle it and rock side to side as if cradling a baby.

Sherry snorts and rolls her eyes then claps her hands together. "Right then, I am off to bed. Jo, you know where the extra pillows and blankets are." She points at Shane and gives him a stern frown. "I better not find you trying to suck my blood while I sleep."

Shane grunts. "I am not goi—"

Sherry raises a brow at him, unknowingly looking like her mother in that moment.

"Yes, ma'am." Shane bows his head.

I snicker and Shane shoots me a look to be quiet which only makes me grin wider.

Chapter 20

Raven is here at exactly ten as promised. She rings the doorbell instead of poofing inside. I appreciate the politeness of the gesture, but it is unnecessary as we are all ready and waiting.

I answer the door and smile my welcome to her as she comes in.

"I have it on good authority that Revelation is there. I called a contact earlier this morning to confirm," Raven says getting straight to business.

Today Raven is dressed in a long, black, pleather coat that flares at the bottom. She has her red hair tied back in a tight updo and her usual raven feather hangs from a string against her chest. She has on fingerless black gloves and combat boots which, combined with her coat, gives her an air of badassery. She looks like she belongs in the Matrix or Underworld movies.

I have got to get me a coat like that.

"We should leave now. I don't know how long he will stay at the House."

"Car or…" I wave my hand in the air to signify her poofing.

"Teleporting will be the quickest, but I can only take one at a time." Raven looks over the two of us then steps to my side. "Jo first."

"Be care—" Sherry starts to say but we disappear before she finishes and suddenly my world goes black.

I stumble when my feet land on hard ground and the black vapors disappear letting light flood my vision once again. Raven tightens her grip on my arm to steady me.

"The first time is always a bit disorienting. Stay here, I'll be back." Raven disappears leaving me alone in a long linoleum hallway.

I assume we are in the Science Museum downtown since that is the headquarters for the House of Discovery, but this area is not one I have seen before. I walk to the nearest door and peer into the room, expecting to see a supernatural strapped to a table while a team of Discovery members poke and prod them. I sigh when all I see is a room with tables full of chemistry sets.

I wander down the hallway to the other doors and find they are all similar. Just science stuff and no people.

"What do you see, Sapphire?" a voice whispers next to my ear as I peer into another room.

I shriek and spin around to find Shane laughing. I swat at his chest, but he moves away before I make contact.

I shake my head at him with a glare then turn to Raven. "Did Sherry say anything?"

Raven has a small smile on her lips. "She says don't let the vampire get probed."

Shane places a hand over his heart. "Aww, I knew she'd come around."

I laugh. My sister may not like the supernatural, her whole job is to fight them after all, but she hates what the House of Discovery does to them more. I know that Sherry doesn't trust Shane yet, but she would never want him to be tortured. She also knows that he kept me safe and has helped us solve mysteries that have been hard to crack. Maybe she is starting to accept Shane as part of our team.

"Where is Revelation?" I ask, looking down the hall in both directions.

"I'm not sure, but if I had to guess, he would be in the lab." Raven starts down the hall. "This way."

I peek into each room we pass and only once we turn the corner do I finally start seeing people. People in lab coats hurry off to some place in the building while others stand in the hall looking over some papers. I only catch glimpses, but I see animals in some rooms and in others are chairs that one would find in a dentist's office with tools and lights hanging over it while people hover over the individual in the seat. The farther we go into the House, the more disturbing it gets. There are rooms where there are no windows on the doors, but I hear growls and screams coming from the other side. I flinch after each scream and Shane's jaw tightens until I think he is going to break something.

I look at Raven wondering how she can work in a place like this. I get nothing from her. Her face is devoid of all emotion, starkly different than when we first got here. I guess after a while in this place, one learns to build up walls.

Finally, after another turn, the noises grow faint and Raven stops at a door without a window. A sign on the door reads 'authorized personnel only' and a yellow caution sign below it warns of hazardous materials.

"Should we be going in there? If Revelation is in there can you just tell him to meet us out here?" I ask warily eyeing the caution sign.

"If he is busy then we will have to talk while he works, that is usually how it goes. Come on." Raven waves for us to follow then enters the room.

I look to Shane, hesitant to go in. He shares my hesitation but for a different reason. I can see the haunted look in his eyes from the screams we heard. His hands are fisted and his body is turned halfway toward the path we came from. We both know that those were supernaturals in those rooms and he probably feels like they are his responsibility. However, there is nothing we can do about them at the moment. Later, after our meeting with Revelation, maybe we can talk to the Council about the treatment being done here.

I grab his hand and gently tug him toward the room. "C'mon."

"Jo—!" Raven's voice calls before it is cut off and the door slams shut.

I share a wide-eyed look with Shane then we burst into action. Shane's speed lets him reach the door first and he throws it open.

Inside there are five people, two of them hold Raven and two others advance on us. Shane steps forward to meet them but suddenly a heavy force pushes down on us. It becomes difficult to hold myself up and I strain to keep standing. I cry out as the force becomes too much and I fall to my knees, the pressure lessening only slightly. Shane collapses next me, growling. It's as if gravity became heavier and pulled us down. We can move but it is like swimming through quicksand with ten pound weights attached to each arm. I don't know which one of the people in here has the power to effect gravity like that but it is kicking our butt.

I manage to shift enough to check on Shane and see that his eyes are completely black. That more than anything sends panic spiking through me. If they see that, then they will know he is a supernatural and will take him away.

My blue sparks react but before I can do anything a pair of thick, metal cuffs are wrapped around my wrists. They prick my skin causing the power inside me to cut off and disappear. I gasp at the emptiness it leaves behind.

I didn't realize how much my power has become a part of me until now. A pair of power cuffs are placed on Shane's wrists and his black eyes revert to their deep blue. The pressure disappears and my body jerks to the side, getting used to the sudden change in gravity. The two Discovery cronies yank us up and hold our arms tightly so we cannot escape. I see now why Raven didn't disappear. She must have power cuffs on too.

My gaze falls on the fifth man in the back of the room with his hands in his pockets and a smirk on his face. I frown, utterly confused.

My eyes drop to the trench coat he is wearing, and my frown deepens as a memory comes to mind. I remember being paralyzed, only able to see things in my direct line of sight or in my peripheral vision. The man who I pegged as a leader of sorts among the Rogues in the warehouse got close enough to me to see what he was wearing. A long trench coat. The exact trench coat Revelation is wearing now.

Coincidence? I think not!

How did I not make the connection sooner? I mean, really? How many people do I know wear trench coats?

"That's him," I whisper.

"Revelation?" Shane asks, spotting the man in the back of the room.

"Yes, but he is also the one from the warehouse."

Shane curses.

Harmony once told me there is a Council member for each House except the House of Rogues. Little did we know all of the Houses *are* represented. A Rogue among the Council.

"What's the meanin' of this?" Raven shouts, red tendrils of hair having escaped her tight updo to hang in front of her face.

"Take her away," Revelation says, waving his hand at Raven.

"No! Don't you dare!" Raven kicks and screams all the way out of the room. I can still hear her when the door closes but the sound fades the farther away they get.

Revelation steps closer to us and chuckles. "Jolene Maski. I saw you coming."

I frown at his words, confused, but then I remember. Specter and Harmony told me at the Gala that Revelation can see anything and anyone in the present.

"That was a lucky escape. You are more powerful than we imagined." He starts pacing the room. "I have been watching you since I saw you in the warehouse. I knew I should have kept tabs on you after our first meeting, but I didn't think anything of your unhelpful, insignificant power. But oh, how wrong I had been. They aren't insignificant at all are they?" He turns to me and tilts his head, studying me. The look in his eyes sends shivers down my spine. He is looking at me like a bug under a microscope. An experiment.

He turns his attention to Shane and grins. "Ah! Prince Shane of the Besondere."

My eyes widen. How does he know about Shane and the Besondere?

Revelation walks closer and peers into Shane's face. "I heard about you. The lost Prince. You'd be surprised by what I can learn from the monsters in this place." He gives him a sly smirk.

Shane jerks forward with a snarl, his eyes back to black and his fangs descend as he bares his teeth at the Councilman.

A second later the cuffs spark at his wrists and Shane cries out in pain, the fangs and black eyes disappearing just as quickly as they came.

I eye the power cuffs on Shane's wrists. I didn't know the supernatural can still access their powers when the cuffs were on. I thought it suppressed them. But maybe with enough emotion or focus, one can still access their powers. I want to access mine but the pain on Shane's face doesn't make me eager to try.

Revelation wags a finger in Shane's face, unconcerned by the vampire. "Ah, ah, ah," he scolds.

Shane jerks forward again, trying to headbutt him this time.

"Now, now. Don't hurt yourself." Revelation nods his head at the cronies holding us. "Strap them."

The woman holding me pushes me toward a door on the side of the room that I hadn't noticed before. Through the door are two dentist chairs like the ones we saw in other rooms on the way here. A light hangs above each chair and some kind of machine sits in between them.

I struggle to get away but the grip on this lady is strong. However, I am sure now that she is not the one with the gravity power. Anytime Shane struggles against the man holding him, his legs crumple a bit from an invisible force pushing down on him.

In no time, the two Discovery cronies have us on the chairs and hold us in place with straps hanging off the edge. The cuffs bite into my wrists and my body is turned to the side slightly from the angle of my arms behind my back and the backpack that makes for an uncomfortable lump. It is all quite painful.

"What are you going to do?"

I don't bother to ask why he is doing all this. If he is a Rogue leader he must be working with King Jerran. I have read enough books and seen enough movies to know the bad guy is usually after more power or if they are a lackey then they are usually promised something. Whether it is power or a promise from King Jerran, Revelation's motives are not the most pressing concern at the moment. The fact that I am strapped to a chair with a suspicious machine next to me and a crazed Council member circling me takes priority.

"He's going to drain you," Shane says from the chair next to mine. He hangs his head, sounding defeated.

I gasp and look anew at the machine. Is that how he does it? Is this where all those innocent Heroes were taken?

Revelation chuckles and starts messing with the machine. "Indeed. Once I heard about what you did to that portal in Pittsburgh, I started asking around. I have never heard of a power that helps the monsters and keeps portals open. After some…persuasion, I was told enough to piece it together. Apparently, your power comes from Besondere energy, the Keeper of the portals to be exact." Shane stiffens and makes a distressed noise. Revelation tilts his head toward Shane with raised eyebrows but keeps his knowing eyes on me. "The Prince of Lightning."

A whirring noise fills the room as the machine turns on and Revelation fiddles with some buttons on top.

I feel as if someone just punched me in the gut. All the pieces start falling into place faster than I can handle. My breathing comes in quick bursts, my lungs unable to hold it before needing more.

My mind flashes with memories. The Council explaining how humans are effected with interdimensional energy which Astra confirmed later. The Council telling me there was no portal that day I exhibited my powers. Shane on the train telling me about how long it has been since he saw his brother. Shane and Nessa in the floral shop explaining how Alstorians lose their energy when they come through the portals to our world.

It seems impossible but…

I look over to see Shane staring at me with a pleading look. "Jo…"

"Is it true? Is this your power? Your energy? Is that why you sought me out and seemed to be following me after that day with the incubus?"

Revelation grabs a needle and starts to fill the syringe with something from a small bottle.

"Were you there when my…when my parents…" I can't finish the sentence, but Shane knows what I am trying to say.

He hangs his head but says nothing.

I choke on a sob, picturing that swirling blue-black portal opening up in the middle of the road. Our car swerving to avoid going in. Our car flipping from the truck hitting us. If it wasn't for Sherry's blast lessening the blow, we would all be dead.

It was Shane's portal that caused that. It was him who came through and caused all that damage.

Except…that is not fair.

He must have only been a teenager at the time, and it wasn't his fault that he was tossed through. His family may not have died that day but he lost his home and his brother when he was thrown into an unfamiliar world. My heart aches to know Shane kept this all from me but it isn't fair to blame him for my loss.

Somehow, I gained his energy rather than energy from the portal and it has lain dormant until now. It now makes sense why he isn't affected when I shock him and how he knows what I can do with it. I have so many questions to ask Shane but now is not the time.

Revelation flicks the syringe then moves to my side. One of the silent cronies, the woman in a lab coat, holds my shoulder down while Revelation injects me with whatever he put in it.

"What is that?" I ask panicked. It better not be another paralyzing serum. For all I know, Reptilia gave him a bottle of it.

He ignores me, instead continuing with our conversation, if you can call it that. He is really living up to his name.

"King Jerran thought the Prince was dead. Lucky for me to have found him and his power in the same place. The King will be pleased. Using the other energy we have collected combined with your power, we will be able to open portals whenever for as long as we need. Just in time too. In two days, King Jerran's army will be ready to march."

He grabs a tube with an oxygen mask attached to one end and places it over my head. I expect to inhale anesthesia or something to put me to sleep but nothing comes out. Instead, every exhale I give, a blue mist forms in the mask before being sucked into the machine through the tube.

My heart is beating so fast as panic spreads through my body. Shane stares at me with such a remorseful expression on his face.

I'm sorry, he mouths silently.

His apology ignites something inside of me. It is the same feeling I had when I watched Blast fight off two monsters. When the wyvern tail was about to stab her. Back when I was just a regular human with only a tactical backpack. That desperation not to lose her fills me now as I look at Shane. That hopeless feeling I had when I knew I couldn't reach her in time fills me now with every exhale I take as more energy is drained from me. My body fills with pressure to the point of pain.

Shane must see something in my eyes because he straightens and yanks at his straps. The man with the gravity power tries to hold him in place and the other two in the room look over at the commotion.

With a yell to expel the pressure, blue energy explodes out of me. Bolts of electricity hit the machine causing it to spark and shut off. I scream as pain cuts into my wrists from the cuffs, but I don't stop. The light above me explodes sending glass fragments raining down. I shut my eyes and feel bits fall into my hair and nick my skin.

The woman touches me to try and stop my attack. Stupid woman. She shouts in pain then collapses from a major electric shock.

"Use your power!" Revelation shouts at the other man.

Shane suddenly turns his head to the side where the Discovery crony has his hand at his shoulder and bites into the man's wrist with his vampire teeth, ripping away the skin there. Blood spurts from the man and he screams, backing away from the chair holding his injured wrist.

I smell burning and look down to see my energy electrifying the straps holding me down enough to burn them. The material blackens and heat presses against my chest and belly, but I can't stop. When they are weak, I push forward until they snap and I fall forward. The mask is ripped from my face causing the strings to snap at my cheeks. It stings but it is nothing compared to the pain from the cuffs as my power continues to defy them.

Blue sparks cover every part of my skin racing up and down and jumping out to reach anything within a two-foot radius. I glare at Revelation and take a step forward. He narrows his eyes and his lips thin.

"There is no where you can hide." With that, he darts for the door and disappears into the other room.

I think about following him, but I can't fight a whole building of Discovery members like this, I will pass out before I reach him. I try to stop the electric energy so the pain will stop but it doesn't go away. It is reacting to my body, still feeling threatened and desperate to protect me and Shane. I grit my teeth and try to think of other things, but my mind keeps going back to Revelation and everything he said.

"Jo."

I look up and meet Shane's black, pupilless eyes.

"Jo," he tries again, "come here."

I move closer, my sparks immediately jumping for him. Blood leaves a trail down his chin from his vicious bite and fangs peek out from his mouth.

I am not scared of him though. And I am not angry about the information I learned about him. I am hurt and there will be words, but right now I am happy he is ok and that we are free. Well, somewhat free.

"Come here, Sapphire," he says again when I am only a foot from his chair.

I lean forward and rest my forehead against his. The sparks dance across his skin and he inhales, the black eyes and fangs disappearing as strength and control return to him. He gives me a soft yet sad smile. His presence soothes me enough for me to stop the power. Immediately the cuffs cease their stabbing.

Chapter 21

A soft sob makes me turn around. It's the man, now in a bloodstained lab coat, holding his wrist as he creeps for the door. His eyes widen when he sees he has been spotted and he lets out a squeak. He doesn't even try to use his power, the pain and blood loss probably too much for him to focus.

"Please don't hurt me," he pleads.

I nod my head toward Shane. "Unstrap him and uncuff us."

The man backs away and shakes his head.

I narrow my eyes and take a menacing step forward. There is no way I can produce my energy again, but he doesn't need to know that.

He closes his eyes in fear then peeks them open when he hears that I haven't stepped forward more.

"F-fine. Just, p-p-please don't kill me."

I don't tell him that he is already close to death from the blood loss in his wrist. If he doesn't treat it soon, he surely will die.

He creeps forward, keeping me in his sights as he reaches Shane's chair. He has to let go of his wrist long enough to unstrap Shane. He sways when he is finished and wraps his wrist in part of his lab coat again.

Shane hops up from the chair and stands by my side, glaring at the Discovery man. "Keys?" I say in an impatient tone.

He reaches into his coat pocket and produces a key. I assume the lady either dead or passed out on the ground has the other one. Thankfully one key fits all so he doesn't need to go digging through someone else's pockets.

He undoes mine first. Once the restraints are off, I roll my wrists, hissing at their tenderness. The skin is red and raw where the power cuffs were but otherwise visually fine. I hold out my hand for the key, seeing that Gravity-man had not undone Shane's yet.

He hands it over then backs up until his back hits the wall. I undo Shane's cuffs and he rolls them the same way I did. He looks at me with that same sad expression he had since I learned about my power coming from his energy.

"Thanks." He nods his head toward the man. "What do we do with him?"

I step forward and ball my hands into fists. "If you want to make sure you get out of here alive, you will tell us where they took Raven."

He jumps and nods his head vigorously. "They took her to a containment room."

I hold out my hand toward the door. "Show us the way."

Just then an alarm blares and a red light flashes from the ceiling. Revelation must have sounded the alarm. Any moment now we will be swarmed with people in lab coats.

"Hurry," Shane growls at the man.

We rush from the room, but the Gravity-man's movements are still too slow for my liking. He takes us down the hall and around a couple corners. Luckily, we do not run into anyone yet, though I can hear the shouting and panicked footsteps of people in rooms and down other halls.

We pass by a room with a window and I glance inside as we rush by but something inside pulls me to a stop. I backtrack and peer into the window. It looks like whoever was in here dropped everything once the siren started and ran off. However, what caught my attention is not the disarray but the creature standing in the back of the room. It has no cage or chains around it. It is free and unsupervised yet all it does is stand there. More than that, I think I know the creature.

Shane notices I am not following and pulls Gravity-man to a stop. He drags him to where I am standing at the door.

"Jo, come on, we must go," he urges. He glances up and down the hall, looking for enemies.

I point and Shane looks through the window to see what I am looking at. His eyes widen then he shakes his head.

"That can't be the same one. We don't have time, let's go."

Shane tries to tug on my arm but I yank it away. I shoot him pleading eyes. "I have to check."

Before he can stop me, I step into the room and approach the creature. The golem stands as still as a statue. When I am within three feet of it, I see its skin is cracked and armor-like and its muscles, if I can call them that, are big.

I let out a shout of joy. "It's him, it's really him."

At the sound of my voice, it suddenly animates and turns to me with an expectant stare.

Shane appears next to me in the blink of an eye. He studies the golem with unbelieving eyes, but he comes to the same conclusion. "That's impossible."

"If you want to get out of here with that woman then you better hurry," Gravity-man says in a weak voice.

Raven! I almost forgot.

I bite my bottom lip and look from the golem to the door.

"Try giving it an order. It should have dissolved in Pittsburgh after delivering that Rogue but since it is still alive, maybe it will continue to follow your orders."

"Um, Golem, follow me."

It doesn't move but neither have I. I run to the door and spin around to see the golem. Without hesitation, the clay creature comes to stand in front of me.

I grin at Shane and he shakes his head, still having a hard time believing the golem is still alive and here of all places. I feel the same, but I am also ecstatic.

I nod for the Discovery member to continue on and we follow him down another hall with the golem in tow.

Finally, he stops at a door and leans against the wall next to it, looking ready to pass out. He nods his head to the door. "She should be in there. I doubt Revelation has gotten to her yet."

I scowl at the man. How can he work for someone like that? How is he ok with draining people and torturing others?

I start for the doorknob, but Shane holds out a hand to stop me. I look up at him and he stares back with determination.

"Let me go first."

I roll my eyes at his protectiveness but let him open the door. We don't have time to argue.

Footsteps thunder around the corner and five people come to a stop.

"There they are!" one of them shouts.

I don't wait for Shane to check if it is safe inside. I push him through, leaving Gravity-man outside. The others can take care of him. The golem follows and I give it an order to hold the door closed. Hopefully, no one on the other side has a power to bust in.

Pounding on the door ensues and demands for our surrender are shouted through the hard wood.

We need to get out of here.

"Jo!"

My eyes land on Raven, her red hair even more ruffled than earlier. She must have been fighting hard against her abductors. I produce the key to the power cuffs from my pocket and rush over to her.

"How did you escape?" She asks, turning her head to see me over her shoulder.

I shrug. "I got a little zappy."

She chuckles and looks to the ceiling. "I'm so glad you have that power."

Yeah, but how long will I have this power before he asks for it back? I glance at Shane who is keeping an eye on the door even though it looks like the golem has it covered. Isn't that why he has been following me?

The cuffs fall from Raven's wrists and she immediately starts massaging the area where they rubbed against her skin.

"Let's get out of here." Raven reaches for me, but I step back.

"Make sure to come back for the golem."

Raven frowns and turns to the clay creature. "That? Why do you want that?"

I press my lips into a determined line and put my hands on my hips. "He's mine."

Raven's eyes widen. "Alrighty then, we'll take the golem." She reaches for me again and this time I let her touch me. In an instant we disappear from the House of Discovery to arrive in relative safety.

"I guess I have to go back to save the vampire and golem then?" She asks with fake reluctance. We share a smile then she disappears leaving behind a black cloud.

A second later Shane appears in the living room and Raven is gone again before I get a good look at her through the cloud, then reappears a second later with the golem. Raven bends over to put her hands on her knees, breathing heavily.

I reach over and pat her back. "You ok?"

She nods. "Yes, just a lot of power usage in such a short amount of time. I'll be fine." She takes a deep breath then straightens and lets it out slowly. "Now what?"

I frown and grit my teeth. "There is nowhere we can hide where Revelation cannot find us. His power lets him see anyone and anything in the present." I cover my face with my hands and groan.

"Do you know if he sees through the person's eyes or if he sees everything as if he is hovering above it all?" Raven asks.

I know what she is trying to get at, but I shake my head. "I don't think blindfolding us and taking us to a secret location will work."

She twists her mouth and frowns in thought.

"I think we should tell everyone what we learned," Shane says.

Right! Revelation said something about King Jerran's army arriving in two days. Harmony is supposed to be alerting the other Heads and my sister is supposed to be preparing the Heroes for war. Specter, Astra, and Jake are probably preparing their House as well.

"I will text them and let them know to watch out for Revelation." I pull my phone out of my backpack and shoot off a group text, telling them about our discovery and to come home as soon as possible so we can explain everything.

I get three texts back immediately.

Astra: What! He must be behind the disappearance of the Council members. Send Raven to get us.

Jake: *open mouthed emoji* I always knew he was sus. He never let me change my name.

Sherry: I will be right there. Don't do anything stupid.

I scoff at Sherry's text. What stupid thing does she think I will do?

I look up to see Raven and Shane staring at me expectantly.

"Astra wants you to go get them."

She sighs. "I don't know how many more trips I can take. I may need to rest for a bit when I get there before I can bring them back." She hesitates. "Um, will you be okay here?" Her eyes dart to Shane then to the golem.

I smile at her concern but wave it away. "Go, I will be fine."

"What about Revelation?" She asks.

"We can handle it," Shane responds for me. I nod my agreement.

She eyes us for a moment longer, trying to determine if we would be safe, then nods. "Call me if you need me." Then she disappears.

I turn to Shane and point at him with a no-nonsense frown. "Start talking."

He sighs and runs a hand through his hair. "Where do you want me to start?"

I cross my arms. "From the beginning."

Shane sits in the armchair nearest to me. He rests his arms on his knees and stares at the coffee table. "I was fifteen Earth years when I came to this world. King Jerran had an assassin infiltrate our palace."

Assassin? Palace? My eyes widen, but I stay silent, wanting him to continue.

"The assassin was a werewolf, easy to pass as Besondere in their humanoid form but they are more animal in heart and spirit. The werewolf managed to get close to my brother, the King, and in the middle of court he threw a potion of some sort at him. At the time I had power over lightning and threw a bolt of it at the bottle.

"Something in that bottle reacted to my lightning, opening a portal right there in court. I usually had perfect control over the portals but for some reason I could not close this one. The assassin, seeing that his plan failed, shifted into his wolf form, and attacked. In the battle I was knocked to the side, right into the portal.

"At that time, we knew portals were opening randomly to another world and that people from both kingdoms were being drawn into them, however, I thought my power over portals would help me direct it elsewhere." Shane balls his hands into fists and places one over his heart. "But when I went through I felt my power being ripped from me and my body weakening. I kept my vampire abilities but that energy that made me the Prince of Lightning, Keeper of the portals, was lost to the vortex and thrown out into the world."

Finally, he looks at me and shakes his head. "I wandered from the scene, culture shock like never before hitting me. I felt overwhelmed by the cars, technology, noise, and air. Thankfully, a group of supernaturals found me and, recognizing me, took me to a safe house. Then I was transferred to Pittsburgh to live with Nessa until I was old enough to search for my lost energy and a way home."

I try to imagine a young boy from another world being thrown into a portal to arrive in an unfamiliar environment with diminished power and having no idea if the assassin succeeded or not. He must have been so scared.

"Do you…do you know if your brother survived?"

Shane nods and gives me a small smile. "I have met with some Besondere who crossed over in the past few years and they keep me somewhat updated. He survived."

"So…I guess you found your power then." I bite my lip. "How did you know?"

"I heard about a woman who shot a wyvern with blue lightning and tracked her down." He looks at me sheepishly. "Tracked *you* down. I imagine your power was latent because it is different from other powers, it needed time to settle then an emotional charge if you will. The rest you pretty much know."

I shake my head. "What were you planning to do when you found me?"

Shane doesn't answer. He sits there in silence, thinking over my question. I try to wait patiently, knowing this is important.

Finally, he shakes his head. "I honestly don't know. Maybe force both of us to go through a portal, hoping that would reset the energy?" He starts off sure but ends up with a questioning tone. "It may or may not have killed you." He sighs and rubs his face.

"Are…are you still going to do that?" A note of fear enters my voice.

Shane is suddenly gone from the chair and is standing in front of me. I gasp at how quick he moved and the sudden closeness. He reaches out and cups my face, gazing at me with a soft look.

"No, I will not do anything that may hurt you. I admit, when I heard of you I didn't care about the consequences. I was taking you to Pittsburgh to work out a power transfer no matter the cost. Then we danced and started working together. You became someone…special to me. I can't imagine stripping your energy from you. It is a part of you now. I have lived years without it and I still have my vampire abilities. I am not helpless."

"But how will you get home?" I whisper.

He grins. "I will just have to teach you how to open portals."

I gape at him. "What! I can do that?"

He chuckles and tucks a strand of my hair behind my ear. "You should be able to."

Suddenly his face turns serious, and he stares into my eyes with an intense look. "Will you ever forgive me?" He whispers with an almost pleading note.

I stare into his blue eyes, seeing the pain and regret there. He has been through so much and even now when he is so close to everything he wanted he is giving it up to save me once again. Who would have thought a vampire would save a human so many times. That he would become so dear to me.

"There is nothing to forgive," I whisper back.

His eyes dart down to my lips and he leans in. My heart starts to beat rapidly and my breath halts in anticipation. Before his lips can touch mine I lean away.

A look of hurt crosses his face before he masks it with a look of indifference. He nods once and steps back. "My apologies."

I reach out and tug him back. "That's not why I pulled away," I chuckle. "It's just that you have a bit of…" I gesture to the dried blood on his chin and mouth.

He tilts his head and frowns in confusion then his eyes widen when he realizes what I mean. "Oh!"

He speeds to the bathroom and I hear him curse. A second later the water turns on in the sink. I smile in his direction even though he can't see me.

The front door handle jiggles and a spike of fear races through me. Has Revelation come to attack us?

I grab the silver dagger from the side pocket of my backpack and take a stand near the door. Shane comes out of the bathroom and, seeing my pose, narrows his eyes at the door and takes a stand by my side.

The door opens and I raise my dagger. When I see who it is, I breathe out a sigh of relief and drop my dagger onto the side table.

"You nearly gave me a heart attack," I tell my sister.

Sherry smiles sheepishly and hunches her shoulders apologetically. "Sorry, Sis."

Sherry throws her keys onto the side table and moves to go change out of her hero suit. Suddenly she shouts and a blast shakes our house.

Chapter 22

Dust rains from the ceiling and the ground rumbles. Our furniture moves from the force hitting it and a loud crash has me looking over to see the golem thrown across the room into our only coffee table.

I run forward holding out my hands to stop Sherry from attacking again. I place myself in between her and the fallen golem.

Sherry has her hands balled, ready to punch out another blast, and her irises are turning pink from her power. She is in battle mode.

"Sherry, no, he's with us."

"What is that?" She asks. The pink leaves her eyes and she bends around me to see the clay creature. "It broke our table."

"No, *you* broke our table. He was just standing there, harmless, when you attacked."

Her face turns red with embarrassment and she bites the inside of her cheek.

"Sorry," she says to the golem.

I don't know if the golem heard her or understood her because it doesn't acknowledge her words.

"Get up," I tell the golem and watch as it acknowledges *my* words.

Sherry shakes her head in wonder then looks back to me. "What is it?"

"He is a golem. A clay creature made to follow orders essentially. This one is supercharged by my energy, so it doesn't dissolve." Suddenly a thought comes to mind and a jolt of excitement runs through me. I now have a source of information about my power!

"Shane," I say turning to him, "were you able to make the supernatural stronger with the lightning?"

"How would he have the lightning?" Sherry asks.

I glance over my shoulder at her. "This used to be Shane's power when he was in Alstoria."

Sherry frowns and looks between us then throws her hands into the air. "This is too much for me. I am going to change and wait for the others." She stalks away mumbling about vampires and other worlds.

I shift back toward Shane, eager for information.

"I was able to give them a bit more energy but never to the degree that you can. You make them stronger and bigger." He gestures to the golem who is standing like a statue next to my broken coffee table. "I never would have been able to do what you did with this golem. He should have dissolved after completing his task."

"Do you think the altered portal had something to do with it?"

"Must be. That or the lightning is affecting the supernatural differently on this world because of their loss of energy when crossing over."

Interesting.

Ah, now I'm doing it.

A black cloud of vapors appears in the middle of the room and two people step out of it. Raven and Astra. I grin at them, pleased to see my friends are safe. Raven gives me a nod then disappears again to retrieve Jake.

"Oh! What is this?" Astra asks intrigued as she circles around the golem.

Shane explains it to her just as Sherry comes out of her room in a pair of jean shorts and a pink hoodie. She looks more relaxed now that she is out of her hero suit.

The black vapors appear once again and Jake comes through with Raven. Raven bends over and breathes heavily. She did not rest long before bringing them both here. She must be exhausted.

Sherry sees that she needs water and food and guides her to the kitchen.

"Oh! Interesting. A golem," Jake says, going to circle the creature with Astra.

They discuss it quietly and Jake pulls out a notebook and starts scribbling notes. I assume he knows what it is because his given House mission was to solve the mystery of the increased monster appearances. Which means he would need to know all about the supernatural.

I turn away from them and check my phone. Still no message from Harmony. Should I call her?

A knock sounds at the door and I rush over to answer it. Shane suddenly appears in front of me and blocks it. He narrows his eyes at it and shakes his head.

Right, we should be careful.

He peeks through the peephole then relaxes. I take that to mean there is no danger and shoulder passed him to answer the door.

"Harmony, Specter, I was just about to call you."

I move to the side to let them in. Once they are in, I peer outside looking for any suspicious characters hanging around but see no one. I lock the door anyway.

"I talked to the Head of Heroes and alerted him to the battle to come and Revelation's betrayal. I had already left the House of Glamour when you texted me, so I had to call them to explain the new danger. That's why I didn't respond to your message," Harmony explains. "We were about to arrive at the House of Discovery when we decided it would be best to avoid the place after your attack and called the Head there instead. There was no answer."

"What did the other Heads say they would do to prepare?" Astra asks, finally looking away from the clay creature.

"The Heroes and Stars are calling an emergency meeting all across the nation. Soon this city will be swarmed with Heroes, Stars, and Agents."

"Well, we have two days to prepare," I tell them. "Do you think they will be here in time?"

"Two days?" Harmony asks.

"Revelation let slip that the Bestia will be invading in two days," Shane says.

Harmony rubs her temple and looks to Specter with concern. "I don't know if we will have enough people by then."

"We are going to have to go up against a Kingdom of animalistic supernatural and a House full of Rogues. Not to mention the House of Discovery and where they stand," I say. "If only there was a way to get the Besondere to help us."

I shake my head at the thought. It's possible seeing as Revelation somehow found a way to contact King Jerran, but it is unlikely for us to figure out his method in time.

Shane zooms to stand in front of me and grasps my shoulders with a huge grin. "Sapphire, you're a genius!"

"I am?"

"She is?" Sherry asks at the same time as she comes back into the living room with a much-improved Raven.

"You can open a portal and send the golem to give a message to my brother."

My eyes widen. "I can't open portals!"

"Brother?" Jake asks.

Shane ignores him. "With my help you can. I can get you to open a portal right in the palace…I think. We don't have much time. Remember, two days Earth time is only about sixteen hours in Alstoria."

"Palace?" Jake holds up his hands. "Ok, wait, who is your brother?"

"That's less than a day to prepare. Do you think your brother will be ready in that short amount of time?" Harmony asks, sounding doubtful.

Shane nods once. "He will have to."

I search his eyes. He seems so sure I can do this. There is only a slim chance I will get it open and a smaller chance the golem will go through without dissolving and get the message to the King of the Besondere in time for him to send an army through a portal to help. It all seems overwhelming, and I just want to go hide in my room and let it all pass me by. But that's not who I am. These people are counting on me.

"Let's do it."

He grins and takes my hand in his, giving it a squeeze.

"We can't open a portal in here," Sherry says, placing her hands on her hips to show her authority.

"No, we should do it away from civilians in case something comes through," Harmony agrees. "Let's go to the House of Mystery."

"But Revelation will surely be watching us. He will then find out the location and…you know who." Specter points out.

I look between them, trying to figure out who they are talking about but neither of them give anything away.

Harmony gives us all a sly smile. "Let them come. My animals haven't had a good chase in a while."

Animals? As in more than one? Lola scares me enough on her own. I picture a pack of Lolas with hackles raised and fangs bared chasing off Revelation and his people. I chuckle at the image. Thank goodness Harmony is on our side.

"Perfect, let me pack a few things and we can go," Sherry says.

Shane, Jake, and I ride in Sherry's car, while the rest lead us to the House in Harmony's car. Harmony has the biggest vehicle, so the golem rides in the back of her car. Jake asks Shane a million questions on the way and I try to listen since Shane is giving intriguing information about Alstoria to him, but I keep an eye on our surroundings most of all. I can't help but feel we are being watched and don't know if it is Revelation using his power to see us or if we are being tailed.

Luckily, we don't experience any car chases and arrive in the forest parking area without issue. Suddenly Lola pops out of the woods and trots over to Harmony's side of the car.

"Is that a…?" Sherry asks trailing off, her hand on the handle of her door about to open it but paused once she saw the wolf.

"Yup! Don't worry, she won't hurt you," Jake says and gets out confidently.

"Right," Sherry says, sounding unsure. But my sister is brave and gets out of the car with a look of determination.

"Alright, we should hurry. We don't want to linger," Harmony says glancing through the forest. She leans down and whispers into Lola's ear. The wolf perks up then trots off into the woods. Harmony straightens and nods toward the retreating wolf. "Lola will scout the area." Then Harmony leads us on the hidden path to the House of Mystery.

Now that I have walked this path a few times I am able to pick out the signs that we are close then the treehouse once it comes into view. Sherry and Raven haven't spotted it yet, but Shane looks upward the closer we get. How many times has he been here? I remember seeing him that day after the incubus incident. I am surer now that it wasn't an illusion.

"Alright, we are here. We don't have any more time to waste, so let's open it now," Specter says.

"Where is here?" Raven asks spinning in a circle and only seeing trees.

Specter presses a button on a hidden remote around his neck.

I point up and Raven and Sherry follow my direction.

"Oh my!" Raven breathes in wonder.

"Your base is in a treehouse," Sherry laughs then grows serious. "That's awesome."

"You will be able to see inside once we are done. But for now, Jo, Shane, please open the portal," Harmony says with a mixture of hope and doubt.

I know what she feels. I am doubting my ability to open a portal to another world too, but Shane is my hope. He had this power long before me and knows its ins and outs. If he says I can open a portal, then I will just have to believe him.

I glance at the golem then Shane. "You should probably write a message to your brother. If this works, then he will be more likely to help if it comes from you."

I dig through my backpack and retrieve a pen and sticky note. His brow rises at the bright pink paper.

I shrug. "Hey, it's all I've got."

He grins as he takes the pen and paper then jots down a quick message on it. He stuffs it in his pocket for now then turns so he is facing away from the treehouse. He points to a spot not far in front of us.

"We are going to open it there. Visualize where you want it to be."

I turn to face the direction he pointed to then raise a brow at him. There must be more to it than just visualizing a swirling portal in front of me.

He moves closer until his arm is brushing mine. "Now I am going to describe the Besondere palace, and I want you to try and picture everything I tell you. As you do that, imagine a portal opening here and connecting to that place." He leans down and brushes his lips against my temple, resting there a moment longer than expected. "I know you can do it, Sapphire," he whispers.

My body heats at that soft touch.

I shake out my hands and stare hard at a spot in the forest a couple yards away. I imagine a swirling blue-black portal just like the ones I have seen a few times before. The clearest image I have of one in my memories is the one from yesterday in Pittsburgh and I try to picture one just like it opening up in front of me.

Seeing that I am ready, Shane begins describing his home. The others fall into silence and I see them in my peripheral vision leaning in to hear of this mystical place that has been such a mystery to our world.

"Imagine a magnificent building three stories high made of white stone that extends to each side of a large courtyard. The front of the palace has brilliant pointed arch windows and columns. There are three doors set in the middle with a beautiful rose window above them. Along the top of the building are blue and white flags with a blue lightning bolt in the middle. The courtyard is made of blue and white stones and a fountain sits in the middle. Dancing in the air around the fountain are twinkling lights in all kinds of colors. Can you picture it?"

I nod, imagining everything he described. I hope I have it accurate enough for this to work. I push out with my mind and feel a tear in the air in front of me.

Miraculously, a swirling portal the size of an armchair suddenly opens up in the middle of the forest where I have been staring so hard at. The others gasp and start murmuring but I ignore them and try to focus on making it bigger. I raise my hands which have begun to spark with blue energy and spread them apart slowly. As my hands move, so does the portal. It grows until it is as big as a small car and the light around the edges spark just like my lightning. Shane touches my shoulder signaling me to stop and I drop my arms, releasing a breath I hadn't realized I was holding.

I opened a portal! A freaking portal!

I squeal and leap at Shane who catches me in his arms and spins me around, both of us grinning like fools. Whether it is because of the adrenaline affecting me or the way he is looking at me, I don't hesitate to lean forward and kiss him. He presses me closer and kisses me back just as enthusiastically. He is still holding me with my feet off the ground effortlessly and I smile at his strength.

Someone clears their throat reminding me where we are and that we have an audience. Shane continues to stare at me as he lets me slide down to the forest floor, the look in his eyes one of passion and hunger.

I refuse to look at my sister, but I know she saw what happened. Everyone saw that. I will be getting a lecture later, I'm sure.

I straighten my shirt and turn to the golem. "Time to send him then?"

"Yes, that would be wise, but if you want to continue with the vampire Prince I won't object," Jake says, a cheeky smile on his face.

Astra reaches around Raven and smacks him on the arm.

"Hey!" Jake shouts and holds the spot where she hit him.

I have no idea if what I imagined is the exact look of the palace but it is as he describes so I have to hope it is close enough to get us where we need the golem to go.

"Golem, take this message to King…" I look to Shane, realizing he never told me his brother's name.

"Simon."

"King Simon of the Besondere," I finish. "Do it as quickly as possible."

I take the note from Shane and give it to the golem who holds it tightly in one hand. Without any words as usual, the golem strides forward and disappears through the portal with no hesitation.

We wait a moment, for what I don't know, but nothing else happens.

"Should I close it?" I ask uncertainly.

"Yes, we don't want anything unpleasant coming through," Harmony answers with a tone of authority.

I nod and imagine the portal shrinking then winking out of existence. Now that I know the method and feel of the energy, it is easy. I wonder if I will be able to open portals to travel across the Earth like Raven can with her teleportation.

"Now what?" I ask.

"Now, we prepare for battle," Shane answers solemnly.

Chapter 23

Two days.

We had two days to prepare for an army of animalistic supernatural and superpowered Rogues to invade our city.

How do we know they are coming here? We don't. But we assume they are coming here since Revelation is in this city organizing everything and since the main headquarters of every House, presumably even the Rogues, is in this city.

I would like to say we are totally ready to kick butt, but I feel we could never be ready for something like this, especially after only two days. We have been training non-stop with Shane's guidance, gathering weapons, and making plans but other than the likelihood of the Bestia arriving in this city, we have no idea where in the city or when they will arrive. Stars, Agents, and Heroes have been coming from all over ever since the call but there are not nearly enough to make much of a difference.

I twirl my dagger and practice sending energy to dance across the metal while I stare around the empty street outside the House of Heroes tower waiting for an attack. Down the street to my left is Sherry in her Blast outfit and to my right is Shane. The others are stationed around the city with radios.

We have been out here since dawn and it is nearly noon now without a trace of a portal or hint of a Rogue. The Heroes successfully put the city on lockdown for the day which means no one is out and about except for those ready to battle.

My radio crackles and I stop twirling my dagger, my body alert for any news.

"This is Northern Light of House of Glamour, reporting a disturbance in sector five."

Sector five. I try to recall the map we made two days ago that divided the city into eight sectors. Sector five, if I am remembering correctly, is the eastern part of the city near the waterfront.

"What is the disturbance?" Harmony' voice asks over the radio. I know she is in sector three along the highway and forest with Specter and a Hero.

"Um, well, the water is moving," Northern Light answers.

"We are going to need a bit more than that," Harmony responds, sounding annoyed. The stress of the last two days has caused her patience to wear thin.

"The water is spinning. It's forming a whirlpool."

A different voice crackles over the radio. *"I can confirm the water is spinning in an unnatural way, it started out of nowhere."*

"Oh God!" Northern Light exclaims. *"It's a giant octopus!"*

"We have a level eight Kraken sighting. In need of assistance," the other voice says urgently. He must be a Hero if he knows the monster levels and species.

I look to Shane then down the street at Sherry. I raise my hands silently asking them what we should do. Sherry holds up her hand telling me to stay put.

The Head of the House of Heroes deals out orders on the radio immediately. *"A Kraken can be dealt with using three Heroes. Two Heroes from sector six, meet them at the waterfront to deal with it. Either an Agent or a Star needs to go to sector six so the person there is not left alone."*

"This is Trident, I am on my way."

"This is Lilith, on my way."

I have always wanted to see a Kraken. I imagine it is as tall as a three-story building and deadly like in the movies. I hope they can deal with it. It is only one supernatural and no one else has spotted anything yet. However, a Kraken is a Bestia so it could mean the start of an attack.

I lift the radio to my mouth and press the button on the side. "Any other disturbances?"

Sectors three, eight, and four respond with a negative. Since ours is good for now, that leaves three sectors unaccounted for. Seeing as how two people from sector six just left, we can give their lack of response a pass.

"Sector two?" Harmony asks, picking up on the disturbing silence.

Astra is in sector two.

The radio crackles and weird noises come from the other side that sound like rustling fabric and wind, but the line shuts off with no words spoken.

"We didn't quite get that sector two," Harmony prompts.

I bite my lip, urging Astra to answer us. Worry twists my stomach.

The same crackling and weird noises come through, but this time Astra speaks one word. *"Rogues!"*

Sherry and I look to each other alarmed. The attack is happening. But other than the Kraken, where are the Bestia?

"Everyone except for the two teams on standby, go to sector two," the Head of Heroes orders through the radios.

I look to Shane who speeds over to me and both of us race toward Sherry who is ahead of us, heading north to the outskirts of downtown where sector two is located. I wonder why they chose there to invade, then I remember. The Science Museum is in that area, or in other words, the House of Discovery.

The radio buzzes and a shrill female voice shouts, grating on my ears. *"Rogues in sector seven! And a portal just opened up! We need backup pronto."*

I halt in the middle of the road, Shane coming to a stop beside me. Sherry, having heard the message, also stops and glances back at us.

Two separate sectors across the city from each other. This will divide our forces. The Head of Heroes doesn't hesitate like we did. He starts barking orders through the radio and sending out the full forces at our disposal to the two sectors. Harmony and her sector are the farthest from anyone so Raven will have to transport them.

I make a quick decision. Sector two is the closest so we will head there and let others respond to sector seven's alarm. I start forward but suddenly a light bursts into existence in between Sherry and me. In less than a second the light expands to create a swirling blue-black vortex with crackling energy on the edges.

I stare at it with dread.

"Portal in sector one," I hear Blast say on the radio urgently. *"They are going to divide us, sir."*

"It seems that way," her boss responds.

He reorders everyone so that all sectors being attacked are covered. We have a few minutes before the remaining Heroes in the tower spill out. I have no idea what will be coming through, but we need to do something while we wait for reinforcements.

"Can I close that before anything comes through?" I ask Shane.

Shane frowns thinking it over then shakes his head. "We need to make sure you have enough energy to open one for the Besondere."

I gesture to the portal. "Then shouldn't I do that now!" I say as a statement more than a question.

He nods and we move down the street, away from the portal. I know Shane will watch my back so I am not afraid to tune out my surroundings to focus on opening a portal. Shane had me practicing my powers for the last two days, but this is the first time since we sent the golem that I am playing with portals.

I imagine the same palace Shane described before and try to picture opening an interdimensional portal in the same courtyard as last time, hoping that will be where the army is waiting. To my relief and joy, a portal larger than the one down the street opens in front of me. I feel its energy this time and my connection to it. It feels different than the other one on the street. Mine feels sturdier, more consistent, while the other feels weak and unpredictable. I would bet the energy Revelation collected to open these is not enough to keep them open for long.

A blast shakes a building and another one makes a loud *boom* as it hits something beyond my line of sight. Sherry appears from around the enemy's portal facing an unseen threat. That must be the Rogues. The enemy's portal pulses and creatures of all kinds suddenly come marching through.

"Blast!" I shout at my sister.

Sherry sees them and runs toward us, knowing she cannot take on Rogues and Bestia on her own. The three of us face the oncoming threat with my portal open behind us.

"What do we do?" I ask, feeling overwhelmed by the numbers approaching.

"We fight," Sherry says, her eyes flashing pink with power.

I look over the horde of Bestia and try to identify the different creatures. I see large wolves with intelligent eyes which I assume to be werewolves. I see a few gigantic birds that must be rocs and half-bird, half horse creatures known as hippogriffs fly out of the portal and into the air to circle us like prey. Others that I can spot from here are foxes with three tails known as kitsunes, little imp creatures, giant lizards that walk on two legs that I think are kobolds, and, surprisingly, stone creatures with wings and fangs that I take to be gargoyles. I thank the universe when no dragons or wyverns come through.

About twenty Rogues stroll around the portal. Most are in uniform and all have the black mask outlined in silver somewhere on their person. Many of them make a wide berth around the Bestia casting them wary looks. The Rogues may work with them but that doesn't mean they trust the Bestia or are unafraid of the creatures.

"Do you think King Jerran will make an appearance?" I ask Shane, keeping my eyes on the rocs above.

"He is already here."

I snap my head toward the Bestia and look for a crazed man with a crown. I only see creatures, the stuff of nightmares and legends.

"Where?" Sherry asks.

Shane points at a werewolf, larger than the others, with a pure black coat and angry, icy blue eyes. "That's him there."

My body stiffens in fear. The King of the Bestia is a large werewolf, and he is staring at us with bloodlust. Suddenly the King-wolf howls, setting off the other animals who howl or shout battle cries then they all surge forward.

I look to Shane and Sherry then at the horde of beasts thundering toward us. Is this how I die? Where are our reinforcements?

I throw up a wall of lightning in front of us, something Shane taught me to do over the couple days. I know that if they hit the wall, the supernatural will only get bigger and stronger, but I am hoping it intimidates them enough for them to stop before touching it.

And they do.

The beasts halt their advance and pace along the wall of blue electricity, looking for a way in, meanwhile Sherry punches out blast after pink blast of her power at the creatures, sending two or three flying at a time.

I use my gun to shoot at others. I restocked on silver bullets, using most of my savings to do so, but I find that it was worth it as I watch the beasts hiss at the contact and collapse. Whether it is the silver or the bullet tearing into flesh, many of my targets fall from the assault.

Shane uses a sword to slash through the wall, making sure not to touch the energy so the others do not catch on to our ruse. Eventually the beasts back away until we can only stare at each other through the wall of electricity. The rocs screech above but none try to attack, wary of the power that I may throw at them.

Noises behind us make me turn with my gun raised but I lower it and sigh in relief when I see who it is.

The Heroes.

At the sight of the Heroes, King Jerran howls which must be a signal for something because every single beast leaps forward without hesitation into my electric barrier. My eyes widen and at least ten of the Bestia get through before I yank at the energy and draw it back into myself.

Those ten, which include King Jerran, yelp and howl and whine as they writhe on the ground. Blue energy skates over their fur or scaly, leathery skin and their bodies begin to grow. Shane doesn't hesitate and uses that moment to kill a kitsune and an imp while they are in the throes of transformation. I follow his lead and shoot two werewolves with silver.

The Heroes reach us and immediately dive into battle with the Rogues and Bestia who are not effected by my energy. I can see we are still outnumbered but at least now we have a chance to stop the invasion from spreading farther. I hope the other sectors are holding their own. I glance at my open portal, but it is as it was before, a swirling vortex with nothing coming through.

The Bestia on the ground finally cease their whining and stand to their feet. The six left have grown much taller. A kobold which survived now looks dragon-like but without the wings and it towers over the rest of us. A kitsune that once had three tails now has six and fire dances around its paws. An imp that evaded Shane's attack while its brother was not so lucky has lengthened claws and teeth and it moves around much faster than before. The three werewolves of the bunch now stand at shoulder height like massive beasts that can chomp my head off in one bite. Unfortunately, King Jerran is one of those beasts.

He looks at me and smiles, showing all his sharpened teeth then lunges at me. I squeak and raise my gun and fire, but it clicks, letting me know it is out of bullets.

Crap.

Chapter 24

I roll to the side to get out of the way, barely missing the teeth as they slide past my face. I breathe heavily, and stare wide eyed at the beast as it lands a few feet away, amazed that I dodged a werewolf like that. I look at my gun then toss it aside, knowing I don't have time to reload it. I reach around to my backpack and pull my silver dagger from the side pocket. I know I cannot take on this massive King-wolf by myself but that doesn't stop me from taking a fighting stance and glaring at him in challenge.

King Jerran crouches and I know the exact moment when he is about to launch himself at me. I wait for it then drop and roll beneath him as the wolf flies over me once again. This time I hold up my dagger and rake it across the underbelly of the King. He howls and twists in midair, swatting at me with a massive paw which catches me in the arm. We both land opposite of each other, him with bloody fur on his belly and me with four claw marks gouged into my right arm. It hurts to grip the dagger and I have to switch hands or risk dropping it.

I look for Shane and the others, but they are all occupied with the other Bestia and Rogues. It is up to me to deal with this wolf. However, I am not skilled at wielding a dagger with my less dominant hand. This fight will not last long without using my lightning which will only strengthen him more.

What do I do?

An idea forms and I bring my backpack around to my front, hissing at the pain it causes in my arm.

After fighting with Knockoff Batman, I added a few things to my arsenal. I pull one of them out and start spinning it over my head. The wolf doesn't seem concerned and stalks forward. I think he learned its lesson from leaping at me so now he will take a different approach. I cannot let him within biting distance. I throw the bolas in my hand at him. It flies through the air but I don't wait for it to connect. He is too fast for it to have much effect. Instead, I pull one of my two smoke bombs out. While King Jerran is occupied with avoiding the bolas, I toss the smoke bomb at his snout.

Bullseye!

The wolf halts as a cloud of smoke bursts around him and starts wheezing. I immediately jump forward and start slashing at the King. He howls. On instinct he swipes out, but the smoke affected his eyes, and he misses. I twist and stab him in the side. He growls and swipes out again, this time he hits me and I go flying.

I groan at the impact with the asphalt and try to sit up but suddenly I am pinned down by two paws and a giant wolf hovering over me. My dagger slips from my hand at the pressure and that's when I know I am about to die.

I cannot use my lightning. I cannot use my lightning. I cannot! I try to tell my body. I can feel myself going into survival mode which usually triggers the energy. As if wanting to confirm my thoughts about survival I feel my blue sparks light up my hands. Thankfully, they do not spread yet and the wolf is not touched by it.

He bares his teeth and leans down forcing me to smell his rank breath. I cough and turn my head away.

"Jo!" I hear Shane shout, but he sounds far away.

I look for him as best as I can from my position and see him attacking a roc that had swooped down to help a kitsune and werewolf. He is trying to get to me but every time he takes one down, another takes its place. He won't reach me in time.

King Jerran opens his mouth to bite my head off and all I can think is that I hope I am not like a chicken when it happens where its body still moves without its head.

I close my eyes and wait, but the bite never comes. Suddenly, the weight is lifted off and I can breathe fresh air instead of wolf breath. My eyes fly open and I see my golem holding the wolf by the scruff of his neck. King Jerran struggles in its grip and even takes chunks of clay off the golem's body with his claws, but the golem is unperturbed. He stares at the wolf for a moment then throws him, showing strength I didn't know golems possess. King Jerran flies into the crowd of Heroes, Bestia, and Rogues, disappearing from sight.

My eyes roam over the golem then his presence registers in my mind. I gasp and look to the portal.

A grin spreads over my face when I see humanoid creatures walk through the portal. Most of them are in a uniform of blue and white and all have a weapon of some sort, whether it is a sword, a club, or magic at their fingertips.

At first glance I spot a few wood nymphs from the bark and vines on their body and cyclopes from their one eye. Then I see beautiful women with hair of snakes, which reminds me of medusa, so I assume they are gorgons. Others that stand out are half-man, half-goat creatures known as satyrs and long haired, clawed women in gowns which I recognize immediately as banshees. Others look too human for me to know what species they are, but I would bet a few are vampires, especially the man in the front leading the army into our world.

He looks exactly like Shane, except maybe a bit taller and with more facial hair. He wears a crown, and his uniform stands out due to the sashes and medals hanging from his jacket. King Simon takes a moment to look around and take in the situation before raising his hand and giving his people a signal. The Besondere launch into the fray leaving the Rogues and Heroes alone while they push back the Bestia.

King Simon's eyes flit over the crowd, looking for something. His eyes land on whatever it is he is looking for and his eyes widen as his lips part. I follow his gaze and see Shane battling a hippogriff. The creature may be able to fly and have sharp talons, but it is no match for the speed of a vampire with a sword. Shane beheads it and looks right at me, then his gaze slides to his brother near the portal.

The two brothers stare at each other, ignoring the fight around them. I take this moment to stand and check over the golem. He looks fine. The extra armor my energy gave his body saved him. I pat his shoulder.

"Good Golem."

The creature doesn't respond but it's okay, I know he heard me.

I look around to find Sherry, but an angry shout makes me look back at King Simon. He is frowning now and has his sword drawn. I frown in confusion at his change in demeanor and look to Shane to see what caused it.

My hands ball into fists when I see him, or more accurately, who is holding him.

King Jerran shifted back into his human form and somehow snuck up on Shane while he was distracted. He is standing behind Shane with an arm around his torso, holding his arms to his sides, while his other hand is gripping Shane's throat with clawed fingers.

King Jerran looks younger than I expected, maybe early forties, and has a thick black beard and shoulder length hair that matches the coat of his wolf. His eyes are the same icy blue as his wolf too. He is not wearing a shirt or shoes, but I am glad to see he is wearing pants and wonder if he shifted with them on or if he picked them up from one of his people. I see blood on his side from where I cut him in his wolf form however it looks to be healing already.

King Simon takes a step forward and King Jerran shakes his head with a dark chuckle. "Take another step and I will rip out your precious brother's throat."

I gasp and touch my throat. Would he really do that?

I move forward a bit drawing the werewolf's attention to me and he growls, warning me to stay back. I hold my hands up to show him I am unarmed.

For the first time, King Simon looks at me, just now noticing my presence and interest in this matter. He narrows his eyes at me.

"Stay back, human." He turns his attention back to his brother, dismissing me without another thought, and glares at the werewolf-King. "I demand you release him at once, mongrel."

King Jerran chuckles and tightens his hold on Shane's throat. Shane's eyes turn black, and his fangs descend. There is nothing he can do but that doesn't stop his instincts from taking over.

Sparks light up my hands and arms and I think about shooting a ball of energy at him, but that may cause him to hurt Shane.

King Simon looks at my arms with wide eyes. "You..." he whispers just loud enough for me to hear.

Instead of attacking King Jerran, I toss a bolt of lightning at a nearby Rogue, sending him flying with a burnt patch in his uniform. I then send out a ring of blue electricity around me and grab it with my bare hands. It doesn't really affect me, it is more tingly than anything. I snap it at the ground in front of me like a whip and hold it up in a threatening stance. He has been strengthened by my energy, but he doesn't know that I can't hurt him at all. The show of power makes the nearby fighters pause and they step away to give us more room, to give me, specifically, a wide berth.

"Let him go, or you're next," I threaten.

King Jerran looks thoughtful. "Okay." My eyes narrow with suspicion, and rightly so because he continues. "On one condition."

We wait for his demand, knowing if we don't do what he says, he will kill Shane.

"I want you," King Jerran says with a wicked smile, his eyes trained on me.

"Me?" I ask, my lightning whip faltering.

"Her?" King Simon says simultaneously.

"You will come with me to Alstoria," he says.

Shane struggles. "No, don't do it," he growls, though it comes out choked.

Shane has saved me over and over. He has always been there when I needed him. He opened my eyes to a world beyond mine and a power beyond my imagination. He helped us prepare for war against people of his own world and has constantly put himself in danger for me. I thought I lost him once. I can't go through that again. If this would save him, then so be it.

I let the whip die out and the energy along my arms to disappear. I step forward with my chin held high and fists clenched. "Fine. I will go. But you have to release him unharmed."

King Jerran inclines his head in agreement.

"Human, you cannot go. That power…he cannot possess it. It will mean the end of us all," King Simon says, zipping over to me with his vampire speed and grasping me by the upper arm.

I gently extricate my arm and smile up at him sadly. "I must, otherwise he will kill Shane."

King Simon looks back to his brother who struggles and shakes his head. His eyes are pleading with his brother not to let me go. King Simon hesitates. I take advantage of his hesitation and stride toward the werewolf. We all know King Simon could easily stop me, but they also know that I will electrocute him if he tried.

When I am within five feet of King Jerran I stop. "Let him go now."

King Jerran shakes his head. "Go to the portal first."

I glance at the portal beyond all the fighters, the one the Bestia came through. It must lead to his kingdom. I clench and unclench my fists, over and over. Nerves and fear cause sparks to dance along my skin once more.

"No tricks," the werewolf demands, eyeing the energy on my skin.

I look to Shane and see his pleading eyes telling me not to go.

I give him a small smile. "You will be with your brother again."

"Don't—" is all he can get out.

I start to walk toward the portal but I freeze when I spot something behind King Jerran. My heart rate kicks up and fear spreads through my body. My eyes widen and meet golden-brown ones. I want to shake my head at her, to tell her *don't even try it* but that will give her position away. Instead, I focus back on Shane and mouth *ready?*

He frowns, not understanding. King Jerran doesn't get to figure out my odd behavior either because suddenly Blast pops up directly behind him and places her hands on either side of his head. Before he can move or even make a sound, she sends out a blast of power.

Unlike all her other blasts, this one doesn't send him flying. Instead, he starts screaming and releases Shane to hold his head, trying to stop the noise and pressure exploding upon him. The werewolf's face turns red and his eyes squeeze shut. My stomach twists as I imagine his head exploding. I really hope she doesn't make his head explode.

Blood leaks out of the King's nose and eyes. He gives a choked gurgle. Finally, the werewolf-king collapses, his brain turned to mush.

But it's over.

Blast saved us.

I leap at my sister and crush her in a hug. She laughs and hugs me back like it was no big deal what she just did but I feel her body tremble. I know she was scared. I pull back and look for Shane, but he is not where the King last held him. I spin around until my eyes land on the two brothers, hugging it out a few feet away.

I look around the battlefield and see that many of the Bestia are fleeing back to the portal. With the death of their King and the arrival of the Besondere, they are too afraid to keep going. Some stay behind but are quickly taken care of by Heroes or Besondere. Soon there are only Rogues left and even they begin to dwindle.

"I think I should go check on the other sectors and bring some Besondere with me to clear them up," Sherry says, having taken a look around the battlefield too. I nod and she gives me one last hug before walking away, radio in hand as she reports the events in sector one.

I turn to Shane and walk slowly toward the two vampires, suddenly nervous to meet his brother.

King Simon and Shane break apart and the King holds his brother by the shoulders as he looks him over. "My, how you have grown. It has only been a couple of years in Alstoria, yet…" The king gestures to Shane's body.

Shane smiles and rubs his chin. "Yeah, it has been much longer here. I've missed you brother."

King Simon gives Shane a soft smile. "I've missed you too."

King Simon sees me over Shane's shoulder and his smile disappears. He steps back and straightens his shoulders. Suddenly, he looks a lot more intimidating than a second ago.

"Care to tell me how this human has your power?" King Simon asks Shane while keeping his gaze on me.

Shane turns around and a grin breaks out over his face, lighting up his eyes. "Jo!"

Shane zips forward, becoming a blur for a second, then wraps me in a hug. "I'm glad you're okay," he whispers in my ear.

"Ditto." I smile into his shoulder and hug him back.

King Simon is scowling, showing me what an older, grumpy Shane would look like.

Shane doesn't move from my side. He places a hand on my back and turns to his brother. "Simon, this is Jo. She ended up getting my energy when I crossed over. I found her recently and we have been working together."

King Simon eyes me up and down and crosses his arms over his chest. "We must transfer it back now."

I gasp and place a hand on my chest protectively. I knew this was coming but I didn't know that it would cause an ache like this. I haven't lost my power yet and I already long for it. However, it is not mine. King Simon is right. I need to give it back. It is time for Shane to go home.

I step forward and bow my head. "I understand." I hesitate then look up at the vampire King nervously. "Will it hurt?"

"This has never been done before, so I don't know," he says, uncharacteristically soft. "I imagine we must go to Alstoria though."

I look fearfully to the portal I still have open. Shane mentioned that is what we might have to do. I am nervous, curious, and terrified to see this Other world.

"No," Shane says firmly and steps around me to block his brother's view of me with his body. "We will not be risking it. The power is hers now."

I gasp. Shane said this once before, but I thought he would change his mind now that he is faced with his brother and an opportunity to get it back.

King Simon clenches a fist and looks at his brother with exasperation. "Shane, come now, this human cannot keep the power of the lightning."

"Her name is Jo," Shane says calmly but there is an edge to it. "And she is keeping it."

Shane and Simon stare at each other for a long time, having a whole conversation with just a look. I guess it is not just a Sherry-Jo thing. Must be a sibling thing.

Finally, King Simon sighs and shakes his head. He looks at me and frowns but then his features soften, and he says, "I expect you to use it responsibly. We will be keeping an eye on you."

I don't know how he can possibly keep an eye on me if I am the only one who can open portals, that is, assuming Revelation is taken care of, but I nod anyway.

"We must get back to Alstoria. Many of us lost energy coming over to this world." King Simon turns to his people and makes a loud whistle. "I will leave some here to finish with this, but the rest will take the Bestia back and this will be over." King Simon places a hand on Shane's shoulder. "It is time to go home."

He gives me a nod then goes to deal with cleanup and directing his people, leaving me and Shane alone.

"So, you get to go home…" I say, trailing off when I cannot find the words to say next.

He makes a noise, something that almost sounds like a thoughtful *hmm* as he stares after his brother.

"A-Are you excited?" I ask nervously. When he doesn't answer, I touch his arm. He swings his gaze back to me with a smile that doesn't reach his eyes. "Do you regret it?"

He frowns. "Regret what?"

"Letting me keep the lightning power?"

Shane puts his hands on my shoulders and dips his head a bit to stare deep into my eyes. "Not at all. Don't ever think that I regret that decision, Jo."

I bite my lip and nod.

"As for your other question, I haven't been to Alstoria in so long, I don't know how to feel about going back. When I think about it, it doesn't really feel like home anymore." He shakes his head, seeming confused about his feelings. "I don't know."

"Well, I am happy for you."

"You are?"

"Yeah, I will miss you, but I am happy you get to be with your family." A sudden urge comes over me and since I know it will be the last time, I give in to it. I grab Shane's face and bring him to me then press my lips against his.

His eyes widen but then he relaxes and steps closer, putting a hand on my back to bring me in closer against him while his other hand reaches up to cup the back of my head around my ponytail. He tilts my head a little to deepen the kiss and when we pull back, we are both breathing heavily.

I smile up at him, a tinge of sadness in the edges. "Remember me."

His lips quirk up on one side then he looks toward his brother. "Hold that thought," he says suddenly then speeds off.

I blink at the empty space in front of me then look around to see where he had run off to. What did he mean *'hold that thought'*?

I see Shane speaking with his brother, but they are too far away for me to hear anything. Whatever it is, Simon is not pleased. His frown deepens with every word then he shakes his head vigorously. Shane stands up straighter, puffing out his chest a little, then crosses his arms. He says something else and Simon stares at him for a long moment with pursed lips. King Simon's eyes dart to me, their color turning black for a moment before reverting to their regular blue. I get the sense they are talking about me, but why?

Eventually, after more arguing and gesturing, Simon nods although reluctantly, and Shane turns to me with a grin. I don't know what they were talking about but the fact that it had something to do with me and the fact that Simon didn't look pleased makes me nervous. Though, Shane's smile confuses my nerves. If he is smiling, then it can't be bad. Right?

Shane takes his time coming back to me instead of zooming back with his vampire speed.

When he is within six feet I ask, "What was that about?"

He doesn't answer and he doesn't stop moving closer. I back up a step when he is in my personal space but that doesn't dissuade him. He reaches out and grasps my face with both hands then brings our lips together in an even more passionate kiss than before. It lasts for what seems like forever and I am tempted to curl my toes in cliché fashion. It sets my skin tingling and blue sparks erupt over my skin in response.

He chuckles when the sparks tickle him and pulls back.

"Wh-what was that?"

"That was a kiss," he says with a smirk.

I swat his arm. "Well, no kidding, but what did you say to your brother?" And why did it lead to kissing me?

He smiles and something in his eyes as he looks over my face, as if memorizing every detail, sends my heart fluttering.

"I realized something. I feel most at home here, on Earth…with you."

I gasp. What is he saying?

He pulls me in for a hug and whispers in my ear. "I am staying, Sapphire."

My chest lightens and I can't help the smile that spreads over my face. "What about your family?"

I feel him shrug. "I can always see him when I wish, that is if you are willing to open portals for us, but we agree that I am not needed there, I am needed more here."

I have a feeling that agreement was more one sided than he is letting on. I squeeze him tight, and he reciprocates, neither of us wanting to let go.

He is staying.

We don't have to say goodbye.

We can be a team.

We can be together.

Epilogue

An IKEA?

Why is it that the two times I meet the Council it is at the most random place someone can think of and has an acronym for a name? I wouldn't be surprised if the next time we meet it is in a UPS facility.

I open the map that was handed to me by the driver that came to pick me up. It was the same black SUV and even the same driver as last time, however, this time my sister did not accompany me and this time I am not nervous to be meeting the Council. In fact, I am excited and cannot stop smiling in anticipation.

In true mysterious Council fashion, an X marks the spot where I am supposed to meet them. It gives me flashbacks to when I had to follow the X to find the House of Mystery. That was the moment that changed my life forever…well, besides getting powers.

I compare the map in my hand to the one standing near the front entrance inside the IKEA. I will be meeting them in the living room section it seems.

I follow the arrows into the living room area then look around for the five individuals that I must speak to. Customers check out the various couches and coffee tables on one side of the aisle and I look for a familiar face among them but do not spot one. I look to the other side where mock living room set ups are displayed. I try to hide my grin when I spot a familiar blond head in the third display.

I rush over and, without announcing myself or being timid around these powerful people, throw myself onto one of the couches right next to one of the Council members.

"Ah, Jo, you found us."

At his words, I turn to the House of Mystery representative across from me on the other couch and smile at him. After the battle a week ago, it came to light that the last Council member, Father Time, had been hiding away in the House of Mystery's treehouse. All that time I was there preparing for the battle, I never knew it. When he was asked to come back and form a new Council he scowled and threw his hands in the air claiming *I'm too old for this crap.* He chose Harmony to take his place, but she politely declined and recommended someone else.

Looking at Specter now among the other members, I know she chose the perfect person to represent the House.

"You had to choose an IKEA to meet? You all are going to keep up the whole moving-to-different-random-locations-for-every-meeting thing?" I ask, chuckling and looking at each of them in turn for an answer.

"Until we can flush out all the Rogues and Bestia, it is only wise we do so," one of the other Council members answers.

My attention switches to the House of Discovery representative at her words. Once the portals were closed, Revelation was placed in a maximum-security prison run by guards with superpowers and his machine to take people's energy was destroyed. Raven had been offered the position soon after, but she declined. She claimed she doesn't like being tied down by the rules and secrecy, plus she is reevaluating whether she wants to continue being part of that House.

I met this woman when I helped the Heroes and Agents do a complete reorder of the House of Discovery. She ended up being a top member who had been one of the good guys. During the battle, she and many others had fought the Rogues within their House. Her alias is Rays, and she can use X-ray vision to see through anything. I fight the urge to cover myself when she looks at me, but I know she would never use her power like that...or I hope anyway.

"Now that you are here," The House of Heroes representative says, "we want to know what you have decided."

The Head of the House of Heroes, Oz as he calls himself due to his illusion power, stepped down from his position to take this one and passed his previous office on to my sister. Mystico and Aphrodite were found in the House of Discovery, but their power was completely drained. They are still healing but when they recover, they will be normal humans. I don't know what they will do but unfortunately, they can't return to the Council.

A young, white haired woman whose eyelashes look like they always have frost on them and goes by the pseudonym of Winter took over Aphrodite's position of representative for House of Glamour. She sits on the same couch as me but at the other end. She nods at Oz's words and leans over the person in between us to hand me a paper and pen.

"I know you are here to register a name, but my House is always open to you, too," Oz adds. "I know your sister would be happy to instate you."

I smile but shake my head. I had a long discussion with my sister over the week and we both agreed that I would be happier staying with the House of Mystery. I may have solved my personal mystery but there is still so much to uncover, solve, and learn. Plus, I have a new mission that involves documenting everything about Alstoria and the three Kingdoms there. Thankfully, I have a great source to interview whenever I need.

Oz shrugs. "The offer is always open."

"Thank you," I say, and take the paper from Winter.

"What did you choose?" Specter asks, leaning forward and resting his arms on his knees.

I look to the person next to me and give him a knowing smile. A spark lights his blue eyes, and he shares my knowing look.

After the battle, everyone decided we needed a position on the Council for a new set of individuals that needed to be represented. A position to help the Besondere and Bestia get home or acclimate to this world without attacking people. Someone who would have their best interests at heart and who they trusted. Shane was chosen unanimously and has taken on the alias of The Prince since then.

Today he wears a purple vest which I find quite charming. His warmth seeps into my arm which is pressed against him, and his eyes hold a heat all its own the longer he stares at me. It all makes me want to climb into his lap and either kiss him senseless or snuggle against him.

Shane raises his eyebrows and smirks, seemingly reading my mind. He reminds me of why I am here by looking pointedly at the paper in my hands. My small, secretive smile turns into a grin as I take the pen and scrawl my chosen alias across the form next to my real name.

"I choose Sapphire Sparks."

Note from the Author

Ways to help Independent authors (without paying anything!):

--Rate and review the book on Amazon and Goodreads

--Follow them on social networks

--Post about the book

--Recommend to friends, family, and even strangers.

Your support means everything and would be much appreciated.

Acknowledgements

I want to thank Sheila Rougé of Ouroboros Design for designing this amazing book cover. I tried to do it myself, but I am artistically challenged, and she made it totally better. It was fun working with her and she had many great ideas. I am excited to work with her again in the future.

Thank you, Victoria Gillette, for reading my book and being my official/unofficial beta reader. You are #1 and I always love hearing your feedback and just spending hours talking about books with you.

About the Author

Katie Dunn grew up in the hot part of Arizona where she graduated from NAU and became a teacher. She got a taste of the author life after her first YA contemporary fantasy novel Ancient Elements. Finding out she loved writing just as much as reading, teaching, and traveling, she sat down and wrote the first installment of the YA fantasy adventure Skor Stone trilogy: Pirates from Under and other YA/NA books. She has a notebook full of other ideas and will slowly be adding more stories to her author library.

You can check out more about Katie Dunn's books and works in progress at Kdunnauthor.com or social media platforms under Kdunnauthor.

www.ingramcontent.com/pod-product-compliance
Lightning Source LLC
Chambersburg PA
CBHW030148310726
48970CB00005B/1640